The

Or, One Of The "Forty." (L'immortel) - 1877

Alphonse Daudet

Translator

A. W. Verrall And Margaret D. G. Verrall

Alpha Editions

This edition published in 2022

ISBN : 9789356313712

Design and Setting By
Alpha Editions
www.alphaedis.com
Email – info@alphaedis.com

As per information held with us this book is in Public Domain.
This book is a reproduction of an important historical work. Alpha Editions uses the best technology to reproduce historical work in the same manner it was first published to preserve its original nature. Any marks or number seen are left intentionally to preserve its true form.

CHAPTER I.

In the 1880 edition of Men of the Day, under the heading *Astier-Réhu*, may be read the following notice:—

Astier, commonly called Astier-Réhu (Pierre Alexandre Léonard), Member of the Académie Française, was born in 1816 at Sauvagnat (Puy-de-Dôme). His parents belonged to the class of small farmers. He displayed from his earliest years a remarkable aptitude for the study of history. His education, begun at Riom and continued at Louis-le-Grand, where he was afterwards to re-appear as professor, was more sound than is now fashionable, and secured his admission to the Ecole Normale Supérieure, from which he went to the Chair of History at the Lycée of Mende. It was here that he wrote the Essay on Marcus Aurelius, crowned by the Académie Française. Called to Paris the following year by M. de Salvandy, the young and brilliant professor showed his sense of the discerning favour extended to him by publishing, in rapid succession, The Great Ministers of Louis XIV. (crowned by the Académie Française), Bonaparte and the Concordat (crowned by the Académie Française), and the admirable Introduction to the History of the House of Orleans, a magnificent prologue to the work which was to occupy twenty years of his life. This time the Académie, having no more crowns to offer him, gave him a seat among its members. He could scarcely be called a stranger there, having married Mlle. Rèhu, daughter of the lamented Paulin Réhu, the celebrated architect, member of the Académie des Inscriptions et Belles-Lettres, and granddaughter of the highly respected Jean Réhu, the father of the Académie Française, the elegant translator of Ovid and author of the Letters to Urania, whose hale old age is the miracle of the Institute. By his friend and colleague M. Thiers Léonard Astier-Réhu was called to the post of Keeper of the Archives of Foreign Affairs. It is well known that, with a noble disregard of his interests, he resigned, some years later (1878), rather than that the impartial pen of history should stoop to the demands of our present rulers. But deprived of his beloved archives, the author has turned his leisure to good account. In two years he has given us the last three volumes of his history, and announces shortly New Lights on Galileo, based upon documents extremely curious and absolutely unpublished. All the works of Astier-Réhu may be had of Petit-Séquard, Bookseller to the Académie.

As the publisher of this book of reference entrusts to each person concerned the task of telling his own story, no doubt can possibly be thrown upon the authenticity of these biographical notes. But why must it be asserted that Léonard Astier-Réhu resigned his post as Keeper of the Archives? Every one knows that he was dismissed, sent away with no more ceremony than a hackney-cabman, because of an imprudent phrase let slip by the historian of the House of Orleans, vol. v. p. 327: 'Then, as to-day, France, overwhelmed by the flood of demagogy, etc.' Who can see the end of a metaphor? His salary of five hundred pounds a year, his rooms in the Quai d'Orsay (with coals and gas) and, besides, that wonderful treasure of historic documents, which had supplied the sap of his books, all this had been carried away from him by this unlucky 'flood,' all by his own flood! The poor man could not get over it. Even after the lapse of two years, regret for the ease and the honours of his office gnawed at his heart, and gnawed with a sharper tooth on certain dates, certain days of the month or the week, and above all on 'Teyssèdre's Wednesdays.' Teyssèdre was the man who polished the floors. He came to the Astiers' regularly every Wednesday. On the afternoon of that day Madame Astier was at home to her friends in her husband's study, this being the only presentable apartment of their third floor in the Rue de Beaune, the remains of a grand house, terribly inconvenient in spite of its magnificent ceiling. The disturbance caused to the illustrious historian by this 'Wednesday,' recurring every week and interrupting his industrious and methodical labours, may easily be conceived. He had come to hate the rubber of floor, a man from his own country, with a face as yellow, close, and hard as his own cake of beeswax. He hated Teyssèdre, who, proud of coming from Riom, while 'Meuchieu Achtier came only from Chauvagnat,' had no scruple in pushing about the heavy table covered with pamphlets, notes, and reports, and hunted the illustrious victim from room to room till he was driven to seek refuge in a kind of pigeon-hole over the study, where, though not a big man, he must sit for want of room to get up. This lumber-closet, which was furnished with an old damask chair, an aged card-table and a stand of drawers, looked out on the courtyard through the upper circle of the great window belonging to the room below. Through this opening, much resembling the low glass door of an orangery, the travailing historian might be seen from head to foot, miserably doubled up like Cardinal La Balue in his cage. It was here that he was sitting one morning with his eyes upon an ancient scrawl, having been already expelled from the lower room by the bang-bang-bang of Teyssèdre, when he heard the sound of the front door bell.

'Is that you, Fage?' asked the Academician in his deep and resonant bass.

'No, *Meuchieu Achtier*. It is the young gentleman.'

On Wednesday mornings the polisher opened the door, because Corentine was dressing her mistress.

'How's *The Master?*' cried Paul Astier, hurrying by to his mother's room. The Academician did not answer. His son's habit of using ironically a title generally bestowed upon him as a compliment was always offensive to him.

'M. Fage is to be shown up as soon as he comes,' he said, not addressing himself directly to the polisher.

'Yes, *Meuchieu Achtier.*' And the bang-bang-bang began again.

'Good morning, mamma.'

'Why, it's Paul! Come in. Mind the folds, Corentine.'

Madame Astier was putting on a skirt before the looking-glass. She was tall, slender, and still good-looking in spite of her worn features and her too delicate skin. She did not move, but held out to him a cheek with a velvet surface of powder. He touched it with his fair pointed beard. The son was as little demonstrative as the mother.

'Will M. Paul stay to breakfast?' asked Corentine. She was a stout countrywoman of an oily complexion, pitted with smallpox. She was sitting on the carpet like a shepherdess in the fields, and was about to repair, at the hem of the skirt, her mistress's old black dress. Her tone and her attitude showed the objectionable familiarity of the under-paid maid-of-all-work.

No, Paul would not stay to breakfast. He was expected elsewhere. He had his buggy below; he had only come to say a word to his mother.

'Your new English cart? Let me look,' said Madame Astier. She went to the open window, and parted the Venetian blinds, on which the bright May sunlight lay in stripes, just far enough to see the neat little vehicle, shining with new leather and polished pinewood, and the servant in spotless livery standing at the horse's head.

'Oh, ma'am, how beautiful!' murmured Coren-tine, who was also at the window. 'How nice M. Paul must look in it!'

The mother's face shone. But windows were opening opposite, and people were stopping before the equipage, which was creating quite a sensation at this end of the Rue de Beaune. Madame Astier sent away the servant, seated herself on the edge of a folding-chair, and finished mending her skirt for herself, while she waited for what her son had to say to her, not without a suspicion what it would be, though her attention seemed to be absorbed in her sewing. Paul Astier was equally silent. He leaned back in an arm-chair and played with an ivory fan, an old thing which he had known for his mother's ever since he was born. Seen thus, the likeness between them was striking; the same Creole skin, pink over a delicate duskiness, the same supple figure, the same impenetrable grey eye, and in both faces a slight defect hardly to be noticed; the finely-cut nose was a little out of line, giving an expression of slyness, of something not to be trusted. While each watched and waited for the other, the pause was filled by the distant brushing of Teyssèdre.

'Rather good, that,' said Paul.

His mother looked up. 'What is rather good?'

He raised the fan and pointed, like an artist, at the bare arms and the line of the falling shoulders under the fine cambric bodice. She began to laugh.

'Yes, but look here.' She pointed to her long neck, where the fine wrinkles marked her age. 'But after all,'... you have the good looks, so what does it matter? Such was her thought, but she did not express it. A brilliant talker, perfectly trained in the fibs and commonplaces of society, a perfect adept in expression and suggestion, she was left without words for the only real feeling which she had ever experienced. And indeed she really was not one of those women who cannot make up their minds to grow old. Long before the hour of curfew—though indeed there had perhaps never been much fire in her to put out—all her coquetry, all her feminine eagerness to captivate and charm, all her aspirations towards fame or fashion or social success had been transferred to the account of her son, this tall, good-looking young fellow in the correct attire of the modern artist, with his slight beard and close-cut hair, who showed in mien and bearing that soldierly grace which our young men of the day get from their service as volunteers.

'Is your first floor let?' asked the mother at last.

'Let! let! Not a sign of it! All the bills and advertisements no go! "I don't know what is the matter with them; but they don't come," as Védrine said at his private exhibition.'

He laughed quietly, at an inward vision of Védrine among his enamels and his sculptures, calm, proud, and self-assured, wondering without anger at the non-appearance of the public. But Madame Astier did not laugh. That splendid first floor empty for the last two years! In the Rue Fortuny! A magnificent situation—a house in the style of Louis XII.—a house built by her son! Why, what did people want? The same people, doubtless, who did not go to Védrine. Biting off the thread with which she had been sewing, she said:

'And it is worth taking, too!'

'Quite; but it would want money to keep it up.'

The people at the Crédit Foncier would not be satisfied. And the contractors were upon him—four hundred pounds for carpenter's work due at the end of the month, and he hadn't a penny of it.

The mother, who was putting on the bodice of her dress before the looking-glass, grew pale and saw that she did so. It was the shiver that you feel in a duel, when your adversary raises his pistol to take aim.

'You have had the money for the restorations at Mousseaux?'

'Mousseaux! Long ago.'

'And the Rosen tomb?'

'Can't get on. Védrine still at his statue.'

'Yes, and why must you have Védrine? Your father warned you against him.'

'Oh, I know. They can't bear him at the Institute.'

He rose and walked about the room.

'You know me, come. I am a practical man. If I took him and not some one else to do my statue, you may suppose that I had a reason.' Then suddenly, turning to his mother:

'You could not let me have four hundred pounds, I suppose?' She had been waiting for this ever since he came in; he never came to see her for anything else.

'Four hundred pounds? How can you think——' She said no more; but the pained expression of her mouth and eyes said clearly enough:

'You know that I have given you everything—that I am dressed in clothes fit for the rag-bag—that I have not bought a bonnet for three years—that Corentine washes my linen in the kitchen because I should blush to give such rubbish to the laundress; and you know also that my worst misery is to refuse what you ask. Then why do you ask?' And this mute address of his mother's was so eloquent that Paul Astier answered it aloud:

'Of course I was not thinking of your having it yourself. By Jove, if you had, it would be the better for me. But,' he continued, in his cool, off hand way, 'there is *The Master* up there. Could you get it from him? You might. You know how to get hold of him.'

'That is over. There is an end of that.'

'Well, but, you know, he works; his books sell; you spend nothing.'

He looked round in the subdued light at the reduced state of the old furniture, the worn curtains, the threadbare carpet, nothing of later date than their marriage thirty years ago. Where was it then that all the money went?

'I say,' he began again, 'I wonder whether my venerable sire is in the habit of taking his fling?'

It was an idea so monstrous, so inconceivable, that of Léonard Astier-Réhu 'taking his fling,' that his wife could not help smiling in spite of herself. No, on that point she thought there was no need for uneasiness. 'Only, you know, he has turned suspicious and mysterious, and "buries his hoard." We have gone too far with him.'

They spoke low, like conspirators, with their eyes upon the carpet.

'And grandpapa,' said Paul, but not in a tone of confidence, 'could you try him?'

'Grandpapa? You must be mad!'

Yet he knew well enough what old Réhu was. A touchy, selfish man all but a hundred years old, who would have seen them all die rather than deprive himself of a pinch of snuff or a single one of the pins that were always stuck on the lapels of his coat. Ah, poor child! He must be hard up indeed before he could think of his grandfather.

'Well, you would not like me to try —— ——.' She paused.

'To try where?'

'In the Rue de Courcelles. I might get something in advance for the tomb.'

'There? Good Heavens! You had better not!'

He spoke to her imperiously, with pale lips and a disagreeable expression in his eye; then recovering his self-contained and fleeting tone, he said:

'Don't trouble any more about it. It is only a crisis to be got through. I have had plenty before now.'

She held out to him his hat, which he was looking for. As he could get nothing from her, he would be off. To keep him a few minutes longer, she began talking of an important business which she had in hand—a marriage, which she had been asked to arrange.

At the word *marriage* he started and looked at her askance: 'Who was it?' She had promised to say nothing at present. But she could not refuse him. It was the Prince d'Athis.

'Who is the lady?' he asked.

It was her turn now to show him the side view of her crooked nose.

'You do not know the lady. She is a foreigner with a fortune. If I succeed I might help you. I have made my terms in black and white.'

He smiled, completely reassured.

'And how does the Duchess take it?'

'She knows nothing of it, of course.'

'Her *Sammy*,' Her dear prince! And after fifteen years!'

Madame Astier's gesture expressed the utter carelessness of one woman for the feelings of another.

'What else could she expect at her age?' said she.

'Why, what is her age?'

'She was born in 1827. We are in 1880. You can do the sum. Just a year older than myself.'

'The Duchess!' cried Paul, stupefied.

His mother laughed as she said, 'Why, yes, you rude boy! What are you surprised at? I am sure you thought her twenty years younger. It's a fact, it seems, that the most experienced of you know nothing about women. Well, you see, the poor prince could not have her hanging on to him all his life. Besides, one of these days the old Duke will die, and then where would he be? Fancy him tied to that old woman!'

'Well,' said Paul, 'so much for your dear friend!' She fired at this. Her dear friend! The Duchess! A pretty friend! A woman who, with twenty-five thousand a year—intimate as she was with her, and well aware of their difficulties—had never so much as thought of helping them! What was the present of an occasional dress? Or the permission to choose a bonnet at her milliner's? Presents for use! There was no pleasure in them.

'Like grandpapa Réhu's on New Year's day,' put in Paul assenting. 'An atlas, or a globe!'

'Oh, Antonia is, I really think, more stingy still. When we were at Mousseaux, in the middle of the fruit season, if *Sammy* was not there, do you remember the dry plums they gave us for dessert? There is plenty in the orchard and the kitchen garden, but everything is sent to market at Blois or Vendôme. It runs in her blood, you know. Her father, the Marshal, was famous for it at the Court of Louis Philippe; and it was something to be thought stingy at the Court of Louis Philippe! These great Corsican families are all alike; nothing but meanness and pretension! They will eat chestnuts, such as the pigs would not touch, off plate with their arms on it. And as for the Duchess—why, she makes her steward account to her in person! They take the meat up to her every morning; and every evening (this is from a person who knows), when she has gone to her grand bed with the lace, at that tender moment she balances her books!'

Madame Astier was nearly breathless. Her small voice grew sharp and shrill, like the cry of a sea-bird from the masthead. Meanwhile Paul, amused at first, had begun to listen impatiently, with his thoughts elsewhere. 'I am off,' said he abruptly. 'I have a breakfast with some business people—very important.'

'An order?'

'No, not architect's business this time.'

She wanted him to satisfy her curiosity, but he went on, 'Not now; another time; it's not settled.' And finally, as he gave his mother a little kiss, he whispered in her ear, 'All the same, do not forget my four hundred.'

But for this grown-up son, who was a secret cause of division, the Astier-Réhu would have had a happy household, as the world, and in particular the Academic world, measures household happiness. After thirty years their mutual sentiments remained the same, kept beneath the snow at the temperature of what gardeners call a 'cold-bed.' When, about '50, Professor Astier, after brilliant successes at the Institute, sued for the hand of Mademoiselle Adelaide Réhu, who at that time lived with her grandfather at the Palais Mazarin, it was not the delicate and slender beauty of his betrothed, it was not the bloom of her 'Aurora' face, which were the real attractions for him. Neither was it her fortune. For the parents of Mademoiselle Adelaide, who died suddenly of cholera, had left her but little; and the grandfather, a Creole from Martinique, an old beau of the time of the Directory, a gambler, a free liver, great in practical jokes and in duels, declared loudly and repeatedly that he should not add a penny to her slender portion.

No, that which enticed the scion of Sauvagnat, who was far more ambitious than greedy, was the Académie. The two great courtyards which he had to cross to bring his daily offering of flowers, and the long solemn corridors into which at intervals there descended a dusty staircase, were for him rather the path of glory than of love. The Paulin Réhu of the Inscriptions et Belles-Lettres, the Jean Réhu of the 'Letters to Urania,' the Institute complete with its lions and its cupola—this was the Mecca of his pilgrimage, and all this it was that he took to wife on his wedding day.

For this not transient beauty he felt a passion proof against the tooth of time, a passion which took such hold of him that his permanent attitude towards his wife was that of those mortal husbands on whom, in the mythological age, the gods occasionally bestowed their daughters. Nor did he quit this respect when at the fourth ballot he had himself become a deity. As for Madame Astier, who had only accepted marriage as a means of escape from a hard and selfish grandfather in his anecdotage, it had not taken her long to find out how poor was the laborious peasant brain, how narrow the intelligence, concealed by the solemn manners of the Academic laureate and manufacturer of octavos, and by his voice with its ophicleide notes adapted to the sublimities of the lecture room. And yet when, by force of intrigue, bargaining, and begging, she had seated him at last in the Académie, she felt herself possessed by a certain veneration, forgetting that it was herself who had clothed him in that coat with the green palm leaves, in which his nothingness ceased to be visible.

In the dull concord of their partnership, where was neither joy, nor intimacy, nor communion of any kind, there was but one single note of natural human feeling, their child; and this note disturbed the harmony. In the first place the father was entirely disappointed of all that he wished for his son, that he should be distinguished by the University, entered for the general examinations, and finally pass through the Ecole Normale to a professorship. Alas! at school Paul took prizes for nothing but gymnastics and fencing, and distinguished himself chiefly by a wilful and obstinate perversity, which covered a practical turn of mind and a precocious understanding of the world. Careful of his dress and his appearance, he never went for a walk without the hope, of which he made no secret to his schoolfellows, of 'picking up a rich wife.' Two or three times the father had been ready to punish this determined idleness after the rough method of Auvergne, but the mother was by to excuse and to protect. In vain Astier-Réhu scolded and snapped his jaw, a prominent feature which, in the days when he was a professor, had gained him the nickname of *Crocodilus*. In the last resort, he would threaten to pack his trunk and go back to his vineyard at Sauvagnat.

'Ah, Léonard, Léonard!' Madame Astier would say with gentle mockery; and nothing further came of it. Once, however, he really came near to strapping his trunk in good earnest, when, after a three years' course of architecture at the Ecole des Beaux-Arts, Paul refused to compete for the Prix de Rome. The father could scarcely speak for indignation. 'Wretched boy! It is the Prix de Rome! You cannot know; you do not understand. The Prix de Rome! Get that, and it means the Institute!' Little the young man cared. What he wanted was wealth, and wealth the Institute does not bestow, as might be seen in his father, his grandfather, and old Réhu, his great-grandfather! To start in life, to get a business, a large business, an immediate income—this was what he wanted for his part, and not to wear a green coat with palms on it.

Léonard Astier was speechless. To hear such blasphemies uttered by his son and approved by his wife, a daughter of the house of Réhu! This time his trunk was really brought down from the box room; his old trunk, such as professors use in the provinces, with as much ironwork in the way of nails and hinges as might have sufficed for a church door, and high enough and deep enough to have held the enormous manuscript of 'Marcus Aurelius' together with all the dreams of glory and all the ambitious hopes of an historian on the high road to the Académie. It was in vain for Madame Astier to pinch her lips and say, 'Oh, Léonard, Léonard!' Nothing would stop him till his trunk was packed. Two days it stood in the way in the middle of his study. Then it travelled to the ante-room; and there reposed, turned once and for ever into a wood-box.

And at first, it must be said, Paul Astier did splendidly. Helped by his mother and her connection in good society, and further assisted by his own cleverness and personal charm, he soon got work which brought him into notice. The Duchess Padovani, wife of a former ambassador and minister, trusted him with the restoration of her much admired country house at Mousseaux-on-the-Loire, an ancient royal residence, long neglected, which he succeeded in restoring with a skill and ingenuity really amazing in an undistinguished scholar of the Beaux-Arts. Mousseaux got him the order for the new mansion of the Ambassador of the Porte; and finally the Princess of Rosen commissioned him to design the mausoleum of Prince Herbert of Rosen, who had come to a tragic end in the expedition of Christian of Illyria. The young man now thought himself sure of success. Astier the elder was induced by his wife to put down three thousand pounds out of his savings for the purchase of a site in the Rue Fortuny. Then Paul built himself a mansion—or rather, a wing to a mansion, which was itself arranged as a block of elegant 'rooms to let.' He was a practical young fellow, and if he wanted a mansion, without which no artist is *chic*, he meant it to bring him an income.

Unfortunately houses to let are not always so easy to let, and the young architect's way of life, with two horses in his stable (one for harness, one for the saddle), his club, his visiting, his slow reimbursements, made it impossible for him to wait. Moreover, the elder Astier suddenly declared that he was not going to give any more; and all that the mother could attempt or say for her darling son failed to shake this irrevocable decision. Her will, which had hitherto swayed the establishment, was now resisted. Thenceforward there was a continual struggle. The mother used her ingenuity to make little dishonest profits on the household expenses, that she might never have to say 'no' to her son's requests. Léonard suspected her and, to protect himself, checked the accounts. In these humiliating conflicts the wife, who was the better bred, was the first to tire; and nothing less than the desperate situation of her beloved Paul would have induced her to make a fresh attempt.

She went slowly into the dining room. It was a long, melancholy room, ill lighted by tall, narrow windows, having in fact been used as a *table d'hôte* for ecclesiastics until the Astiers took it. There she found her husband already at table, looking preoccupied and almost grumpy. In the ordinary way *'the Master'* came to his meals with a smiling serenity as regular as his appetite, and with teeth which, sound as a foxhound's, were not to be discouraged by stale bread or leathery meat, or by the miscellaneous disagreeables which are the everyday flavouring of life.

'Ah, it's Teyssèdre's day,' thought Madame Astier, as she took her seat, her best dress rustling as she did so. She was a little surprised at not receiving the compliment with which her husband never failed to welcome her 'Wednesday' costume, shabby as it was. Reckoning that this bad temper would go off with the first mouthfuls, she waited before beginning her attack. But, though *the Master* went on eating, his ill humour visibly increased. Everything was wrong; the wine tasted of the cork; the balls of boiled beef were burnt.

'And all because your M. Fage kept you waiting this morning,' cried Corentine angrily from the adjoining kitchen. She showed her shiny pitted face for a moment at the hatch in the wall through which, in the days of the *table d'hôte*, they used to pass the dishes. She shut it with a bang; upon which Astier muttered, 'Really that girl's impudence——' He was in truth much annoyed that the name of Fage had been mentioned before his wife. And sure enough at any other moment Madame Astier would not have failed to say, 'Oh, Fage the bookbinder here again!' and there would have followed a domestic scene; on all which Corentine reckoned when she threw in her artful speech. To-day, however, it was all-important that the master should not be irritated, but prepared by skilful stages for the intended petition. He was talked to, for instance, about the health of Loisillon, the perpetual secretary of the Académie, who, it seemed, was getting worse and worse. Loisillon's post and his rooms in the Institute were to come to Léonard Astier as a compensation for the office which he had lost; and though he was really attached to his dying colleague, still the prospect of a good salary, an airy and comfortable residence, and other advantages had its attractions. He was perhaps ashamed to think of the death in this light, but in the privacy of his household he did so without blinking. But to-day even that did not bring a smile. 'Poor M. Loisillon!' said Madame Astier's thin voice; 'he begins to be uncertain about his words. La vaux was telling us yesterday at the Duchess's, he can only say "a cu-curiosity, a cu-curiosity," and,' she added, compressing her lips and drawing up her long neck, 'he is on the Dictionary Committee.'

Astier-Réhu did not move an eyebrow.

'It is not a bad story,' said he, clapping his jaw with a magisterial air. 'But, as I have said somewhere in my history, in France the provisional is the only thing that lasts. Loisillon has been dying any time this ten years. He'll see every one of us buried yet—every one of us,' he repeated angrily, pulling at his dry bread. It was clear that Teyssèdre had put him into a very bad temper indeed.

Madame Astier went to another subject, the special meeting of all the five Académies, which was to take place within a few days, and to be honoured by the presence of the Grand Duke Leopold of Finland. It so happened that Astier-Réhu, being director for the coming quarter, was to preside at the meeting and to deliver the opening speech, in which his Highness was to receive a compliment. Skilfully questioned about this speech, which he was already planning, Léonard described it in outline. It was to be a crushing attack upon the modern school of literature—a sound thrashing administered in public to these pretenders, these dunces. And at this his eyes, big with his heavy meal, lighted up his square face, and the blood rose under his thick bushy eyebrows. They were still coal-black, and contrasted strangely with the white circle of his beard.

'By the way,' said he suddenly, 'what about my uniform coat? Has it been seen to? The last time I wore it, at Montribot's funeral——'

But do not women think of everything? Madame Astier had seen to the coat that very morning. The silk of the palm leaves was getting shabby; the lining was all to pieces. It was very old. Oh, dear, when did he wear it first? Why, it was as long ago—as long ago—as when he was admitted! The twelfth of October, eighteen-sixty-six! He had better order a new one for the Meeting. The five Académies, a Royal Highness, and all Paris! Such an audience was worth a new coat. Léonard protested, not energetically, on the ground of expense. With a new coat he would want a new waistcoat; knee-breeches were not worn now, but a new waistcoat would be indispensable.

'My dear, you really must!' She continued to press him. If they did not take care they would make themselves ridiculous with their economy. There were too many shabby old things about them. The furniture of her room, for instance! It made her feel ashamed when a friend came in, and for a sum comparatively trifling.

'Ouais! quelque sot,' muttered Astier-Réhu, who liked to quote his classics. The furrow in his forehead deepened, and under it, as under the bar of a shutter, his countenance, which had been open for a minute, shut up. Many a time had he supplied the means to pay a milliner's bill, or a dressmaker's, or to re-paper the walls, and after all no account had been settled and no purchase made. All the money had gone to that Charybdis in the Rue Fortuny. He had had enough of it, and was not going to be caught again. He rounded his back, fixed his eyes upon the huge slice of Auvergne cheese which filled his plate, and said no more.

Madame Astier was familiar with this dogged silence. This attitude of passive resistance, dead as a ball of cotton, was always put on when money was mentioned. But this time she was resolved to make him answer. 'Ah,' she said, 'I see you rolling up, Master Hedgehog. I know the meaning of that. "Nothing to be got! nothing to be got! No, no, no!" Eh?' The back grew rounder and rounder. 'But you can find money for M. Fage.' Astier started, sat up, and looked uneasily at his wife. Money for M. Fage? What did she mean?' Why, of course,' she went on, delighted to have forced the barrier of his silence, 'of course it takes money to do all that binding. And what's the good of it, I should like to know, for all those old scraps?'

He felt relieved; evidently she knew nothing; it was only a chance shot.

But the term 'old scraps' went to his heart: unique autograph documents, signed letters of Richelieu, Colbert, Newton, Galileo, Pascal, marvels bought for an old song, and worth a fortune. 'Yes, madam, a fortune.' He grew excited, and began to quote figures, the offers that had been made him. Bos, the famous Bos of the Rue de l'Abbaye (and he knew his business if any one did), Bos had offered him eight hundred pounds merely for three specimens from his collection—three letters from Charles the Fifth to François Rabelais. Old scraps indeed!

Madame Astier listened in utter amazement. She was well aware that for the last two or three years he had been collecting old manuscripts. He used sometimes to speak to her of his finds, and she listened in a wandering absent-minded way, as a woman does listen to a man's voice when she has heard it for thirty years. But this was beyond her conception. Eight hundred pounds for three letters! And why did he not take it?'

He burst out like an explosion of dynamite.

'Sell my Charles the Fifths! Never! I would see you all without bread and begging from door to door before I would touch them—understand that!' He struck the table. His face was very pale, and his lips thrust out This fierce maniac was an Astier-Réhu whom his wife did not know. In the sudden glow of a passion human beings do thus take aspects unknown to those who know them best The next minute the Academician was quite calm, again, and was explaining, not without embarrassment, that these documents were indispensable to him as an author, especially now that he could not command the Records of the Foreign Office. To sell these materials would be to give up writing. On the contrary, he hoped to make additions to them. Then, with a touch of bitterness and affection, which betrayed the whole depth of the father's disappointment, he said, 'After my time, my fine gentleman of a son may sell them if he chooses; and since all he wants is to be rich, I will answer for it that he will be.'

'Yes; but meanwhile——'

This 'meanwhile' was said in a little flute-like voice so cruelly natural and quiet that Léonard, unable to control his jealousy of this son who left him no place in his wife's heart, retorted with a solemn snap of the jaw, 'Meanwhile, madam, others can do as I do. I have no mansion, I keep no horses and no English cart. The tramway does for my going and coming, and I am content to live on a third floor over an *entresol*, where I am exposed to Teyssèdre. I work night and day, I pile up volume after volume, two and three octavos in a year. I am on two committees of the Académie; I never miss a meeting; I never miss a funeral; and even in the summer I never accept an invitation to the country, lest I should miss a single tally. I hope my son, when he is sixty-five, may be as indefatigable.'

It was long since he had spoken of Paul, and never had he spoken so severely. The mother was struck by his tone, and in her look, as she glanced sidelong, almost wickedly, at her husband, there was a shade of respect, which had not been there before.

'There is a ring,' said Léonard eagerly, rising as he spoke, and flinging his table napkin upon the back of his chair. 'That must be my man.'

'It's some one for you, ma'am; they are beginning early to-day,' said Corentine, as, with her kitchen-maid's fingers wiped hastily on her apron, she laid a card on the edge of the table. Madame Astier looked at it. 'The Vicomte de Freydet.' A gleam came into her eyes. But her delight was not perceptible in the calm tone in which she said, 'So M. de Freydet is in Paris?'

'Yes, about his book.'

'Bless me! His book! I have not even cut it. What is it about?'

She hurried over the last mouthfuls, and washed the tips of her white fingers in her glass while her husband in an absent-minded way gave her some idea of the new volume. 'God in Nature,' a philosophic poem, entered for the Boisseau prize.

'Oh, I do hope he will get it. He must, he must. They are so nice, he and his sister, and he is so good to the poor paralysed creature. Do you think he will?'

Astier would not commit himself. He could not promise, but he would certainly recommend Freydet, who seemed to him to be really improving. 'If he asks you for my personal opinion, it is this: there is still a little too much for my taste, but much less than in his other books. You may tell him that his old master is pleased.'

Too much of what? Less of what? It must be supposed that Madame Astier knew, for she sought no explanation, but left the table and passed, quite happy, into her drawing room—as the study must be considered for the day. Astier, more and more absorbed in thought, lingered for some minutes, breaking up with his knife what remained in his plate of the Auvergne cheese; then, being disturbed in his meditations by Corentine, who, without heeding him, was rapidly clearing the table, he rose stiffly and went up, by a little staircase like a cat-ladder, to his attic, where he took up his magnifying glass and resumed the examination of the old manuscript upon which he had been busy since the morning.

CHAPTER II.

SITTING straight, with the reins well held up in the most correct fashion, Paul Astier drove his two-wheeled cart at a stiff pace to the scene of his mysterious breakfast 'with some business people.' 'Tclk! tclk!' Past the Pont Royal, past the quays, past the Place de la Concorde. The road was so smooth, the day so fine, that as terraces, trees, and fountains went by, it would have needed but a little imagination on his part to believe himself carried away on the wings of Fortune. But the young man was no visionary, and as he bowled along he examined the new leather and straps, and put questions about the hay-merchant to his groom, a young fellow perched at his side looking as cool and as sharp as a stable terrier. The hay-merchant, it seemed, was as bad as the rest of them, and grumbled about supplying the fodder.

'Oh, does he?' said Paul absently; his mind had already passed to another subject. His mother's revelations ran in his head. Fifty-three years old! The beautiful Duchess Antonia, whose neck and shoulders were the despair of Paris! Utterly incredible! 'Tclk! tclk!' He pictured her at Mousseaux last summer, rising earlier than any of her guests, wandering with her dogs in the park while the dew was still on the ground, with loosened hair and blooming lips; she did not look made up, not a bit. Fifty-three years old? Impossible!

'Tclk, tclk! Hi! Hi!' That's a nasty corner between the Rond Pont and the Avenue d'Antin.—All the same, it was a low trick they were playing her, to find a wife for the Prince. For let his mother say what she would, the Duchess and her drawing-room had been a fine thing for them all. Perhaps his father might never have been in the Académie but for her; he himself owed her all his commissions. Then there was the succession to Loisillon's place and the prospect of the fine rooms under the cupola—well, there was nothing like a woman for flinging you over. Not that men were any better; the Prince d'Athis, for instance. To think what the Duchess had done for him! When they met he was a ruined and penniless rip; now what was he? High in the diplomatic service, member of the Académie des Sciences Morales et Politiques, on account of a book not a word of which he had written himself, 'The Mission of Woman in the World'. And while the Duchess was busily at work to fit him with an Embassy, he was only waiting to be gazetted before taking French leave and playing off this dirty trick on her, after fifteen years of uninterrupted happiness. 'The mission of woman in the world!' Well, the Prince understood what the mission of woman was. The next thing was to better the lesson. 'Tclk! tclk! Gate, please.'

Paul's soliloquy was over, and his cart drew up before a mansion in the Rue de Courcelles. The double gates were rolled, back slowly and heavily as if accomplishing a task to which they had long been unused.

In this house lived the Princess Colette de Rosen, who had shut herself up in the complete seclusion of mourning since the sad occurrence which had made her a widow at twenty-six. The daily papers recorded the details of the young widow's sensational despair: how the fair hair was cut off close and thrown into the coffin; how her room was decorated as for a lying in state; how she took her meals alone with two places laid, while on the table in the anteroom lay as usual the Prince's walking stick, hat, and gloves, as though he were at home and just going out. But one detail had not been mentioned, and that was the devoted affection and truly maternal care which Madame Astier showed for the 'poor little woman' in these distressing circumstances.

Their friendship had begun some years ago, when a prize for an historical work had been adjudged to the Prince de Rosen by the Académie, 'on the report of Astier-Réhu.' Differences of age and social position had however kept them apart until the Princess's mourning removed the barrier. When the widow's door was solemnly closed against society, Madame Astier alone escaped the interdict. Madame Astier was the only person allowed to cross the threshold of the mansion, or rather the convent, inhabited by the poor weeping Carmelite with her shaven head and robe of black; Madame Astier was the only person admitted to hear the mass sung twice a week at St. Philip's for the repose of Herbert's soul; and it was she who heard the letters which Colette wrote every evening to her absent husband, relating her life and the way she spent her days. All mourning, however rigid, involves attention to material details which are degrading to grief but demanded by society. Liveries must be ordered, trappings provided for horses and carriages, and the heartbroken mourner must face the hypocritical sympathy of the tradesman. All these duties were discharged by Madame Astier with never-failing patience. She undertook the heavy task of managing the household, which the tear-laden eyes of its fair mistress could no longer supervise, and so spared the young widow all that could disturb her despair, or disarrange her hours for praying, weeping, writing 'to him,' and carrying armfuls of exotic flowers to the cemetery of Père Lachaise, where Paul Astier was superintending the erection of a gigantic mausoleum in commemorative stone brought at the express wish of the Princess from the scene of the tragedy.

Unfortunately the quarrying of this stone and its conveyance from Illyria, the difficulties of carving granite, and the endless plans and varying fancies of the widow, to whom nothing seemed sufficiently huge and magnificent to suit her dead hero, had brought about many hitches and delays. So it happened that in May 1880, two years and more after the catastrophe and the commencement of the work, the monument was still unfinished. Two years is a long time to maintain the constant paroxysms of an ostentatious grief, each sufficient to discharge the whole. The mourning was still observed as rigidly as ever, the house was still closed and silent as a cave. But in the place of the living statue weeping and praying in the furthest recesses of the crypt was now a pretty young woman whose hair was growing again, instinct with life in every curl and wave of its soft luxuriance. The reappearance of this fair hair gave a touch of lightness, almost of brightness, to the widow's mourning, which seemed now no more than a caprice of fashion. In the movements and tones of the Princess was perceptible the stirring of spring; she had the air of relief and repose noticeable in young widows in the second period of their mourning. It is a delightful position. For the first time after the restraints of girlhood and the restraints of marriage, a woman enjoys the sweets of liberty and undisputed possession of herself; she is freed from contact with the coarser nature of man, and above all from the fear of maternity, the haunting terror of the young wife of the present day. In the case of the Princess Colette the natural development of uncontrollable grief into perfect peacefulness was emphasised by the paraphernalia of inconsolable widowhood with which she was still surrounded. It was not hypocrisy; but how could she give orders, without raising a smile on the servants' faces, to remove the hat always waiting in the ante-room, the walking stick conspicuously handy, the place at table always laid for the absent husband; how could she say, 'The Prince will not dine to-night'? But the mystic correspondence 'with Herbert in heaven' had begun to fall off, growing less frequent every day, till it ended in a calmly written journal which caused considerable, though unexpressed, amusement to Colette's discerning friend.

The fact was that Madame Astier had a plan. The idea had sprung up in her practical little mind one Tuesday night at the Théâtre Français, when the Prince d'Athis had said to her confidentially in a low voice: 'Oh, my dear Adelaide, what a chain to drag! I am bored to death.' She at once planned to marry him to the Princess. It was a new game to play, crossing the old game, but not less subtle and fascinating. She had not now to hold forth upon the eternal nature of vows, or to hunt up in Joubert or other worthy philosophers such mottoes as the following, which the Princess had written out at the beginning of her wedding book: 'A woman can be wife and widow with honour but once.' She no longer went into raptures over the manly beauty of the young hero, whose portrait, full length and half length, profile and three quarters, in marble and on canvas, met you in every part of the house.

It was her system now to bring him gradually and dexterously down. 'Do you not think, dear,' she would say, 'that these portraits of the Prince make his jaw too heavy? Of course I know the lower part of his face was rather pronounced, a little too massive.' And so she administered a series of little poisonous stabs, with an indescribable skill and gentleness, drawing back when she went too far, and watching for Colette's smile at some criticism a little sharper than the rest. Working in this way she at last brought Colette to admit that Herbert had always had a touch of the boor; his manners were scarcely up to his rank; he had not, for instance, the distinguished air of the Prince d'Athis, 'whom we met a few Sundays ago on the steps of St. Philip's. If you should fancy him, dear, he is looking for a wife.' This last remark was thrown out as a jest; but presently Madame Astier recurred to it and put it more definitely. Well, why should the Princess not marry him? It would be most suitable; the Prince had a good name, a diplomatic position of some importance; the marriage would involve no alteration of the Princess's coronet or title—a practical convenience not to be overlooked. 'And, indeed, if I am to tell you the truth, dear, the Prince entertains towards you an affection which'... &c. &c.

The word 'affection' at first hurt the Princess's feelings, but she soon grew used to hear it. They met the Prince d'Athis at church, then in great privacy at Madame Astier's in the Rue de Beaune, and Colette soon admitted that he was the only man who might have induced her to abandon her widowhood. But then poor dear Herbert had loved her so devotedly—she had been his all.

'Really,' said Madame Astier with the quiet smile of a person who knows. Then followed allusions, hints, and all the devices by which one woman poisons the mind of another.

'Why, my dear, there is no such thing in the world. A man of good breeding—a gentleman—will take care, for the sake of peace, not to give his wife pain or distress. But——'

'Then you mean that Herbert——'

'Was no better than the rest of them.' The Princess, with an indignant protest, burst into tears; painless, passionless tears, such as ease a woman, and leave her as fresh as a lawn after a shower. But still she did not give way, to the great annoyance of Madame Astier, who had no conception of the real cause of her obduracy.

The truth was that frequent meetings to criticise the scheme of the mausoleum, much touching of hands and mingling of locks over the plans and sketches of cells and sepulchral figures, had created between Paul and Colette a fellow feeling which had gradually grown more and more tender, until one day Paul Astier detected in Colette's eyes as she looked at him an expression that almost confessed her liking. There rose before him as a possibility the miraculous vision of Colette de Rosen bringing him her million as a marriage gift. That might be in a short time, after a preliminary trial of patience, a regularly conducted beleaguering of the fortress. In the first place it was most important to-betray no hint to 'mamma,' who, though very cunning and subtle, was likely to fail through excess of zeal, especially when the interests of her Paul were at stake. She would spoil all the chances in her eagerness to hasten the successful issue. So Paul concealed his plans from Madame Astier, in entire ignorance that she was running a countermine in the same line as his. He acted on his own account with great deliberation. The Princess was attracted by his youth and fashion, his brightness and his witty irony, from which he carefully took the venom. He knew that women, like children and the mob, and all impulsive and untutored beings, hate a tone of sarcasm, which puts them out, and which they perceive by instinct to be hostile to the dreams of enthusiasm and romance.

On this spring morning it was with feelings of more confidence than usual that young Astier reached the house. This was the first time that he had been asked to breakfast at the Rosen mansion; the reason alleged was a visit which they were to make together to the cemetery, in order to inspect the works on the spot. With an unexpressed understanding they had fixed on a Wednesday, the day when Madame Astier was 'at home,' so as not to have her as a third in the party. With this thought in his mind the young man, self-controlled as he was, let fall as he crossed the threshold a careless glance which took in the large courtyard and magnificent offices almost as if he were entering on the possession of them. His spirits fell as he passed through the ante-room, where the footmen and lacqueys in deep mourning were dozing on their seats. They seemed to be keeping a funeral vigil round the hat of the defunct, a magnificent grey hat, which proclaimed the arrival of spring as well as the determination with which his memory was kept up by the Princess. Paul was much annoyed by it; it was like meeting a rival. He did not realise the difficulty which prevented Colette from escaping the self-forged fetters of her custom. He was wondering angrily whether she would expect him to breakfast in company with *him*, when the footman who relieved him of his walking stick and hat informed him that the Princess would receive him in the small drawing-room. He was shown at once into the rotunda with its glass roof, a bower of exotic plants, and was completely reassured by the sight of a little table with places laid for two, the arrangement of which Madame de Rosen was herself superintending.

'A fancy of mine,' she said, pointing to the table, 'when I saw how fine it was. It will be almost like the country.'

She had spent the night considering how she could avoid sitting down with this handsome young man in the presence of *his* knife and fork, and, not knowing what to say to the servants, had devised the plan of abandoning the situation and ordering breakfast, as a sudden whim, 'in the conservatory.'

Altogether the 'business' breakfast promised well. The *Romany blanc* lay to keep cool in the rocky basin of the fountain, amidst ferns and water plants, and the sun shone on the pieces of spar and on the bright smooth green of the outspread leaves. The two young people sat opposite one another, their knees almost touching: he quite self-possessed, his light eyes cold and fiery; she all pink and white, her new growth of hair, like a delicate wavy plumage, showing without any artificial arrangement the shape of her little head. And while they talked on indifferent topics, both concealing their real thoughts, young Astier exulted each time that the silent servants opened the door of the deserted dining-room, when he saw in the distance the napkin of the departed, left for the first time cheerless and alone.

CHAPTER III.

From the Vicomte de Freydet

To Mademoiselle Germaine de Freydet,

Clos Jallanges, near Mousseaux, Loir et Cher.

My dear Sister,—I am going to give you a precise account of the way I spend my time in Paris. I shall write every evening, and send you the budget twice a week, as long as I stay here.

Well, I arrived this morning, Monday, and took up my quarters as usual in my quiet little hotel in the Rue Servandoni, where the only sounds of the great city which reach me are the bells of Saint Sulpice, and the continual noise from a neighbouring forge, a sound of the rhythmical beating of iron, which I love because it reminds me of our village. I rushed off at once to my publisher. 'Well, when do we come out?'

'Your book? Why, it came out a week ago.'

Come out, indeed, and gone in too—gone into the depths of that grim establishment of Manivet's, which never ceases to pant and to reek with the labour of giving birth to a new volume. This Monday, as it happened, they were just sending out a great novel by Herscher, called *Satyra*. The copies struck off—how many hundreds of thousands of them I don't know—were lying in stacks and heaps right up to the very top of the establishment. You can fancy the preoccupation of the staff, and the lost bewildered look of worthy Manivet himself, when I mentioned my poor little volume of verse, and talked of my chances for the Boisseau prize. I asked for a few copies to leave with the members of the committee of award, and made my escape through *streets*—literally streets—of *Satyra*, piled up to the ceiling. When I got into my cab, I looked at my volume and turned over the pages. I was quite pleased with the solemn effect of the title, 'God in Nature.' The capitals are perhaps a trifle thin, when you come to look at them, not quite as black and impressive to the eye as they might be. But it does not matter. Your pretty name, 'Germaine,' in the dedication will bring us luck. I left a couple of copies at the Astiers' in the Rue de Beaune. You know they no longer occupy their rooms at the Foreign Office. But Madame Astier has still her 'Wednesdays.' So of course I wait till Wednesday to hear what my old master thinks of the book; and off I went to the Institute.

There again I found them as busy as a steam factory. Really the industry of this big city is marvellous, especially to people like us, who spend all the year in the peace of the open country. Found Picheral—you remember Picheral, the polite gentleman in the secretary's office, who got you such a good place three years ago, when I received my prize—well, I found Picheral and his clerks in the midst of a wild hubbub of voices, shouting out names and addresses from one desk to another, and surrounded on all sides by tickets of every kind, blue, yellow, and green, for the platform, for the outer circle, for the orchestra, Entrance A, Entrance B, &c. They were in the middle of sending out the invitations for the great annual meeting, which is to be honoured this year by the presence of a Royal Highness on his travels, the Grand Duke Leopold. 'Very sorry, my lord'—Picheral always says 'my lord,' having learnt it, no doubt, from Chateaubriand—' but I must ask you to wait.' 'Certainly, M. Picheral, certainly.'

Picheral is an amusing old gentleman, very courtly. He reminds me of Bonicar and our lessons in deportment in the covered gallery at grandmamma's house at Jallanges. He is as touchy, too, when crossed, as the old dancing master used to be. I wish you had heard him talk to the Comte de Bretigny, the ex-minister, one of the grandees of the Académie, who came in, while I was waiting, to rectify a mistake about the number of his tallies. I must tell you that the tally attesting attendance is worth five shillings, the old crown-piece. There are forty Academicians, which makes two hundred shillings per meeting, to be divided among those present; so, you see, the fewer they are, the more money each gets. Payment is made once a month in crown-pieces, kept in stout paper bags, each with its little reckoning pinned on to it, like a washing bill. Bretigny had not his complete number of tallies; and it was the most amusing sight to see this man of enormous wealth, director of Heaven knows how many companies, come there in his carriage to claim his ten shillings. He only got five, which sum, after a long dispute, Picheral tossed to him with as little respect as to a porter. But the 'deity' pocketed them with inexpressible joy; there is nothing like money won by the sweat of your brow. For, my dear Germaine, you must not imagine that there is any idling in the Académie. Every year there are fresh bequests, new prizes instituted; that means more books to read, more reports to engross, to say nothing of the dictionary and the orations. 'Leave your book at their houses, but do not go in,' said Picheral, when he heard I was competing for the prize. 'The extra work, which people are always putting on the members, makes them anything but gracious to a candidate.'

I certainly have not forgotten the way Ripault-Babin and Laniboire received me, when I called on them about my last candidature. Of course, when the candidate is a pretty woman, it is another story. Laniboire becomes jocose, and Ripault-Babin, still gallant in spite of his eighty years, offers the fair canvasser a lozenge, and says in his quavering voice, 'Touch it with your lips, and I will finish it.' So they told me in the secretary's office, where the deities are discussed with a pleasing frankness. 'You are in for the Boisseau prize. Let me see; you have for awarders two Dukes, three Mouldies, and two Players.' Such, in the office, is the familiar classification of the Académie

Française! 'Duke' is the name applied to all members of the nobility and episcopacy; Mouldies' includes the professors and the learned men generally; while a 'Player' denotes a lawyer, dramatic author, journalist, or novelist.

After ascertaining the addresses of my Dukes, Mouldies, and Players, I gave one of my 'author's copies' to the friendly M. Picheral, and, for form's sake, left another for poor M. Loisillon, the Permanent Secretary, who is said to be all but dead. Then I set to work to distribute the remaining copies all over Paris. The weather was glorious. As I passed through the Bois de Boulogne on my way back from the house of Ripault-Babin (which reminded me of the lozenges), the place was sweet with may and violets. I almost fancied myself at home again on one of those first days of early spring when the air is fresh and the sun hot; and I was inclined to give up everything and come back to you at Jallanges. Dined on the boulevard alone and gloomy, and then spent the rest of my evening at the Comédie Française, where they were playing Desminières' '*Le Dernier Frontin.*' Desminières is one of the awarders of the Boisseau prize, so I shall tell no one but you how his verses bored me. The heat and gas gave me a headache. The actors played as if Louis XIV. had been listening; and while they spouted alexandrines, suggestive of the unrolling of a mummy's bands, I was still haunted by the scent of the hawthorn at Jallanges, and repeated to myself the pretty lines of Du Bellay, a fellow-countryman, or a neighbour at least:

More than your marbles hard I love the tender slate,

Than Tiber more the Loire, and France than Rome,

Mine own dear hills than Palatinus' state,

More than the salt sea breeze the fragrantair of home.

Tuesday.—Walked about the town all the morning, stopping in front of the booksellers' shops to look for my book in the windows. *Satyra, Satyra, Satyra! Satyra* and nothing else to be seen everywhere, with a paper slip round it, 'Just out.' Here and there, but very seldom, there would be a poor miserable *God in Nature* tucked away out of sight. When no one was looking I put it on the top of the heap, well in view; but people did not stop. One man did, though, in the Boulevard des Italiens, a negro, a very intelligent-looking fellow. He turned over the pages for five minutes, and then went away without buying the book. I should have liked to present it to him.

Breakfasted in the corner of an English eating-house, and read the papers. Not a word about me, not even an advertisement. Manivet is so careless, very likely he has not so much as sent the orders, though he declared he had. Besides, there are so many new books. Paris is deluged with them. But for all that it is depressing to think that verses, which ran like fire through one's fingers, which seemed, in the feverish delight of writing them, beautiful enough to fill the world with brightness, are more lost now that they are gone into circulation, than when they were but a confused murmuring in the brain of their author. It reminds one of a ball-dress. When it is tried on in the sympathetic family circle, it is expected to outshine and eclipse every dress in the room; but under the blaze of the gas it is lost in the crowd. Well, Herscher is a lucky fellow. He is read and understood. I met ladies carrying snugly under their arms the little yellow volume just issued. Alas, for us poor poets! It is all very well for us to rank ourselves above and beyond the crowd. It is for the crowd, after all, that we write. When Robinson Crusoe was on his desert island, cut off from all the world and without so much as the hope of seeing a sail on the horizon, would he have written verses, even if he had been a poetic genius? Thought about this a great deal as I tramped through the Champs Elysées, lost, like my book, in an unregarding stream.

I was coming back to my hotel, pretty glum, as you may imagine, when on the Quai d'Orsay, just in front of the grass-grown ruin of the Cour des Comptes, I knocked against a big fellow, strolling along in a brown study. 'Hullo, Freydet!' said he. 'Hullo, Védrine!' said I. You'll remember my friend Védrine who, when he was working at Mousseaux, came with his sweet young wife to spend an afternoon at Clos-Jallanges. He is not a bit altered, except that he is a trifle grey at the temples. He held by the hand the fine boy with the beaming eyes, whom you used to admire. His head was erect, his movements slow and eloquent, his whole carriage that of a superior being. A little way behind was Madame Védrine pushing a perambulator, in which was a laughing little girl, born since their visit to Touraine.

'That makes three for her, counting me,' said Védrine, with a wave of his hand towards his wife; and the look of Madame when her eye rests on her husband really does express the tender satisfaction of motherhood; she is like a Flemish Madonna contemplating her Divine Child. Talked a long time, leaning against the parapet of the quay; it did me good to be with these honest folk. That is a man, anyhow, who cares nothing whatever for success, and the public, and the prizes! With his connections (he is cousin to Loisillon and to the Baron d'Huchenard), if he chose—if he just put a little water into his strong wine—he might have orders, and get the Biennial Prize, and be in the Institute in no time. But nothing tempts him, not even fame. 'Fame,' he said, 'I have had a taste of it. I know what it is. When a man's smoking, he sometimes gets his cigar by the wrong end. Well, that's fame: just a cigar with the hot end and ash in your mouth.'

'But, Védrine,' said I, 'if you work neither for fame nor for money—— yes, yes; I know you despise it; but, that being so, I say, why do you take so much trouble?'

'For myself and my personal satisfaction. It's the desire for creation and self-expression.'

Clearly here is a man who would have gone on with his work in the desert island. He is a true artist, ever in quest of a new type, and in the intervals of his labour endeavours by change of material and change of conditions to satisfy his craving for a fresh revelation. He has made pottery, enamels, mosaics, the fine mosaics so much admired in the guard-room at Mousscaux. When the thing is done, the difficulty overcome, he goes on to something else. At the present moment his great idea is to try painting; and the moment he has finished his warrior, a great bronze figure for the Rosen tomb, he intends, as he says, 'to put himself to oil.' His wife always gives her approval, and rides behind him on each of his hobbies. The right wife for an artist taciturn, admiring, saving the grown-up boy from all that might spoil his dream or catch his feet as he goes star-gazing along. She is the sort of woman dear Germaine, to make a man want to be married. If I knew another such, I should certainly bring her to Clos-Jallanges, and I am sure you would love her. But do not be alarmed. There are not many of them; and we shall go on to the end, living just by our two selves, as we do now.

Before we parted we fixed another meeting for Thursday, not at their house at Neuilly, but at the studio on the Quai d'Orsay, where the whole family spend the day together. This studio would seem to be the strangest place. It is in a corner of the old Cour des Comptes. He has got permission to do his work there, in the midst of wild vegetation and mouldering heaps of stone. As I went away I turned to watch them walking along the quay, father, mother, and children, all enveloped in the calm light of the setting sun, which made a halo round them like a Holy Family. Strung together a few lines on the subject in the evening at my hotel; but I am put out by having neighbours, and do not like to spout. I want my large study at Jallanges, with its three windows looking out oh the river and the sloping vineyards.

And now we come to *Wednesday*, the great day and the great event! I will tell you the story in full. I confess that I had been looking forward to my call on the Astiers with much trepidation, which increased to-day as I went up the broad moist steps of the staircase in the Rue de Beaune. What was I going to hear said about my book? Would my old master have had time to glance at it? His opinion means for me so very much. He inspires me still with the same awe as when I was in his class, and in his presence I shall always feel myself a schoolboy. His unerring and impartial judgment must be that of the awarders of the prize. So you may guess the tortures of impatience which I underwent in the master's large study, which he gives up to his wife for her reception.

It's sadly different from the room at the Foreign Office. The table at which he writes is pushed away into a recess behind a great screen covered in old tapestry, which also hides part of the bookshelves. Opposite, in the place of honour, is a portrait of Madame Astier in her young days, wonderfully like her son, and also like old Réhu, whose acquaintance I have just had the honour of making. The portrait has a somewhat depressing air of elegance, cold and polished, like the large uncarpeted room itself, with its sombre curtains and its outlook on a still more sombre courtyard. But in comes Madame Astier, and her friendly greeting brightens all the surroundings. What is there in the air of Paris which preserves the beauty of a woman's face beyond the natural term, like a pastel under its glass? The delicate blonde with her keen eyes looked to me three years younger than when I saw her last. She began by asking after you, and how you were, dearest, showing great interest in our domestic life. Then suddenly she said: 'But your book, let us talk about your book. How splendid! You kept me reading all night.' And she showered upon me well-chosen words of praise, quoted two or three lines with great appropriateness, and assured me that my old master was delighted; he had begged her to tell me so, in case he should not be able to tear himself from his documents.

Red as you know I always am, I must have turned as scarlet as after a hunt dinner. But my joy soon passed away when I heard what the poor woman was led on into confiding to me about their embarrassments. They have lost money; then came Astier's dismissal; now the master works night and day at his historical books, which take so long to construct and cost so much to produce, and then are not bought by the public. Then they have to help old Réhu, the grandfather, who has nothing but his fees for attendance at the Académie; and at his age, ninety-eight, you may imagine the care and indulgence necessary. Paul is a good son, hardworking, and on the road to success, but of course the initial expenses of his profession are tremendous. So Madame Astier conceals their narrow means from him as well as from her husband. Poor dear man! I heard his heavy even step overhead while his wife was stammering out, with trembling lips and hesitating, reluctant words, a request that if I could——

Ah, the adorable woman! I could have kissed the hem of her dress!

Now, my dear sister, you will understand the telegram you must have received a little while ago, and who the £400 were for that I asked for by return of post. I suppose you sent to Gobineau at once. The only reason I did not telegraph direct to him is that, as we 'go shares' in everything, our freaks of liberality ought, like the rest, to be common to both. But it is terrible, is it not, to think of the misery concealed under these brilliant and showy Parisian exteriors?

Five minutes after she had made these distressing disclosures people arrived and the room was full; Madame Astier was conversing with a complete self-possession and an appearance of happiness in voice and manner which made my flesh creep. Madame Loisillon was there, the wife of the Permanent Secretary. She would be much better employed in looking after her invalid than in boring society with the charms of their delightful suite, the most comfortable in the Institute, 'with three rooms more than it had in Villemain's time.' She must have told us this ten times, in the pompous voice of an auctioneer, and in the hearing of a friend living uncomfortably in rooms lately used for a *table d'hôte!*

No fear of such bad taste in Madame Ancelin, a name often to be seen in the Society papers. A good fat round lady, with regular features and high complexion, piping out epigrams, which she picks up and carries round: a friendly creature, it must be allowed. She too had sat up all night reading me. I begin to think it is the regular phrase. She begged me to come to her house whenever I liked. It is one of the three recognised meeting-places of the Académie. Picheral would say that Madame Ancelin, mad on the theatre, welcomes more especially the 'Players,' Madame Astier the 'Mouldies,' while the Duchess Padovani monopolises the 'Dukes,' the aristocracy of the Institute. But really these three haunts of fame and intrigue communicate one with another, for on Wednesday in the Rue de Beaune I saw a whole procession of deities of every description. There was Danjou the writer of plays, Rousse, Boissier, Dumas, de Brétigny, Baron Huchenard of the Inscriptions et Belles-Lettres, and the Prince d'Athis of the Sciences Morales et Politiques. There is a fourth circle in process of formation, collected round Madame Eviza, a Jewess with full cheeks and long narrow eyes, who flirts with the whole Institute and sports its colours; she has green embroideries on the waistcoat of her spring costume, and a little bonnet trimmed with wings *à la* Mercury. She carries her flirtations a little too far. I heard her say to Danjou, whom she was asking to come and see her, 'The attractions of Madame Ancelin's house are for the palate, those of mine for the heart.'

'I require both lodging and board,' was the cold reply of Danjou. Danjou, I believe, covers the heart of a cynic under his hard impenetrable mask and his black stiff thatch, like a shepherd of Latium. Madame Eviza is a fine talker, and is mistress of considerable information; I heard her quoting to the old Baron Huchenard whole sentences from his 'Cave Man,' and discussing Shelley with a boyish magazine writer, neat and solemn, with a pointed chin resting on the top of a high collar.

When I was young it was the fashion to begin with verse-writing, whatever was to follow, whether prose, business, or the bar. Nowadays people begin with literary criticism, generally a study on Shelley. Madame Astier introduced me to this young gentleman, whose views carry weight in the literary world;

but my moustaches and the colour of my skin, as brown as that of a sapper-and-miner, probably failed to please him. We spoke only a few words, while I watched the performance of the candidates and their wives or relatives, who had come to show themselves and to see how the ground lay. Ripault-Babin is very old, and Loisillon cannot last much longer; and around these seats, which must soon be vacant, rages a war of angry looks and poisoned words.

Dalzon the novelist, your favourite, was there; he has a kindly, open, intellectual face, as you would expect from his books. But you would have been sorry to see him cringing and sniggering before a nobody like Brétigny, who has never done anything, but occupies in the Academic the seat reserved for the man of the world, as in the country we keep a place for the poor man in our Twelfth Night festivities. And not only did he court Brétigny, but every Academician who came in. There he was, listening to old Rehu's stories, laughing at Danjou's smallest jokes with the 'counterfeited glee' with which at Louis-le-Grand we rewarded what Védrine used to call 'usher's wit.' All this to bring his twelve votes of last year up to the required majority.

Old Jean Réhu looked in at his granddaughter's for a few minutes, wonderfully fresh and erect, well buttoned up in a long frock coat. He has a little shrivelled face, looking as if it had been in the fire, and a short cottony beard, like moss on an old stone. His eyes are bright and his memory marvellous, but he is deaf, and this depresses him and drives him into long soliloquies about his interesting personal recollections, To-day he told us about the household of the Empress Joséphine at Malmaison; his 'compatriote,' he calls her, both being Creoles from Martinique. He described her, in her muslins and cashmere shawls, smelling of musk so strongly as to take one's breath away, and surrounded with flowers from the colonies. Even in war time these flowers, by the gallantry of the enemy, were allowed to pass the lines of their fleet. He also talked of David's studio, as it was under the Consulate, and did us the painter, rating and scolding his pupils with his mouth all awry and the remains of his dinner in his cheek. After each extract from the long roll of his experience, the patriarch shakes his head solemnly, gazes into space, and says in his firm tones, 'That's a thing that I have seen.' It is his signature, as it were, put at the bottom of the picture to prove it genuine. I ought to say that, with the exception of Dalzon, who pretended to be drinking in his words, I was the only person in the room who attended to the old man's tales. They seemed to me much more worth hearing than the stories of a certain Lavaux, a journalist, or librarian, or something—a dreadful retailer of gossip, whatever else he may be. The moment he came in there was a general cry, 'Ah, here's Lavaux!' and a circle was formed round him at once, all laughing and enjoying themselves. Even the frowning 'deities' revel in his anecdotes. He has a smooth-shaven, quasi-clerical face and goggle eyes. He prefaces all his tales and witticisms with such remarks as 'I was saying to

De Broglie,' or 'Dumas told me the other day,' or 'I have it from the Duchess herself,' backing himself up with the biggest names and drawing his instances from all quarters. He is a pet of the ladies, whom he posts up in all the intrigues of the Académie and the Foreign Office, the world of letters and the world of fashion. He is very intimate with Danjou, and a constant companion of the Prince d'Athis, with whom he came in. Dalion and the young critic of Shelley he patronises; and indeed he exercises a power and authority quite inexplicable to me.

In the medley of stories which he produced from his inexhaustible chops—most of them were riddles to a simple rustic like myself—one only struck me as amusing. It was the mishap which occurred to a young Count Adriani, of the Papal Guard. He was going through Paris, in attendance upon a reverend personage, to take a cardinal's hat and cap to some one or other, and the story is that he left the insignia at the house of some fair lady whom he met with as he left the train, and of whom he knew neither the name nor the address, being, poor young man! a stranger in Paris. So he had to write off to the Papal Court for new specimens of the ecclesiastical headgear to replace the first, which the lady must find entirely superfluous. The best part of the story is that the little Count Adriani is the Nuncio's own nephew, and that at the Duchess's last party—she is called 'the Duchess' in Academic circles just as she is at Mousseaux—he told his adventure quite naively in his broken French. Lavaux imitates it wonderfully.

In the midst of the laughter and the exclamations, 'Charming! Ah, what a man Lavaux is!' etc., I asked Madame Ancelin, who was sitting near me, who Lavaux was, and what he did. The good lady was amazed. 'Lavaux? You don't know him? He is the Duchess's zebra.' Thereupon she departed in pursuit of Danjou, and left me much the wiser! Really Parisian society is a most extraordinary thing; its vocabulary alters every season. Zebra—a zebra—what can it possibly mean? But I began to see that I was staying much too long, and that my old master was not going to appear; it was time I went. I made my way through the chairs to say good-bye to my hostess, and as I passed saw Mademoiselle Moser whimpering before Brétigny's white waistcoat. Poor Moser became a candidate ten years ago, and now has lost all hopes. So he goes nowhere himself, but sends his daughter, a lady of a certain age, not at all pretty, who plays the part of Antigone, climbs up to the top floors, makes herself general messenger and drudge to the Academicians and their wives, corrects proofs, nurses the rheumatic, and spends her forlorn maidenhood in running after the Academic chair which her father will never get. Dressed quietly in black, with an unbecoming bonnet, she stood in the doorway; and near her was Dalzon, very much excited, between two members of the Académie who looked judicial. He was protesting violently and with a choking voice. 'It's not true, it's a shame, I never wrote it!' Here was a mystery; and Madame Astier, who might have enlightened me, was herself engaged in close confabulation with Lavaux and the Prince d'Athis. You must have seen the Prince d'Athis driving about Mousseaux with the Duchess. 'Sammy,' as he is called, is a long, thin, bald man, with stooping shoulders, a crinkled face as white as wax, and a black beard reaching half down his chest, as if his hair, falling from his head, had lodged upon his chin. He never speaks, and when he looks at you seems shocked at your daring to breathe the same air as he. He is high in the service, has a close, mysterious, English air which reminds you that he is Lord Palmerston's great-nephew, and is in high repute at the Institute and on the Quai d'Orsay. He is said to be the only French diplomatist whom Bismarck never dared to look in the face. It is supposed that he will very shortly have one of the great Embassies. Then what will become of the Duchess? To leave Paris and follow him would be a serious thing for a leader of society. And then abroad the world might refuse to accept their equivocal relations, which here are looked upon almost as marriage, in consideration of the propriety of their conduct and their respect for appearances, and considering also the sad state of the Duke, half paralysed and twenty-years older than his wife, who is also his niece.

The Prince, was no doubt discussing these grave matters with Lavaux and Madame Astier when I drew near. A man just arrived in any society, no matter where, soon finds how much he is 'out of it,' He understands neither the phrases current nor the thoughts, and is a nuisance. I was just leaving when that kind Madame Astier called me back, saying, 'Will you not go up and see him? He will be so glad.' So I went up a narrow staircase in the wall to see my old master. I heard his loud voice from the end of the passage, 'Is that you, Fage?'

'No, sir,' said I.

'Why, it's Freydet! Take care; keep your head down.'

It was in fact impossible to stand upright under the sloping roof. What a different place from the Foreign Office, where I last saw him, in a lofty gallery lined with portfolios.

'A kennel, is it not?' said the worthy man with a smile; 'but if you knew what treasures I have here,'—and he waved his hand towards a large set of pigeonholes containing at least 10,000 important MS. documents, collected by him during the last few years. 'There is history in those drawers,' he went on, growing more animated and playing with his magnifying glass; 'history new and authentic, let them say what they will.' But in spite of his words he seemed to me gloomy and uncomfortable. He has been treated very badly. First came that cruel dismissal; and now, as he has continued to publish historical works based on new documents, people say that he has plundered from the Bourbon papers. This calumny was started in the Institute, and is traced to Baron Huchenard, who calls his collection of MSS. 'the first in France,' and hates to be outdone by that of Astier. He tries to revenge himself by treacherous criticisms, launched, like an assegai, from the bush. 'Even my letters of Charles V.,' said Astier, 'even those they want now to prove false. And on what ground if you please? For a mere trifling error, "Maître Rabelais" instead of "Frère Rabelais." As if an emperor's pen never made a slip! It's dishonest, that's what it is!' And, seeing that I shared his indignation, my good old master grasped me by both hands and said, 'But there! enough of these slanders. Madame Astier told you, I suppose, about your book? There is still a little too much for my taste; but I am pleased with it on the whole.' What there is 'too much' of in my poetry is what he calls 'the weed' of the fancy. At school he was always at it, plucking it out, and rooting it up. Now, dear Germaine, attend. I give you the last part of our conversation, word for word.

I. Do you think, sir, that I have any chance of the Boisseau prize?

M. A. After such a book as that, my dear boy, it is not a prize you deserve, but a seat. Loisillon is hard hit; Ripault cannot last much longer. Don't move; leave it to me; henceforward I look upon you as a candidate.

I don't know what I said in reply. I was so confused that I feel still as if I were dreaming. Me, me, in the Académie Française! Take good care of yourself, dearest, and get your naughty legs well again; for you must come to Paris on the great occasion, and see your brother, with his sword at his side and his green coat embroidered with palms, take his place among all the greatest men of France! Why, it makes me dizzy now! So I send you a kiss, and am off to bed.

Your affectionate brother,

ABEL DE FREYDET.

You may imagine that among all these doings I have quite forgotten the seeds, matting, shrubs, and all the rest of my purchases. But I will see about them soon, as I shall stay here some time. Astier-Réhu advised me to say nothing, but to go about in Academic society. To show myself and be seen is the great point.

CHAPTER IV.

'Don't trust them, my dear Freydet. I know that trick; it's the recruiting trick. The fact is, these people feel that their day is past, and that under their cupola they are beginning to get mouldy. The Académie is a taste that is going out, an ambition no longer in fashion. Its success is only apparent. And indeed for the last few years the distinguished company has given up waiting at home for custom, and comes down into the street to tout. Everywhere, in society, in the studios, at the publishers', in the greenroom, in every literary or artistic centre, you will find the Recruiting-Academician, smiling on young budding talent. "The Académie has its eye on you, my young friend." If a man has got some reputation, and has just written his third or fourth book, like you, then the invitation takes a more direct form. "Don't forget us, my dear fellow; now's your time." Or perhaps, brusquely, with a friendly scolding, "Well, so you don't mean to be one of us." When it's a man in society who is to be caught a translator of Ariosto or a writer of amateur plays, there is a gentler and more insinuating way of playing off the trick. And if our fashionable writer protests that he is not a gun of sufficient calibre, the Recruiting-Academidan brings out the regular phrase, that "the Académie is a club." Lord bless us, how useful that phrase has been! "The Académie is a club, and its admission is not only for the work, but the worker." Meantime the Recruiting-Academician is welcomed everywhere, made much of, asked to dinner and other entertainments. He becomes a parasite, fawned upon by those whose hopes he arouses—and is careful to maintain.'

But at this point kind-hearted Freydet protested indignantly. Never would his old master lend himself to such base uses. Védrine shrugged his shoulders: 'Why, the worst of the lot is the recruiter who is sincere and disinterested. He believes in the Académie; his whole life is centred in the Académie; and when he says to you, "If you only knew the joy of it," with a smack of the tongue like a man eating a ripe peach, he is saying what he really means, and so his bait is the more alluring and dangerous. But when once the hook has been swallowed and struck, then the Academician takes no more notice of the victim, but leaves him to struggle and dangle at the end of the line. You are an angler; well, when you have taken a fine perch or a big pike, and you drag it along behind your boat, what do you call that?'

'Drowning your fish.'

'Just so. Well, look at Moser! Does he not look like a drowned fish? He has been carried along in tow for these ten years. And there's De Salèle, and Guérineau, and I don't know how many others, who have even given up struggling.'

'But still people do get into the Académie sooner or later.'

'Not those once taken in tow. And suppose a man does succeed, where's the good? What does it bring you? Money? Not as much as your hay-crop. Fame? Yes, a hole-and-corner fame within a space no bigger than your hat. It would be something if it gave talent, but those who have talent lose it when once they get inside and are chilled by the air of the place. The Académie is a club, you know; so there is a tone that must be adopted, and things which must be left unsaid, or watered down. There's an end to originality, an end to bold neck-or-nothing strokes. The liveliest spirits never move for fear of tearing their green coats. It is like putting children into their Sunday clothes and saying "Amuse yourselves, my dears, but don't get dirty." And they do amuse themselves, I can tell you. Of course, they have the adulation of the Academical taverns, and their fair hostesses. But what a bore it is! I speak from experience, for I have let myself be dragged there occasionally. I can say with old Réhu, "That's a thing I have seen." Silly pretentious women have favoured me with ill-digested scraps from magazine articles, coming out of their little beaks like the written remarks of characters in a comic paper. I have heard fat, good natured Madame Ancelin, a woman as stupid as anything, cackle with admiration at the epigrams of Danjou, regular stage manufacture, about as natural as the curling of his wig.'

Here was a shock for Freydet: Danjou, the shepherd of Latium, had a wig!

'A half-wig, what they call a *breton*. At Madame Astier's,' he went on, 'I have gone through lectures on ethnology enough to kill a hippopotamus; and at the table of the Duchess, the severe and haughty Duchess, I have seen that old monkey Laniboire, seated in the place of honour, do and say things for which, if he had not been a "deity," he would have been turned out of the house, with a good-bye in her Grace's characteristic style. And the joke is, that it was she who got him into the Académie. She has seen that very Laniboire at her feet, begging humbly, piteously, importunately, to get himself elected, "Elect him," she said to my cousin Loisillon, "elect him, do; and then I shall be rid of him." And now she looks up to him as a god; he is always next her at table; and her contempt has changed into an abject admiration. It is like a savage, falling down and quaking before the idol he has carved. I know what Academic society is, with all its foolish, ludicrous, mean little intrigues. You want to get into it! What for, I should like to know? You have the happiest life in the world. Even I, who am not set upon anything, was near envying you, when I saw you with your sister at Clos-Jallanges: a perfect house on a hill-side, airy rooms, chimney-corners big enough to get into, oakwoods, cornfields, vineyards, river; the life of a country gentleman, as it is painted in the novels of Tolstoi; fishing and shooting, a pleasant library, a neighbourhood not too dull, the peasants reasonably honest; and to prevent you from growing callous in the midst of such unbroken satisfaction, your companion, suffering and smiling, full of life and keenness, poor thing, in her arm-chair, delighted to listen, when you came in from a ride and read her a good sonnet, genuine poetry, fresh from nature, which you had pencilled on your saddle, or lying flat in the grass, as we are now—only without this horrible din of waggons and trumpets.'

Védrine stopped perforce. Some heavy drays, loaded with iron, and shaking ground and houses as they went by, a piercing alarum from the neighbouring barracks, the harsh screech of a steam-tug's whistle, an organ, and the bells of Sainte-Clotilde, all united at the moment, as from time to time the noises of a great town will do, in a thundering *tutti*; and the outrageous babel, close to the ear, contrasted strangely with the natural field of grass and weed, overshadowed by tall trees, in which the two old classmates were enjoying their smoke and their familiar chat.

On the ruined terrace of the old Cour des Comptes   Page 72.

It was at the corner of the Quai d'Orsay and the Rue de Bellechasse, on the ruined terrace of the old Cour des Comptes, now occupied by sweet wild plants, like a clearing in the forest at the coming of spring. Clumps of lilac past the flowering and dense thickets of plane and maple grew all along the balustrades, which were loaded with ivy and clematis: and within this verdant screen the pigeons lighted, the bees wandered, and under a beam of yellow light might be seen the calm and handsome profile of Madame Védrine, nursing her youngest, while the eldest threw stones at the numerous cats, grey, black, yellow, and tabby, which might be called the tigers of this Parisian jungle.

'And as we are talking of your poetry, you will wish me to speak my mind, won't you, old boy? Well, I have only just looked into your last book, but it has not that smell of bluebells and thyme that I found in the others. Your "God in Nature" has rather a flavour of the Academic bay; and I am much afraid you have made a sacrifice of your "woodnotes wild," you know, and thrown them, by way of pass-money, into the mouth of *Crocodilus*.'

This nickname 'Crocodilus,' turning up at the bottom of Védrine's schoolboy recollections, amused them for a moment. They pictured once more Astier-Réhu at his desk, with streaming brow, his cap well on the back of his head, and a yard of red ribbon relieved against the black of his gown, emphasising with the solemn movements of his wide sleeves the well-worn joke from Racine or Molière, or his own rounded periods in the style of Vic't-d'Azir, whose seat in the Académie he eventually filled. Then Freydet, vexed with himself for laughing at his old master, began to praise his work as an historian. What a mass of original documents he had brought out of their dust!

'There's nothing in that,' retorted Védrine with unqualified contempt. In his view, the most interesting documents in hands of a fool had no more meaning than has the great book of humanity itself, when consulted by a stupid novelist. The gold all turns into dead leaves. 'Look here,' he went on with rising animation, 'a man is not to be called an historian because he has expanded unpublished material into great octavo volumes, which are shelved unread among the books of information, and should be labelled, "For external application only. Shake the bottle." It is only French frivolity that attaches a serious value to compilations like those. The English and Germans despise us. "Ineptissimus vir Astier-Réhu," says Mommsen somewhere or other in a note.'

'Yes, and it was you, you heartless fellow, who made the poor man read out the note before the whole class.'

'And a terrible jaw he gave me. It was nearly as bad as when one day I got so tired of hearing him tell us that the will was a lever, a lever with which you might lift anything anywhere, that I answered him from my place in his own voice: "Could you fly with it, sir—could you fly with it?"'

Freydet, laughing, abandoned his defence of the historian, and began to plead for Astier-Réhu as a teacher. But Védrine went off again.

'A teacher! What is he? A poor creature who has spent his life in "weeding" hundreds of brains, or, in plain terms, destroying whatever in them was original and natural, all the living germs which it is the first duty of an educator to nourish and protect. To think how the lot of us were hoed, and stubbed, and grubbed! One or two did not take kindly to the process, but the old fellow went at it with his tools and his nails, till he made us all as neat and as flat as a schoolroom bench. And see the results of his workmanship! A few rebels, like Herscher, who, from hatred of the conventional, go for exaggeration and ugliness, or like myself, who, thanks to that old ass, love roughness and contortion so much, that my sculpture, they say, is "like a bag of walnuts." And the rest of them levelled, scraped, and empty!'

'And pray, what of me?' said Freydet, with an affected despair.

'Oh, as for you, Nature has preserved you so far; but look out for yourself if you let Crocodilus clip you again. And to think that we have public schools to provide us with this sort of pedagogue, and that we reward him with endowments, and honours, and a place (save the mark) in the National Institute!'

Stretched at his ease in the long grass, with his head on his arm and waving a fern, which he used as a sun-screen, Védrine calmly uttered these strong remarks, without the slightest play of feature in his broad face, pale and puffy like that of an Indian idol. Only the tiny laughing eyes broke the general expression of dreamy indolence.

His companion was shocked at such treatment of what he was accustomed to respect 'But,' he said, 'if you are such an enemy of the father, how do you manage to be such a friend of the son?'

'I am no more one than the other. I look upon Paul Astier, with his imperturbable *sang-froid* and his pretty-miss complexion, as a problem. I should like to live long enough to see what becomes of him.'

'Ah, Monsieur de Freydet,' said Madame Védrine, joining in the conversation from the place where she sat, 'if you only knew what a tool he makes of my husband! All the restorations at Mousseaux, the new gallery towards the river, the concert-room, the chapel, all were done by Védrine. And the Rosen tomb too. He will only be paid for the statue; but the whole thing is really his—conception, arrangement, everything.'

'There, there, that will do,' said the artist quietly. 'As for Mousseaux, the young fellow would certainly have been hard put to it to rediscover a fragment of the design under the layers of rubbish that the architects have been depositing there for the last thirty years. But the neighbourhood was charming, the Duchess amiable and not at all tiresome, and there was friend Freydet, whom I had found out at Clos-Jallanges. Besides, the truth is I have too many ideas, and am just tormented with them. To relieve me of a few is to do me a real service. My brain is like a railway junction, where the engines are getting up steam on all the lines at once. The young man saw that. He has not many ideas. So he purloins mine, and brings them before the public, quite certain that I shall not protest But he does not take me in. Don't I know when he is going to filch! He preserves his little indifferent air, with no expression in his eyes, until suddenly there comes a little nervous twitch at the corner of his mouth. Done! Nabbed! I have no doubt he thinks to himself, "Good Lord, what a simpleton Védrine is!" He has not the least notion that I watch him and enjoy his little game. Now,' said the sculptor as he got up, 'I will show you my Knight, and then we will go over the ruin. It is worth looking at, you will find.'

Passing from the terrace into the building, they mounted a semicircle of steps and went through a square room, formerly the apartment of the Secretary to the Conseil d'Etat. It had no floor and no ceiling, all the upper storeys had fallen through and showed the blue sky between the huge iron girders, now twisted by the fire, which had divided the floors. In a corner, against a wall to which were attached long iron pipes overgrown with creepers, lay in three pieces a model of the Rosen tomb, buried in nettles and rubbish.

'You see,' said Védrine, 'or rather you can't see.' And he began to describe the monument. The little Princess's conception of a tomb was not easy to come up to. Several things had been tried—reminiscences of Egyptian, Assyrian, and Ninevite monuments—before deciding on Védrine's plan, which would raise an outcry among architects, but was certainly impressive. A soldier's tomb: an open tent with the canvas looped back, disclosing within, before an altar, the wide low sarcophagus, modelled on a camp bedstead, on which lay the good Knight Crusader, fallen for King and Creed; beside him his broken sword, and at his feet a great greyhound.

The difficulty of the work and the hardness of the Dalmatian granite, which the Princess insisted on having, had obliged Védrine to take mallet and chisel himself and to work like an artisan under the tarpaulin at the cemetery. Now, at last, after much time and trouble, the canopy was up, 'and that young rascal, Astier, will get some credit from it,' added the sculptor with a smile in which was no touch of bitterness. Then he lifted up an old carpet hanging over a hole in the wall, which had once been a door, and led Freydet into the huge ruined hall which served him for a studio, roofed with planks and decorated with mats and hangings.

It looked with all its litter like a barn, or rather a yard under cover, for in a sun-lit corner climbed a fine fig-tree with its twining branches and elegant leaves, while close by was the bulk of a broken stove, garlanded with ivy and honeysuckle, so as to resemble an old well. Here he had been working for two years, summer and winter, in spite, of the fogs of the neighbouring river and the bitter cold winds, without a single sneeze (his own expression), having the healthful strength of the great artists of the Renaissance, as well as their large mould of countenance and fertile imagination. Now he was as weary of sculpture and architecture as if he had been writing a tragedy. The moment his statue was delivered and paid for, wouldn't he be off, nursery and all, for a journey up the Nile in a dahabeeah, and paint and paint from morning to night! While he spoke he moved away a stool and a bench, and led his friend up to a huge block in the rough. 'There's my warrior. Frankly now, what do you think of him?'

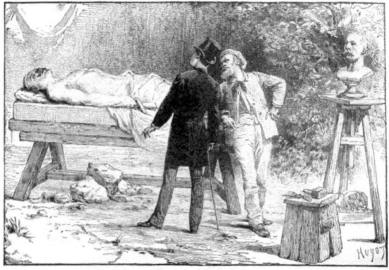

"There's my warrior." Page 79.

Freydet was somewhat startled and amazed at the colossal dimensions of the sleeping hero. The scale was magnified in proportion to the height of the canopy, and the roughness of the plaster exaggerated the anatomical emphasis characteristic of Védrine. Rather than smooth away the force, he gives his work an unfinished earthy surface, as of something still in the rock. But as the spectator gazed and began to grasp, the huge form became distinct with that impressive and attractive power which is the essence of fine art.

'Splendid!' he exclaimed, with the tone of sincerity. The other winked his merry little eyes, and said:

'Not at first sight, eh? My style does not take till you are accustomed to it; and I do not feel sure of the Princess, when she comes to look at this ugly fellow.'

Paul Astier was to bring her in a few days, as soon as it had been rubbed down and smoothed and was ready to go to the foundry; and the sculptor looked forward to the visit with some uncertainty, knowing the taste of great ladies, as it is displayed in the stereotyped chatter, which at the Salon on five-shilling days runs up and down the picture-rooms, and breaks out round the sculpture. Oh, what hypocrisy it is! The only genuine thing about them is the spring costume, which they have provided to figure on this particular occasion.

'And altogether, old fellow,' continued Védrine, as he drew his friend out of the studio, 'of all the affectations of Paris, of all the hypocrisies of society, the most shameless, the most amusing, is the pretended taste for art. It's enough to make you die of laughing; everyone performing a mummery, which imposes on nobody. And music, the same! You should just see them at the Pop!'

They went down a long arcaded passage, full of the same odd vegetation, sown there by all the winds of heaven, breaking out in green from the hard-beaten ground, and peeping among the paintings on the shrivelled and smoke-blackened walls, Presently they came to the principal court, formerly gravelled, but now a field, in which were mingled wild grasses, plantain, pimpernel, groundsel, and myriads of tiny stems and heads. In the middle, fenced off with boards, was a bed of artichokes, strawberries, and pumpkins, looking like the garden of some squatter at the edge of a virgin forest; and, to complete the illusion, beside it was a little building of brick.

'It's the bookbinder's garden, and that is his shop,' said Védrine, pointing to a board over the half-open door, displaying in letters a foot long the inscription,

 ALBIN FAGE,

 Bookbinding in all its branches.

Fage had been bookbinder to the Cour des Comptes and the Conseil d'Etat, and having obtained leave to keep his lodge, which had escaped the fire, was now, with the exception of the caretaker, the sole tenant of the building. 'Let us go in for a minute,' said Védrine; 'you will find him a remarkable specimen.' He went nearer and called, 'Fage! Fage!' but the humble workshop was empty. In front of the window was the binder's table, on which, among a heap of parings, lay his shears. Under a press were some green ledgers capped with copper. Strange to remark, everything in the room—the sewing-press, the tressel-table, the empty chair in front of it, the shelves piled with books, and even the shaving-mirror hung upon the latch—was on a diminutive scale, adapted to the height and reach of a child of twelve years old. It might have been taken for the house of a dwarf, or of a bookbinder of Lilliput.

'He is a humpback,' whispered Védrine to Frey-det, 'and a lady's man into the bargain, all scent and pomade.' A horrible smell like a hairdresser's shop, otto of roses and macassar, mingled with the stifling fumes, of glue. Védrine called once more in the direction of the back of the shop where the bedroom was; then they left, Freydet chuckling at the idea of a humpbacked Lovelace.

'Perhaps he's at a tryst,' he said.

'You are pleased to laugh; but, my dear fellow, the humpback is on the best of terms with all the beauties of Paris, if one may believe the testimony of his bedroom walls, which are covered with photographs bearing the owners' names, and headed "To Albin," "To my dear little Fage." There is never any lady to be seen here, but he sometimes comes and tells me about his fine octavo, or his pretty little duodecimo, as he calls his conquests, according to their height and size.'

'And he is ugly, you say?'

'A perfect monster.'

'And no money?'

'A poor little bookbinder and worker in cardboard, living on his work and his bit of a garden, but very intelligent and learned, with a marvellous memory. We shall probably find him wandering about in some corner of the building. He is a great dreamer is little Fage, like all sentimentalists.—This way, but look where you step; there are some awkward places.'

They were going up a huge staircase, of which the lower steps still remained, as did the balustrade, rusty, split, and in places twisted. Then suddenly they turned off by a fragile wooden bridge, resting on the supports of the staircase, between high walls on which were dimly visible the remains of huge frescoes, cracked, decayed, and blackened with soot, the hind legs of a horse, a woman's torso undraped, with inscriptions almost illegible on panels that had lost their gilding, 'Meditation,' 'Silence,' 'Trade uniting the nations of the world.'

On the first floor a long gallery with a vaulted roof, as in the amphitheatre at Aries or Nîmes, stretched away between smoke-stained walls, covered with huge fissures, remains of plaster and iron work, and tangled vegetation. At the entrance to this passage was inscribed on the wall, 'Corridor des Huissiers.' On the next floor they found much the same thing, only that here, the roof having given way, the gallery was nothing but a long terrace of brambles climbing up to the undestroyed arcades and falling down in disordered waving festoons to the level of the courtyard. From this second floor could be seen the roofs of the neighbouring houses, the whitewashed walls of the barracks in the Rue de Poitiers, and the tall plane trees of the Padovani mansion, with the rooks' nests, abandoned till the winter, swinging in their top branches. Below was the deserted court in full sunlight, with the little garden and tiny house of the bookbinder.

'Just look, old boy, there's a good lot of it here,' said Védrine to his friend, pointing to the wild exuberant vegetation of every species which ran riot over the whole building. 'If Crocodilus saw all these weeds, what a rage he would be in!' Suddenly he started, and said, 'Well, I never!'

At this moment, near the bookbinder's house below, came into sight Astier-Réhu, recognisable by his long frock-coat of a metallic green and his large wide 'topper.' Most people in the neighbourhood knew this hat, which, set on the back of a grey curly head, distinguished, like a halo, the hierarch of erudition. It was Crocodilus himself!

He was talking earnestly to a man of very small stature, whose bare head shone with hair-oil, and whose tight-fitting, light-coloured coat showed in all its elegance the deformity of his back. Their words were not audible, but Astier seemed much excited. He brandished his stick and bent himself forward over the face of the little creature, who for his part was perfectly calm, and stood, as if his mind was made up, with his two large hands behind him folded under his hump.

'The cripple does work for the Institute, does he?' said Freydet, who remembered now that his master had uttered the name of Fage. Védrine did not answer. He was watching the action of the two men, whose conversation at this moment suddenly stopped, the humpback going into his house with a gesture which seemed to say, 'As you please,' while Astier with angry strides made for the gate of the building towards the Rue de Lille, then paused, turned back to the shop, went in, and closed the door behind him.

'It's odd,' muttered the sculptor. 'Why did Fage never tell me? What a mysterious little fellow it is! But I dare say they have the same taste for the "octavo" and the "duodecimo"!'

'For shame, Védrine!'

The visit done, Freydet went slowly up the Quai d'Orsay, thinking about his book and his aspirations towards the Académie, which had received a severe shock from the home truths he had been hearing. How like the man is to the boy! How soon the character is in its essence complete! After an interval of twenty-five years, beneath the wrinkles and grey hairs and other changes, with which life disguises the outer man, the schoolfellows found each other just what they were when they sat together in class: one wilful, high-spirited, rebellious; the other obedient and submissive, with a tendency to indolence, which had been fostered by his quiet country life. After all Védrine was perhaps right. Even if he was sure of succeeding, was the thing worth the trouble? He was particularly anxious about his invalid sister, who, while he went about canvassing, must be left all alone at Clos-Jallanges. A few days' absence had already made her feel nervous and low, and the morning's post had brought a miserable letter.

He was by this time passing before the dragoon barracks; and his attention was caught by the appearance of the paupers, waiting on the other side of the street for the distribution of the remains of the soup. They had come long before for fear of missing their turn, and were seated on the benches or standing in a line against the parapet of the quay. Foul and grimy, with the hair and beard of human dogs, and dressed in the filthiest rags, they waited like a herd, neither moving nor speaking to each other, but peering into the great barrack-yard to catch the arrival of the porringers and the adjutant's signal to come up. It was horrible to see in the brilliant sunlight the silent row of savage eyes and hungry faces, fixed with the same animal look upon the wide-open gate.

'What are you doing there, my dear boy?' said a voice, and Astier-Réhu, in high spirits, took his pupil's arm. The poet pointed to the pathetic group on the opposite pavement. 'Ah, yes,' said the historian, 'Ah, yes.' He had in truth no eyes for anything outside books, nor any direct and personal perception of the facts of life. Indeed, from the way in which he took Freydet off, saying as he did so, 'You may as well go with me as far as the Institute,' it was clear that he did not approve the habit of mooning in the streets when you ought to be better employed. Leaning gently on his favourite's arm, he began to tell him of his rapturous delight at having chanced upon a most astonishing discovery, a letter about the Académie from the Empress Catherine to Diderot, just in time for his forthcoming address to the Grand-Duke. He meant to read the letter at the meeting and perhaps to present his Highness, in the name of the Society, with the original in the handwriting of his ancestress. Baron Huchenard would burst with envy.

'And, by the way, about my Charles the Fifths, you know! It's absolutely false. Here is something to confute the old backbiter,' and he clapped with his thick short hand a heavy leather pocket-book. He was so happy that he tried to arouse an answering happiness in Freydet by leading the conversation to the topic of yesterday—his candidature for the first place in the Académie that should be vacant. It would be delightful when the master and the scholar sat together under the dome! 'And you will find how pleasant it is, and how comfortable. It cannot be imagined till you are there.' The moment of entrance, he seemed to say, put an end to the miseries of life. At that threshold they might beat in vain. You soared into a region of peace and light, above envy, above criticism, blessed for ever! All was won, and nothing left to desire. Ah, the Académie! Those who spoke ill of it spoke in ignorance, or in jealousy, because they could not get in. The apes, the dunces!

His strong voice rose till it made everyone turn as he went along the quay. Some recognised him and mentioned his name. The booksellers and the vendors of engravings and curiosities, standing at their stalls, and accustomed to see him go by at his regular hours, stepped back and bowed respectfully.

'Freydet, look at that,' said his master, pointing to the Palais Mazarin, to which they had now come. 'There it is! There's the Institute as I saw it on the Didot books when I was a lad. I said to myself then, "I will get into that;" and I have got in. Now, my boy, it is your turn to use your will. Good luck to you.' He stepped briskly in at the gate to the left of the main building, and went on into a series of large paved courts, silent and majestic, his figure throwing a lengthening shadow upon the ground.

He disappeared; but Freydet was gazing still, struck motionless. And on his kindly round brown face and in his soft, full-orbed eyes was the same expression as had been on the visages of the human dogs who waited before the barracks for their soup. Henceforward, whenever he looked at the Institute, that expression would always come over his face.

CHAPTER V.

A select reception at the Padovani mansion. Page 90.

It was the evening of a great dinner, to be followed by a select reception, at the Padovani mansion. The Grand-Duke Leopold was entertaining at the table of his 'respected friend,' as he called the Duchess, some members selected from the various departments of the Institute, and so making his return to the five Académies for their courteous reception of him and for the complimentary harangue of the President. Diplomatic society was, as usual, well represented at the house of a lady whose husband had been Ambassador; but the Institute had the chief place, and the arrangement of the guests showed the object of the dinner. The Grand-Duke, seated opposite the hostess, had Madame Astier on his right, and on his left the Countess Foder, wife of the First Secretary of the Finnish Embassy, acting as Ambassador. On the right of the Duchess sat Léonard Astier, and on her left Monsignor Adriani, the Papal Nuncio. Then came successively Baron Huchenard, representing the Inscriptions et Belles-Lettres; Mourad Bey, the Ambassador of the Porte; Delpech the chemist, Member of the Académie des Sciences; the Belgian Minister; Landry the musician, of the Beaux-Arts; Danjou the dramatist, one of Picherals 'Players'; and, lastly, the Prince d'Athis, whose twofold claims to distinction as diplomatist and Member of the Académie des Sciences Morales et Politiques combined the characteristics of the two sets in the circle. At the ends of the table were the General acting as Aide-de-camp to His Highness, the young Count Adriani, nephew of the Nuncio, and Lavaux, whose presence was indispensable at every social gathering.

The feminine element was lacking in charm. The Countess Foder, red-haired, small, and lively, enveloped in lace to the tip of her little pointed nose, looked like a squirrel with a cold in its head. Baroness Huchenard, a lady of no particular age and with a moustache, produced the effect of a very fat old gentleman in a low dress. Madame Astier, in a velvet dress partly open at the neck, a present from the Duchess, had sacrificed on the altar of friendship the pleasure she would have had in displaying her arms and shoulders, the remains of her beauty; and thanks to this delicate attention the Duchess Padovani looked as if she were the only woman at dinner. The Duchess is elegantly dressed, tall and fair, with a tiny head and fine eyes of a golden hazel colour—eyes whose shifting haughty glance, from under long dark brows almost meeting, shows their power of expressing kindness, affection, or anger. Her nose is short, her mouth emotional and sensitive, and her complexion has the brilliancy of a young woman's, owing to her custom of sleeping in the afternoon when she is going out in the evening or receiving friends at her own house. A long residence abroad at Vienna, St. Petersburg, and Constantinople, where as the wife of the French Ambassador it had been her duty to set the fashion to French society, has left in her manners a certain air of superior information, which the ladies of Paris find it hard to forgive. She talks graciously to them as though they were foreigners, and explains things to them which they understand as well as she. In her house in the Rue de Poitiers the Duchess still acts as though representing Paris among the Kurds. It is the sole defect of this noble and splendid lady.

Though there were, so to speak, no women, no bright dresses showing arms and shoulders and breaking the monotony of black coats with a blaze of jewels and flowers, still the table was not without colour. There was the violet cassock of the Nuncio with his broad silk sash, the purple *Chechia* of Mourad Bey, and the red tunic of the Papal Guard with its gold collar, blue embroideries, and gold braid on the breast, decorated also with the huge brilliant cross of the Legion of Honour, which the young Italian had received that very morning, the President thinking it proper to reward the successful delivery of the Cardinal's hat. Scattered about, too, were ribbons green, blue, and red, and the silvery gleam and sparkling stars of decorations and orders.

Ten o'clock. The dinner is almost over, but not one of the flowers elaborately arranged round plates and dishes has been disturbed, there have been no raised voices or animated gestures. Yet the fare is excellent at the Padovani mansion, one of the few houses in Paris where they still have wine. The dinner betrays the presence in the house of an epicure, and the epicure is not the Duchess, who, like all leaders of French fashion, thinks the dinner good if she has on a becoming dress and the table is carefully and tastefully decorated. No; the epicure is the lady's humble servant, the Prince d'Athis, a man of cultivated palate and fastidious appetite, spoilt by club cooking and not to be satisfied by silver plate or the sight of fine liveries and irreproachable white calves. It is for his sake that the fair Antonia admits among her occupations the care of the *menu*, it is for him that she provides highly seasoned dishes and fiery wines of Burgundy, which it must be admitted have not on this particular occasion dispelled the coldness of the guests.

At dessert there is the same deadness, stiffness, and restraint that marked the first course; hardly has a tinge of colour touched the ladies' cheeks or noses. It is a dinner of wax dolls, official,-magnificent, with the magnificence which comes chiefly of ample room, lofty ceilings, and seats placed so far apart as to preclude all friendly touching of chairs. A gloomy chilly underground feeling separates the guests, in spite of the soft breath of the June night floating in from the gardens through the half-open shutters and gently swelling the silk blinds. The conversation is distant and constrained, the lips scarcely move and have an unmeaning smile. Not a remark is real, not one makes its way to the mind of the hearer; they are as perfectly artificial as the sweetmeats among which they are dropped. The speeches, like the faces, are masked, and it is lucky they are, for if at this moment the mask were to be taken off, and the true thoughts disclosed, how dismayed the noble company would be!

The Grand-Duke, who has a broad pale face framed by extra-black trim round whiskers, just such a royal personage as you see in an illustrated paper, is questioning Baron Huchenard with much interest about his recent book, and thinking to himself: 'Oh dear, how this learned gentleman does bore me with his primitive dwellings! How much better off I should be at *Roxelane*, where sweet little Déa is dancing in the ballet! The author of *Roxelane* is here, I understand, but he is a middle-aged man, very ugly and very dull. And to think of the ankles of little Déa!'

The Nuncio, who has an intellectual face of the Roman type, large nose, thin lips, black eyes and sallow complexion, has leant on one side to listen to the history of the habitations of Man. He is looking at his nails, which shine like shells, and is thinking: 'At the Embassy this morning I ate a delicious *misto fritto* and I haven't got rid of it. Gioachimo has pulled my sash too tight; I wish I could get away from the table.'

The Turkish Ambassador, thick-lipped, yellow, and coarse, with his fez over his eyes and a poke in his neck, is filling the glass of Baroness Huchenard and saying, 'How disgusting in these Westerns to bring their women into society, when they are as dilapidated as this! I had rather be impaled right off than exhibit that fat creature as my wife.' The Baroness is thanking His Excellency with a mincing smile, which covers the thought 'This Turk is a revolting beast.'

Nor are Madame Astier's spoken thoughts any more in harmony with her internal reflections: 'I only hope Paul will not have forgotten to go for grandpapa. It will be an effective scene when the old man comes in, supported on the arm of his great-grandson. Perhaps we may get an order out of His Highness.' Then, as she looks affectionately at the Duchess, she thinks: 'She is looking very handsome this evening. Some good news no doubt about the promised Embassy. Make the best of your time, my dear; in a month Sammy will be married.'

Madame Astier is not mistaken. The Grand-Duke on arriving announced to his 'respected friend' the President's promise to appoint D'Athis within the next few days. The Duchess is filled with à repressed delight, which shines through as it were, and gives her a marvellous brilliance. To this height she has raised the man of her choice! And already she is making plans for removing her own establishment to St. Petersburg, to a mansion not too far from the Embassy; while the Prince, with his pale sunk cheeks and rapt look—the look whose penetration Bismarck could never sustain—checks upon his contemptuous lips the smile at once mysterious and dogmatic, compounded of diplomacy and learning, and thinks to himself: 'Now Colette must make up her mind. She could come out there, we could be married quietly at the Chapelle des Pages, and all would be done and past recall before the Duchess heard of it.'

And thus many a reflection ludicrously inappropriate to the occasion passes from guest to guest under the same safe wrapper. Here you have the pleased beatitude of Léonard Astier, who has this very morning received the order of Stanislas (second class), as a return for presenting to His Highness a copy of his speech with the autograph letter of Catherine pinned to the first page and very ingeniously worked into the complimentary address. This letter was the great thing at the meeting, had been mentioned in the papers two days running, and heard of all over Europe, giving to the name of Astier, to his collection, and to his work, that astounding and disproportionate echo with which the Press now multiplies any passing event. Now Baron Huchenard might do his best to bite, might mumble as he pleased in his insinuating tones,

'I ask you, my dear colleague, to observe.' But no one would listen. And the 'first collector in France' was perfectly aware of it. See what a savage look he casts at his dear colleague in the pauses of his scientific harangue! What venom is in every deeply graven hollow of his porous, pumice-stone face!

Handsome Danjou is also furious, but for other reasons than the Baron. The Duchess has not asked his wife. The exclusion is painful to his feelings as a husband, a part of a man no less sensitive than the original *ego*; and in spite of his wish to shine before the Grand-Duke, the witticisms as good as new, which he was prepared with, will not go off. Another who does not feel comfortable is Delpech the chemist, whom His Highness, when he was presented, congratulated on his interpretation of the cuneiform character, confounding him with his colleague of the Académie des Inscriptions. It should be said that, with the exception of Danjou, whose comedies are popular abroad, the Grand-Duke has never heard of any of the Academic celebrities introduced to him at this dinner. Lavaux this very morning, in concert with the Aide-de-camp, arranged a set of cards bearing each the name of a guest with the titles of his principal works. The fact that His Highness did not get more confused among the list than he did proves much presence of mind and an Imperial memory. But the evening is not over, and other stars of learning are about to appear. Already may be heard the muffled rolling of wheels and the slamming of carriages putting down at the door. The Prince will have more chances yet.

Meanwhile, in a weak, slow voice, seeking for words and losing half of them in his nose, His Highness is discussing with Astier-Réhu a point of history suggested by the letter of Catherine II. The ewers have long completed the round, no one is eating or drinking any more, no one is even breathing, for fear of interrupting the conversation; all the company are in a hypnotic trance, and—a remarkable effect of lévitation—are literally hanging upon the Imperial lips. Suddenly the august nose is silent, and Léonard Astier, who has made a show of resistance in order to improve the effect of his opponent's victory, throws up his arms like broken foils and says with an air of surrender, 'Ah, Your Highness has mated me!' The charm is broken, the company feel the ground under them again, everyone rises in a slight flutter of applause, the doors are thrown open, the Duchess takes the arm of the Grand-Duke, Mourad Bey that of the Baroness, and while, with a sound of sweeping-dresses and chairs pushed Lack, the assembly files out, Firmin, the *maître d'hôtel*, solemn and dignified, is privately doing a sum. 'In any other house this dinner would have been worth to me forty pounds: with her, I'll warrant, it won't be a dozen;' to which he adds aloud, as if he would spit his anger upon Her Grace's train, 'Grr! you hag!'

'With Your Highness's permission—my grandfather, M. Jean Réhu, the oldest member in the whole Institute.'

The high notes of Madame Astier's voice ring in the great drawing-room, not nearly filled, though the guests invited to the reception have already arrived.

She speaks very loud to make grandpapa understand to whom he is being introduced and answer accordingly. Old Réhu looks grand, drawing up his tall figure and still carrying high his little Creole face darkened and cracked with age. Paul, graceful and pleasing, supports him on one side, his granddaughter on the other; Astier-Réhu is behind. The family makes a sentimental group in the style of Greuze. It would look well on one of the pale-coloured tapestries with which the room is decorated, tapestries—a strange thing to think of—scarcely older than Réhu himself. The Grand-Duke, much affected, tries to say something happy, but the author of the Letters to Urania is not upon his cards. He gets out of it by a few vague complimentary phrases, in answer to which old Réhu, supposing that he is being asked as usual about his age, says, 'Ninety-eight years in a fortnight, Sir.' His next attempt does not fit much better with His Highness's gracious congratulations. 'Not since 1803, Sir; the town must be much changed.' During the progress of this singular dialogue, Paul is whispering to his mother, 'You may see him home if you like; I won't have anything more to do with him; he's in an awful temper. In the carriage he was kicking me all the time in the legs, to work off his fidgets, he said.' The young man himself had an unpleasant ring in his voice this evening, and in his charming face something set and hard, which his mother knew well, and noticed immediately on coming into the room. What is the matter? She watched him, trying to read the meaning in his light eyes, which, however, harder and keener than usual, revealed nothing.

But the chill, the ceremonious chill, prevailed here no less than at the dinner-table. The guests kept apart in groups, the few ladies in a circle upon low chairs, the gentlemen standing or walking about with a pretence of serious conversation, but obviously engaged in attracting His Highness's attention. It was for His Highness that Landry the musician stood pensive by the chimney-piece, gazing upward with his inspired brow and his apostolic beard; for him that on the other side Delpech the chemist stood meditative with his chin upon his hand, poring intently with gathered brows as if watching the precipitation of a compound.

Laniboire the philosopher, famous for his likeness to Pascal, was wandering round, perpetually passing before the sofa, where, unable to escape from Jean Réhu, sat the Prince. The hostess had forgotten to present him, and his fine nose looked longer than usual and seemed to be making a desperate appeal: 'Cannot you see that this is the nose of Pascal?'

At the same sofa Madame Eviza was shooting between her scarcely parted eyelids a look which asked His Highness to name his own price if he would but be seen at her reception next Monday. Ah! change the scene as you will, it is always the same performance—pretension, meanness, readiness to bow down, the courtier's appetite for self-humiliation and self-abasement. We need not decline the visits of majesty; we are provided with all the properties required for the occasion.

'General.'

'Your Highness.'

'I shall never be in time for the ballet.'

'But why are we staying, Sir?'

'I don't know; there's to be a surprise when the Nuncio is gone.'

While these few words passed in an undertone between the pair, they neither looked at each other nor changed a muscle of their ceremonial countenances. The Aide-de-camp had copied from his master the nasal intonation, the absence of gesture, the fixed attitude on the edge of the seat with the bowed arm against the side. He was rigid as on parade or in the Imperial box at the Théâtre Michel. Old Réhu stood before them, he would not sit down; he was still talking, still exhibiting the dusty stores of his memory, the people he had known, the many fashions in which he had dressed. The more distant the time, the clearer his recollection. 'That is a thing I have seen,' says he, as he pauses at the end of a story, with his eyes fixed, as it were, upon the flying past, and then off upon a fresh subject. He had been with Talma at Brunoy, he had been in the drawing-room of Josephine, full of musical boxes and artificial humming-birds covered with jewels, which sang and clapped their wings.

Out of doors on the terrace, in the warm darkness of the garden, was heard low conversation and stifled laughter, coming from the place where the cigars were visible as a ring of red dots. Lavaux was amusing himself by getting the young Guardsman to tell Danjou and Paul Astier the story of the Cardinal's hat. 'And the lady, Count—the lady at the station.' 'Cristo, qu'elle était bella!' said the Italian in a low voice, and added correctively, 'sim-patica, surtout, simpatica.' Charming and responsive—this was his general idea of the ladies of Paris. He only wished he need not go back. The French wine had loosed his tongue, and he began describing his life in the Guards, the advantages of the profession, the hope which they all had on entering it that they might find a rich wife—that at one of His Holiness's audiences they would dazzle some wealthy English Catholic or a fanatical Spaniard from South America come to bring her offering to the Vatican. 'L'ouniforme est zouli, comprenez; et pouis les en-fortounes del Saint Père, cela nous donne à nous autres ses soldats oun prestigio roumanesque, cava-leresque, qualque sose qui plaît aux dames zénérale-menté.' It must be allowed that with his youthful manly face, his gold braid shining softly in the moonlight, and his white leather breeches, he did recall the heroes of Artosto or Tasso.

'Well, my dear Pepino,' said fat Lavaux, in his mocking and disagreeable tone, 'if you want a good match, here it is at your elbow.'

'How so? Where?'

Paul Astier started and became attentive. The mention of a good match always made him fear that some one was stealing his.

'The Duchess, of course. Old Padovani can't stand another stroke.'

'But the Prince d'Athis?'

'He'll never marry her.'

Lavaux was a good authority, being the friend of the Prince, and of the Duchess, too, for that matter; though, seeing that the establishment must shortly split, he stood on the side which he thought the safest 'Go in boldly, my dear Count; there's money, lots of it, and a fine connection, and a lady still well enough.'

'Cristo, qu'elle est bella!' said the Italian, with a sigh.

'E simpatica,' said Danjou, with a sneer. At which the Guardsman after a moment's amazement, delighted to find an Academician with so much perception, exclaimed: 'Si, simpatica, précisamenté!'

'And then,' continued Lavaux, 'if you are fond of dyes, and enamel, and padding, you'll get it. I believe she's a marvel of construction, the best customer that Charrière has.'

He spoke out loud and quite freely, right in front of the dining-room. The garden door was slightly open, and through the crack the light fell upon the broad red impudent face of the parasite, and the warm air floated laden with the rich smell of the dinner which he had eaten and was repaying in mean dirty slanders. There's for your *truffes farcies*; there's for your *gelinottes*, and your *'chateaux'* at fifteen shillings a glass! Danjou and he have got together on purpose to play this popular game of running-down; and a great deal they know and a great deal they tell. Lavaux serves the ball and Danjou returns. And the simple Guardsman, not knowing how much to believe, tries to laugh, with a horrid fear lest the Duchess should catch them, and is much relieved when he hears his uncle calling him from the other end of the terrace. The Papal Embassy shuts up early, and since his little misfortune he has been kept strictly to hours.

'Good night, gentlemen.'

'Good luck to you, young man.'

The Nuncio is gone; now for the surprise. At a signal from the Duchess, the author of *Roxelane* took his place at the piano and swept his beard over the keys as he struck two penetrating chords. Immediately at the far end of the rooms the curtains were drawn from the door, and down the vista of brilliant apartments, tripping along on the tips of her little gilt slippers, came a charming brunette in the close bodice and puffed skirts of the ballet, conducted at arm's-length by a gloomy person with hair in rolls and a cadaverous countenance divided by a dead black moustache. It is Déa! Déa, the folly of the hour, the fashionable toy, accompanied by her instructor, Valère, the ballet-master at the opera. *Roxelane* was taken first this evening; and the girl, warm from her triumphant performance, had come to give her dance again for the benefit of the Duchess's Imperial guest. A more delightful surprise his respected friend could not have devised. What more exquisite than to have all to yourself, close to yourself, and within an inch of your face, the pretty whirl of muslin and the panting of the fresh young breath, and to hear the sinews of the little creature strain like the sheets of a sail! His Highness was not alone in this opinion. The moment the dance began the men drew together, selfishly making a close ring of black coats and leaving the few ladies present to see what they could from outside. Even the Grand-Duke is hustled and shoved in the press: for as the dance quickens the circle narrows, till there is scarcely room for the movement. Men of letters and of politics, breathing hard, thrust their heads forward, while their decorations swing like cow-bells, and grinning from ear to ear show their watery lips and toothless jaws with grotesque animal cachinnations. Even the Prince d'Athis stoops with less contempt for humanity, as he gazes upon this marvel of youth and fairy grace, who with the tips of her toes takes off the masks of convention; and the Turk, Mourad Bey, who has sat the whole evening without a word in the depths of an armchair, is now gesticulating in the front row with open nostrils and staring eyes.

As easy as the hovering of a dragon-fly. Page 107.

In the midst of the wild shouts of applause the girl springs and leaps with so harmonious a concealment of the muscular working of her frame, that her dance might seem as easy as the hovering of a dragon-fly, but for the few drops on her firm rounded neck and the smile, forced, tense, and almost painful, at the corner of her mouth, which betray the exhausting effort of the exquisite little creature, Paul Astier, who did not care for dancing, had stayed on the terrace to smoke. The applause and the thin sounds of the piano, audible in the distance, made an accompaniment to his reflections, which took shape little by little, even as his outward eyes, growing accustomed to the dark, made out by degrees in the garden the trunks of the trees and their quivering leaves, and far away at the end the delicate tracery of an old-fashioned trellis against the wall. It was so hard to succeed; one must hold on so long to reach the desired point, always close at hand and always receding. Why was it that Colette seemed every moment on the point of falling into his arms, and yet when he went back he had to begin again from the beginning? It looked as if in his absence some one for amusement pulled down his work. Who was it? It was that dead fellow, confound him! He ought to be at her side from morning to night; but how could he, with the perpetual necessity of running after money?

There came a light step, a soft sound of velvet. It was his mother looking for him. Why did he not come into the drawing-room with all the rest? She leaned over the balustrade beside him and wanted to know what he was thinking about.

'Oh, nothing, nothing.' But further pressed he came out with it. Well, the fact was—the fact was—that he had had enough of starving. Dun, dun, dun. One hole stopped and another opened. He would not stand any more of it, so there!

From the drawing-room came loud exclamations and wild laughter, together with the expressionless voice of Valère, directing the dancer in the imitation of an old-fashioned ballet figure.

'How much do you want?' whispered the mother trembling. She had never seen him like this before.

'No, it's no use; it's more than you could possibly manage.'

'How much?' she asked again.

'Eight hundred.' And the agent must have it tomorrow by five o'clock, or else he would take possession. There would be a sale and all sorts of horrors. Sooner than that—and here he ground his cigar between his teeth as he said the last words—'better make a hole in my frontispiece.'

The mother had heard enough. 'Hush! hush!' she said. 'By five o'clock to-morrow? Hush!' And she flung herself upon him, and she pressed her hands in agony upon his lips, as if she would arrest there the appalling sentence of death.

CHAPTER VI.

That night she could not sleep. Eight hundred pounds! eight hundred pounds! The words went to and fro in her head. Where were they to be found? To whom could she apply? There was so little time. Names and faces flashed before her, passing for a moment where the pale gleam of the nightlight fell on the ceiling, only to disappear and be replaced by other names and other faces, which vanished as quickly in their turn. Freydet? She had just made use of him. Sammy? Had nothing till he married. Besides, did anybody do such a thing as to borrow or lend eight hundred pounds? No one but a poet from the country. In Parisian society money never appears on the scene; it is assumed that you have it and are above these details, like the people in genteel comedy. A breach of this convention would banish the transgressor from respectable company.

And while Madame Astier pursued her feverish thoughts she saw beside her the round back of her husband rising and falling peacefully. It was one of the depressing incidents of their joint life that they had lain thus side by side for thirty years, having nothing in common but the bed. But never had the isolation of her surly bedfellow so strongly aroused her indignation. What was the use of waking him, of talking to him about the boy and his desperate threat? She knew perfectly well that he would not believe her, nor so much as move the big back which protected his repose. She was inclined for a minute to fall upon him, to pummel him, and scratch him, and rouse him out of his selfish slumbers by shouting in his ear: 'Léonard, your papers are on fire!' And as the thought of the papers flashed madly across her mind she almost leaped out of bed. She had got her eight hundred! The drawers upstairs! How was it she had not thought of them before? There she lay, till day dawned and the night-light went out with a sputter, content and motionless, arranging what she should do, with the look of a thief in her open eyes.

Before the usual hour she was dressed, and all the morning prowled about the rooms, watching her husband. He talked of going out, but changed his mind, and went on with his sorting till breakfast. Between his study and the attic he went to and fro with armfuls of pamphlets, humming a careless tune. He had not feeling enough to perceive the constrained agitation which surcharged the air with nervous electricity and played among the furniture in the cupboards, and upon the handles of the doors. He worked on undisturbed. At table he was talkative, told idiotic stories, which she knew by heart, interminable as the process of crumbling with his knife his favourite cheese. Piece after piece of cheese he took, and still one anecdote followed another. And when the time came for going to the Institute, where the Dictionary Committee was to sit before the regular meeting, how long he took to start! and in spite of her eagerness to get him off quick, what an age he spent over every little thing!

The moment he turned the corner of the street, without waiting to shut the window, she darted to the serving-hatch, crying, 'Corentine, call a cab, quick!' He was gone at last, and she flew up the little staircase to the attic.

Crouching down to keep clear of the low ceiling she began to try a bunch of keys in the lock which fastened the bar of the drawers. She could not fit it. She could not wait. She would have forced away, without scruple, a side of the frame, but her fingers gave way and her nails broke. She wanted something to prise with. She opened the drawer of the card-table: and there lay three yellow scrawls. They were the very things she was looking for—the letters of Charles V.! Such miracles do happen sometimes!

She bent down to the low-arched window to make sure, and read: 'François Rabelais, maître en toutes sciences et bonnes lettres.' Enough! She started up, hitting her head hard as she did so, and was not aware of it till she was in the cab and on her way to the shop of the famous Bos in the Rue de l'Abbaye.

She got down at the corner of the street. It is a short quiet street, overshadowed by St. Germain des Près and by the old red brick buildings of the School of Surgery. A few of the surgeons' carriages, professional broughams with splendid liveries, were in waiting. Scarcely anyone was about. Pigeons were feeding on the pavement, and flew away as she came to the shop opposite the school. It offers both books and curiosities, and exhibits an archaic inscription, highly appropriate to such a nook of Old Paris: 'Bos: Antiquary and Palaeographer.'

The shop-front displayed something of all sorts: old manuscripts, ancient ledgers with mould spots on the edges, missals with damaged gilding, book-clasps and book-covers. To the upper panes were fastened assignats, old placards, plans of Paris, ballads, military franks with spots of blood, autographs of all ages, some verses by Madame Lafargue, two letters from Chateaubriand to 'Pertuzé, Boot-maker, names of celebrities ancient and modern at the foot of an invitation to dinner, or perhaps a request for money, a complaint of poverty, a love letter, &c, enough to cure anyone of writing for ever. All the autographs were priced; and as Madame Astier paused for a moment before the window she might see next to a letter of Rachel, price 12L., a letter from Léonard Astier-Réhu to Petit Séquard, his publisher, price 2s. But this was not what she came for: she was trying to discover, behind the screen of green silk, the face of her intended customer, the master of the establishment. She was seized with a sudden fear: suppose he was not at home after all!

The thought of Paul waiting gave her determination, and she went into the dark, close, dusty room. She was taken at once into a little closet behind, and began to explain her business to M. Bos, who, with his large red face and disordered hair, looked like a speaker at a public meeting. A temporary difficulty—her husband did not like to come himself—and so—— But before she could finish her lie, M. Bos, with a 'Pray, madame, pray,' had produced a cheque on the Crédit Lyonnais, and was accompanying her with the utmost politeness to her cab.

'A very genteel person,' he said to himself, much pleased with his acquisition, while she, as she took the cheque out of the glove into which it had been slipped, and looked again at the satisfactory figure, was thinking 'What a delightful man!' She had no remorse, not even the slight recoil which comes from the mere fact that the thing is done. A woman has not these feelings. She wears natural blinkers, which prevent her from, seeing anything but the thing which she desires at the moment, and keep her from the reflections which at the critical moment embarrass a man. She thought at intervals, of course, of her husband's anger when he discovered the theft, but she saw it, as it were, dim in the distance. Nay, it was rather a satisfaction to add this to all she had gone through since yesterday, and say to herself, 'I can bear it for my child!'

For beneath her outward calm, her external envelope as a woman of Academic fashion, lay a certain thing that exists in all women, fashionable or not, and that thing is passion. It is the pedal which works the feminine instrument, not always discovered by the husband or the lover, but always by the son. In the dull story with no love in it, which makes up the life of many a woman, the son is the hero and the principal character. To her beloved Paul, especially since he had reached manhood, Madame Astier owed the only genuine emotions of her life, the delightful anguish of the waiting, the chill in the pale cheeks and the heat in the hollow of the hand, the supernatural intuitions which, before the carriage is at the door, give the infallible warning that 'he comes,'—things which she had never known even in the early years of her married life or in the days when people called her imprudent, and her husband used to say with simplicity, 'It's odd; I never smoke, and my wife's veils smell of tobacco.'

When she reached her son's, and the first pull of the bell was not answered, her anxiety rose to distraction. The little mansion showed no sign of life from the ground to the ornamental roof-ridge, and, in spite of its much-admired style, had to her eyes a sinister appearance, as also had the adjoining lodging-house, not less architecturally admirable, but showing bills all along the high mullioned windows of its two upper storeys, 'To let; To let; To let.' At the second pull, which produced a tremendous ring, Stenne, the impudent little man-servant, looking very spruce in his close-fitting sky-blue livery, appeared at last at the door, rather confused and hesitating: 'Oh yes, M. Paul was in, but—but—'

The unhappy mother, haunted ever since yesterday by the same horrible idea, pictured her son lying in his blood, crossed at a bound the passage and three steps, and burst breathless into the study. Paul was standing at work before his desk in the bay window. One pane of the stained glass was open, to throw light upon the half-finished sketch and the box of colours, while the rest of the perfumed apartment was steeped in a soft subdued glow. Absorbed in his work he seemed not to have heard the carriage stop, the bell ring twice, and a lady's dress flit along the passage. He had: but it was not his mother's shabby black dress that he expected, it was not for her that he posed at his desk, nor for her that he had provided the delicate bouquets of fine irises and tulips, or the sweetmeats and elegant decanters upon the light table.

The way in which as he looked round he said, 'Oh, it's you,' would have been significant to anyone but his mother. She did not notice it, lost in the delight of seeing him there, perfectly well, perfectly dressed. She said not a word, but tearing her glove open she triumphantly handed him the cheque. He did not ask her where she got it, or what she had given for it, but put his arms round her, taking care not to crumple the paper. 'Dear old Mum'; that was all he said, but it was enough for her, though her child was not as overjoyed as she expected, but rather embarrassed. 'Where are you going next?' he said thoughtfully, with the cheque in his hand.

'Where next?' she repeated, looking at him with disappointment. Why, she had only just come, and made certain of spending a few minutes with him; but she could go if she was in the way. 'Why, I think I shall go to the Princess's. But I am in no hurry; she wearies me with her everlasting lamentation for Herbert. You think she has done with it, and then it takes a fresh start.'

Paul was on the point of saying something, which he did not say.

'Well,' he said, 'Mammy, will you do something for me? I am expecting somebody. Go and cash this for me, and let the agent have the money in return for my drafts. You don't mind?'

She did not indeed. If she went about his business she would seem to be with him still. While he was signing his name, the mother looked round the room. There were charming carpets and curtains, and nothing to mark the profession of the occupant except an X ruler in old walnut, and some casts from well-known friezes hung here and there. As she thought of her recent agony and looked at the elaborate bouquets and the refreshments laid by the sofa, it occurred to her that these were unusual preparations for a suicide.

She smiled without any resentment. The naughty wretch! She only pointed with her parasol at the bonbons in the box and said:

'Those are to make a hole in your—your—what do you call it?'

He began to laugh too.

'Oh, there's a great change since yesterday.

The business, you know, the big thing I talked to you about, is really coming off this time, I think.'

'Really? So is mine.'

'Eh? Ah yes, Sammy's marriage.'

Their pretty cunning eyes, both of the same hard grey, but, the mother's a little faded, exchanged one scrutinising glance.

'You'll see, we shall be rolling in riches,' he said after a moment. 'Now you must be going,' and he hurried her gently to the door.

That morning Paul had had a note from the Princess to say that she should call for him at his own house to go to the usual place. The usual place was the cemetery. Lately there had been what Madame Astier called 'a fresh start' of Herbert. Twice a week the widow went to the cemetery with flowers, or tapers, or articles for the chapel, and urged the progress of the work; her conjugal feelings had broken out again. The fact was, that after a long and painful hesitation between her vanity and her love, the temptation of keeping her title and the fascinations of the delightful Paul—a hesitation the more painful that she confided it to no one, except in her journal every evening to 'poor Herbert'—the appointment of Sammy had finally decided her, and she thought it proper, before taking a new husband, to complete the sepulture of the first and have done with the mausoleum and the dangerous intimacy of its seductive designer.

Paul, without understanding the flutterings of the foolish little soul, was amused by them, and thought them excellent symptoms, indicating the approach of the crisis. But the thing dragged, and he was in a hurry; it was time to hasten the conclusion and profit by Colette's visit, which had been long proposed but long deferred, the Princess, though curious to see the young man's lodgings, being apparently afraid to meet him in a place much more private than her own house or her carriage, where there were always the servants to see. Not that he had ever been over-bold; he only seemed to surround her with his presence. But she was afraid of herself, her opinion coinciding with that of the young man, who, being an experienced general in such matters, had classed her at once as one of the 'open towns.' It was his name for the sort of fashionable women who, in spite of a high and apparently unassailable position, in spite of a great apparatus of defences in every direction, are in reality to be carried by a bold attack. He did not intend now to make the regular assault, but only a smart approach or so of warm flirtation, sufficient to set a mark upon his prey without hurting her dignity, and to signify the final expropriation of the deceased. The marriage and the million would follow in due time. Such was the happy dream which Madame Astier had interrupted. He was pursuing it still, at the same desk and in the same contemplative attitude, when the whole house resounded with another ring at the bell, followed however only by conversation at the front door. 'What is it?' said Paul impatiently, as he came out.

The voice of a footman, whose tall black figure was conspicuous in the doorway against a background of splashing rain, answered from the steps, with respectful insolence, that my lady was waiting for him in the carriage. Paul, though choking with rage, managed to get out the words, 'I am coming,' But what horrid curses he muttered under his breath! The dead fellow again! Sure enough, it was the remembrance of him that had kept her away. But after a few seconds the hope of avenging himself before long in a highly amusing way enabled him so far to recover countenance, that when he joined the Princess he was as cool as ever, and showed nothing of his anger but a little extra paleness in the cheek.

It was warm in the brougham, the windows having been put up because of the shower. Huge bouquets of violets and wreaths as heavy as pies loaded the cushions round Madame de Rosen and filled her lap.

'Are the flowers unpleasant? Shall I put the window down?' said she, with the cajoling manner which a woman puts on when she has played you a trick and wants not to have a quarrel over it. Paul's gesture expressed a dignified indifference. It was nothing to him whether the window was put down or put up. The Princess, whose deep veil, still worn on such occasions as the present, concealed a blooming face, felt more uncomfortable than if he had reproached her openly. Poor young man! She was treating him so cruelly— so much more cruelly than he knew! She laid her hand gently upon his, and said, 'You are not angry with me?'

He? Not at all. Why should he be angry with her?

'For not coming in. I did say I would, but at the last moment I—I did not think I should hurt you so much.'

'You hurt me very much indeed.'

When a gentleman of severely correct deportment is betrayed into a word or two of emotion, oh, what an impression they make upon a woman's heart! They upset her almost as much as the tears of an officer in uniform.

'No, no,' she said, 'please, please do not distress yourself any more about me. Please say that you are not angry now.'

As she spoke she leaned quite close to him, letting her flowers slip down. She felt quite safe with two broad black backs and two black cockades visible on the box under a large umbrella.

'Look,' she went on; 'I promise you to come once—at least once—before——' but here she stopped in dismay. Carried away by her feelings, she was on the point of telling him that they were soon to part, and that she was going to St. Petersburg. Recovering herself in a moment, she declared emphatically that she would call unannounced some afternoon when she was not going to visit the mausoleum.

'But you go there every afternoon,' he said, with clenched teeth and such a queer accent of suppressed indignation that a smile played beneath the widow's veil, and to make a diversion she put down the window. The shower was over. The brougham had turned into a poor quarter, where the street in its squalid gaiety seemed to feel that the worst of the year was past, as the sun, almost hot enough for summer, lighted up the wretched shops, the barrows at the gutter's edge, the tawdry placards, and the rags that fluttered in the windows. The Princess looked out upon it with indifference. Such trivialities are non-existent for people accustomed to see them from the cushions of their carriage at an elevation of two feet from the road. The comfort of the springs and the protection of the glass have a peculiar influence upon the eyes, which take no interest in things below their level.

Madame de Rosen was thinking, 'How he loves me! And how nice he is!' The other suitor was of course more dignified, but it would have been much pleasanter with this one. Oh, dear! The happiest life is but a service incomplete, and never a perfect set!

By this time they were nearing the cemetery. On both sides of the road were stonemasons' yards, in which the hard white of slabs, images, and crosses mingled with the gold of *immortelles* and the black or white beads of wreaths and memorials.

'And what about Védrine's statue? Which way do we decide?' he asked abruptly, in the tone of a man who means to confine himself to business.

'Well, really——' she began. 'But, oh dear, oh dear, I shall hurt your feelings again?'

'My feelings! how so?'

The day before, they had been to make a last inspection of the knight, before he was sent to the foundry. At a previous visit the Princess had received a disagreeable impression, not so much from Védrine's work, which she scarcely looked at, as from the strange studio with trees growing in it, with lizards and wood-lice running about the walls, and all around it roofless ruins, suggesting recollections of the incendiary mob. But from the second visit the poor little woman had come back literally ill. 'My dear, it is the horror of horrors!' Such was her real opinion, as given the same evening to Madame Astier. But she did not dare to say so to Paul, knowing that he was a friend of the sculptor, and also because the name of Védrine is one of the two or three which the fashionable world has chosen to honour in spite of its natural and implanted tastes, and regards with an irrational admiration by way of pretending to artistic originality. That the coarse rude figure should not be put on dear Herbert's tomb she was determined, but she was at a loss for a presentable reason.

'Really, Monsieur Paul, between ourselves—of course it is a splendid work—a fine *Védrine*—but you must allow that it is a little *triste!*'

'Well, but for a tomb——' suggested Paul.

'And then, if you will not mind, there is this.' With much hesitation she came to the point. Really, you know, a man upon a camp bedstead with nothing on! Really she did not think it fit. It might be taken for a portrait!' And just think of poor Herbert, the correctest of men! What would it look like?'

'There is a good deal in that,' said Paul gravely, and he threw his friend Védrine overboard with as little concern as a litter of kittens. 'After all, if you do not like the figure, we can put another, or none at all. It would have a more striking effect. The tent empty; the bed ready, and no one to lie on it!'

The Princess, whose chief satisfaction was that the shirtless ruffian would not be seen there, exclaimed, 'Oh, how glad I am! how nice of you! I don't mind telling you now, that I cried over it all night!'

As usual, when they stopped at the entrance gate, the footman took the wreaths and followed some way behind, while Colette and Paul climbed in the heat a path made soft by the recent showers. She leaned upon his arm, and from time to time 'hoped that she did not tire him.' He shook his head with a sad smile. There were few people in the cemetery. A gardener and a keeper recognised the familiar figure of the Princess with a respectful bow. But when they had left the avenue and passed the upper terraces, it was all solitude and shade. Besides the birds in the trees they heard only the grinding of the saw and the metallic clink of the chisel, sounds perpetual in Père-la-Chaise, as in some city always in building and never finished.

Two or three times Madame de Rosen had seen her companion glance with displeasure at the tall lacquey in his long black overcoat and cockade, whose funereal figure now as ever formed part of the love-scene. Eager on this occasion to please him, she stopped, saying, 'Wait a minute,' took the flowers herself, dismissed the servant, and they went on all alone along the winding walk. But in spite of this kindness, Paul's brow did not relax; and, as he had hung upon his free arm three or four rings of violets, *immortelles*, and lilac, he felt more angry with the deceased than ever. 'You shall pay me for this,' was his savage reflection. She, on the contrary, felt singularly happy, in that vivid consciousness of life and health which comes upon us in places of death. Perhaps it was the warmth of the day, the perfume of the flowers, mixing their fragrance with the stronger scent of the yews and the box trees and the moist earth steaming in the sun, and with another yet, an acrid, faint, and penetrating scent, which she knew well, but which, to-day, instead of revolting her senses, as usual, seemed rather to intoxicate them.

Suddenly a shiver passed over her. The hand which lay on the young man's arm was suddenly grasped in his, grasped with force and held tight, held as it were in an embrace, and the little hand dared not take itself away. The fingers of his hand were trying to get between the delicate fingers of hers and take possession of it altogether. Hers resisted, trying to clench itself in the glove by way of refusal. All the time they went on walking, arm in arm, neither speaking nor looking, but much moved, resistance, according to the natural law, exciting the relative desire. At last came the surrender; the little hand opened, and their fingers joined in a clasp which parted their gloves, for one exquisite moment of full avowal and complete possession. The next minute the woman's pride awoke. She wanted to speak, to show that she was mistress of herself, that she had no part in what was done, nor knowledge of it at all. Finding nothing to say, she read aloud the epitaph on a tomb lying flat among the weeds, 'Augusta, 1847,' and he continued, under his breath, 'A love-story, no doubt.' Overhead the thrushes and finches uttered their strident notes, not unlike the sounds of the stone-cutting, which were heard uninterruptedly in the distance.

They were now entering the Twentieth Division, the part of the cemetery which may be called its 'old town,' where the paths are narrower, the trees higher, the tombs closer together, a confused mass of ironwork, pillars, Greek temples, pyramids, angels, genii, busts, wings open and wings folded. The tombs were various as the lives now hidden beneath—commonplace, odd, original, simple, forced, pretentious, modest. In some the floor-stones were freshly cleaned and loaded with flowers, memorials, and miniature gardens of a Chinese elegance in littleness. In others the mossy slabs were mouldering or parting, and were covered with brambles and high weeds. But all bore well-known names, names distinctly Parisian, names of lawyers, judges, merchants of eminence, ranged here in rows as in the haunts of business and trade. There were even double names, standing for family partnerships in capital and connection, substantial signatures, known no more to the directory or the bank ledger, but united for ever upon the tomb.

And Madame de Rosen remarked them with the same tone of surprise, almost of pleasure, with which she would have bowed to a carriage in the Park, 'Ah! the So-and-So's! Mario? was that the singer?' and so forth, all by way of seeming not to know that their hands were clasped.

But presently the door of a tomb near them creaked, and there appeared a large lady in black, with a round fresh face. She carried a little watering-pot, and was putting to rights the flower-beds, oratory, and tomb generally, as calmly as if she had been in a summer-house. She nodded to them across the Enclosure with a kindly smile of unselfish good will, which seemed to say, 'Use your time, happy lovers; life is short, and nothing good but love.' A feeling of embarrassment unloosed their hands. The spell was broken, and the Princess, with a sort of shame, led the way across the tombs, taking the quickest and shortest line to reach the mausoleum of the Prince.

It stood on the highest ground in 'Division 20,' upon a large level of lawn and flowers, inclosed by a low rich rail of wrought iron in the style of the Scaliger tombs at Verona. Its general appearance was designedly rough, and fairly realised the conception of an antique tent with its coarse folds, the red of the Dalmatian granite giving the colour of the bark in which the canvas had been steeped. At the top of three broad steps of granite was the entrance, flanked with pedestals and high funereal tripods of bronze blackened with a sort of lacquer. Above were the Rosen arms upon a large scutcheon, also of bronze, the shield of the good knight who slept within the tent.

Entering the inclosure, they laid the wreaths here and there, on the pedestals and on the slanted projections, representing huge tent-pegs, at the edge of the base. The Princess went to the far end of the interior, where in the darkness before the altar shone the silver fringes of two kneeling-desks, and the old gold of a Gothic cross and massive candlesticks, and there fell upon her knees—a good place to pray in, among the cool slabs, the panels of black marble glittering with the name and full titles of the dead, and the inscriptions from Ecclesiastes or the Song of Songs. But the Princess could find only a few indistinct words, confused with profane thoughts, which made her ashamed. She rose and busied herself with the flower-stands, retiring gradually far enough to judge the effect of the sarcophagus or bed. The cushion of black bronze, with silver monogram, was already in its place, and she thought the hard couch with nothing upon it had a fine and simple effect. But she wanted the opinion of Paul, who could be heard pacing the gravel as he waited without. Mentally approving his delicacy, she was on the point of calling him in, when the interior grew dark, and on the trefoil lights of the lantern was heard the patter of another shower. Twice she called him, but he did not move from the pedestal, where he sat exposed to the rain, and without speaking declined her invitation.

'Come in,' she said, 'come in.'

Still he stayed, saying rapidly and low, 'I do not want to come. You love him so.'

'Come,' she still said, 'come/ and taking his hand drew him to the entrance. Step by step the splashing of the rain made them draw back as far as the sarcophagus, and there, half sitting, half standing, they remained side by side, contemplating beneath the low clouds the 'old town' of the dead, which sloped away at their feet with its crowding throng of pinnacles and grey figures and humbler stones, rising like Druid architecture from the bright green. No birds were audible, no sound of tools, nothing but the water running away on all sides, and from the canvas cover of a half-finished monument the monotonous voices of two artisans discussing their worries. The rain without made it all the warmer within, and with the strong aroma of the flowers mingled still that other inseparable scent The Princess had raised her veil, feeling the same oppression and dryness of the mouth that she had felt on the way up. Speechless and motionless, the pair seemed so much a part of the tomb, that a little brown, bird came hopping in to shake its feathers and pick a worm between the slabs. 'It's a nightingale,' murmured Paul in the sweet overpowering stillness. She tried to say, 'Do they sing still in this month?' But he had taken her in his arms, he had set her between his knees at the edge of the granite couch, and putting her head back, pressed upon her half-open lips a long, long kiss, passionately returned.

He had taken her in his arms. Page 132.

'Because love is more strong than death,' said the inscription from the Canticle, written above them upon the marble wall.

When the Princess reached her house, where Madame Astier was awaiting her return, she had a long cry in the arms of her friend, a refuge unhappily not more trustworthy than those of her friend's son. It was a burst of lamentation and broken words. 'Oh, my dear, oh, my dear, how miserable I am! If you knew,' she said, 'if you only knew!' She felt with despair the hopeless difficulty of the situation, her hand solemnly promised to the Prince d'Athis, and her affections just plighted to the enchanter of the tombs, whom she cursed from the depths of her soul. And, most distressing of all, she could not confide her weakness to her affectionate friend, being sure that, the moment she opened her lips, the mother would side with her son against 'Sammy,' with love against prudence, and perhaps even compel her to the intolerable degradation of marrying a commoner.

'There then, there then,' said Madame Astier, unaffected by the torrent of grief. 'You are come from the cemetery, I suppose, where you have been working up your feelings again. But you know, dear, there must be an end to *Artemisia!*' She understood the woman's weak vanity, and insisted on the absurdity of this interminable mourning, ridiculous in the eyes of the world, and at all events injurious to her beauty And after all, it was not a question of a second love-match! What was proposed was no more than an alliance between two names and titles equally noble. Herbert himself, if he saw her from heaven, must be content.

'He did understand things, certainly, poor dear,' sighed Colette de Rosen, whose maiden name was Sauvadon. She was set on becoming 'Madame l'Ambassadrice,' and still more on remaining 'Madame la Princesse.'

'Look, dear, will you have a piece of good advice? You just run away. Sammy will start in a week. Do not wait for him. Take Lavaux. He knows St. Petersburg, and will settle you there meanwhile. And there will be this advantage, that you will escape a painful scene with the Duchess. A Corsican, you know, is capable of anything.'

'Ye-es, perhaps I had better go,' said Madame de Rosen, to whom the chief merit of the plan was that she would avoid any fresh attack, and put distance between her and the folly of the afternoon.

'Is it the tomb?' asked Madame Astier, seeing her hesitate. 'Is that it? Why, Paul will finish it very well without you. Come, pet, no more tears. You may water your beauty, but you must not over-water it.' As she went away in the fading light to wait for her omnibus, the good lady said to herself, 'Oh dear, D'Athis will never know what his marriage is costing me!' And here her feeling of weariness, her longing for a good rest after so many trials, reminded her suddenly that the most trying of all was to come, the discovery and confession at home. She had not yet had time to think about it, and now she was going fast towards it, nearer and nearer with every turn of the heavy wheels. The very anticipation made her shudder: it was not fear; but the frantic outcries of Astier-Réhu, his big rough voice, the answer that must be given, and then the inevitable reappearance of his trunk—oh, what a weariness it would be! Could it not be put off till to-morrow? She was tempted not to confess at once, but to turn suspicion upon some one else, upon Teyssèdre for instance, till the next morning. She would at least get a quiet night.

'Ah, here is Madame! Something has happened/ cried Corentine, as she ran to the door in a fluster, excitement making more conspicuous than usual the marks of her smallpox. Madame Astier made straight for her own room; but the door of the study opened, and a peremptory 'Adelaide!' compelled her to go in. The rays of the lamp-globe showed her that the face of her husband had a strange expression. He took her by the two hands and drew her into the light. Then in a quivering voice he said, 'Loi-sillon is dead,' and he kissed her on both cheeks.

Not found out! No, not yet. He had not even gone up to his papers; but had been pacing his study for two hours, eager to see her and tell her this great news, these three words which meant a change in their whole life, 'Loisillon is dead!'

CHAPTER VII.

Mlle. Germaine de Freydet,

Clos Jallanges.

My DEAREST SISTER,—Your letters distress me much. I know you are lonely and ill, and feel my absence; but what am I to do? Remember my master's advice to show myself and be seen. It is not, as you may suppose, at Clos Jallanges, in my tweed suit and leggings, that I could get on with my candidature. I cannot but see that the time is near. Loisillon is sinking visibly, dying by inches; and I am using the time to make friendships among the Academicians, which may mean votes hereafter. Astier has already introduced me to several of them. I often go to fetch him after the meetings. It is charming to see them come out of the Institute, almost all laden with years as with honours, and walk away arm-in-arm in groups of three or four, bright and happy, talking loud and filling the pavement, their eyes still wet after the hearty laughs they have had within. 'Paille-ron is very smart,' says one; 'But Danjou gave it him back,' says another. As for me, I fasten on to the arm of Astier-Réhu and, ranked with the deities, seem almost a deity myself. One by one at this or that bridge the groups break up. 'See you next Thursday,' is the last word. And I go back to the Rue de Beaune with my master, who gives me encouragement and advice, and in the confidence of success says, with his frank laugh, 'Look at me, Freydet; I am twenty years younger after a meeting!'

I really believe the dome does keep them fresh. Where is there another old man as lusty as Jean Réhu, whose ninety-eighth birthday we celebrated yesterday evening by a dinner at Voisin's? Lavaux suggested it, and if it cost me 40L., it gave me the opportunity of counting my men. We were twenty-five at table, all Academicians, except Picheral, Lavaux, and myself. I have the votes of seventeen or eighteen; the rest are uncertain, but well disposed. Dinner very well served, and very chatty.

By the way, I have asked Lavaux to come to Clos Jallanges for his holiday. He is librarian of the Bibliothèque Mazarine. He shall have the large room in the wing, looking out on the pheasants. I don't think highly of his character, but I must have him; he is the Duchess's 'zebra'! Did I tell you that a zebra in ladies' language is a bachelor friend, unoccupied, discreet, and quick, kept always at hand for errands and missions too delicate to be trusted to a servant? In the intervals of his diplomacy a young zebra may sometimes get particular gratifications, but as a rule the animal is tame and wants little, content with small promotion, a place at the bottom of the table, and the honour of showing his paces before the lady and her friends. Lavaux, I fancy, has made his place profitable in other ways. He is so clever and, in spite of his easy manner, so much dreaded. He knows, as he says, 'the servants' hall' of two establishments, literature and politics, and he shows me the holes and traps of which the road to the Institute is full. Astier, my master, does not know them to this day. In his grand simplicity he has climbed straight up, unaware of danger, with his eyes upon the dome, confident in his strength and his labour. A hundred times he would have broken his neck, if his wife, the cleverest of clever women, had not guided him unperceived.

It was Lavaux who dissuaded me from publishing between this and the next vacancy my 'Thoughts of a Rustic.' 'No, no,' said he to me, 'you have done enough. You might well even let it be understood that you will not write any more. Your work is over, and you are a mere gentleman at large. The Académie loves that.' I put that with the valuable hint from Picheral: 'Do not take them your books.'

The fewer your works, I see, the better your claim. Picheral has much influence; he too must come to us this summer. Put him on the second floor, in what was the box-room, or somewhere. Poor Germaine, it is a great bother for you, and ill as you are! But where's the help? It is bad enough not to have a house in town for the winter and give parties, like Dalzon, Moser, and all my competitors. Do, do take care of yourself and get well.

To go back to my dinner party. There was naturally much talk of the Académie, its elections and duties, its merits and demerits in public estimation. The 'deities' hold that those who run down the institution are all, without exception, poor creatures who cannot get in. For the strong apparent instances to the contrary, there was a reason in each case. I ventured to mention the great name of Balzac, a man from our country. But the playwright Desminières, who used to manage the amateur theatricals at Compiègne, burst out with 'Balzac! But did you know him? Do you know, sir, the sort of man he was? An utter Bohemian! A man, sir, who never had a guinea in his pocket! I had it from his friend Frédéric Lemaître. Never one guinea! And you would have had the Académie——' Here old Jean Réhu, having his trumpet to his ear, got the notion that we were talking of 'tallies,' and told us the fine story of his friend Suard coming to the Académie on January 21, 1793, the day the king was executed, and availing himself of the absence of his colleagues to sweep off the whole fees for the meeting.

He tells a story well, does the old gentleman, and but for his deafness would be a brilliant talker. When I gave his health, with a few complimentary verses on his marvellous youth, the old fellow in a gracious reply called me his dear colleague. My master Astier corrected him—'future colleague.' Laughter and applause. 'Future colleague' was the title which they all gave me as they said goodbye, shaking my hand with a significant pressure, and adding, 'We shall meet before long,' or 'See you soon,' in reference to my expected call. It is not a pleasant process, paying these calls, but everyone goes through it. Astier-Réhu told me, as we came away from the dinner, that when he was elected old Dufaure let him come ten times without seeing him. Well, he would not give up, and the eleventh time the door was thrown open. Nothing like persistence.

In truth, if Ripault-Babin or Loisillon died (they are both in danger, but even now I have most hopes of Ripault-Babin), my only serious competitor would be Dalzon. He has talent and wealth, stands well with the 'dukes,' and his cellar is capital; the only thing against him is a youthful peccadillo lately discovered, 'Without the Veil,' a poem of 600 lines printed 'at Eropolis,' anonymously, and utterly outrageous. They say that he has bought up and suppressed the whole, but there are still some copies in circulation with signature and dedication. Poor Dalzon contradicts the story and makes a desperate fight. The Académie reserves judgment pending the inquiry. That is why my respected master said to me gravely one evening without giving reasons, 'I shall not vote again for M. Dalzon.' The Académie is a club, that is the important thing to remember. You cannot go in without proper dress and clean hands. For all that I have too much gallantry and too much respect for my opponent to make use of such concealed weapons; and Fage, the bookbinder in the Cour des Comptes, the strange little humpback whom I sometimes meet in Védrine's studio—Fage, I say, who has much acquaintance with the curiosities of bibliography, got a good snub when he offered me one of the signed copies of 'Without the Veil.' 'Then it will go to M. Moser,' was his calm reply.

Talking of Védrine, I am in an awkward position. In the warmth of our first few meetings I made him promise to bring his family to stay with us in the country. But how can we have him along with people like Astier and Lavaux, who detest him? He is so uncivilised, such an oddity! Just imagine! He is by descent Marquis de Védrine, but even at school he suppressed the title and the 'de,' additions coveted by most people in this democratic age, when everything else may be got. And what is his reason? Because, do you see, he wants to be liked for his own sake! The latest of him is that the Princess de Rosen will not take the knight, which he has done for the Prince's tomb. It was mentioned every minute in the family, where money is not plenty. 'When we have sold the knight, I am to have a clockwork horse,' said the boy. The poor mother too counted upon the knight for refurnishing her empty presses, and to Védrine himself the price of the master-piece meant just three months' holiday in a Nile-boat. Well! the knight not sold, or to be paid for heaven knows when, after a lawsuit and a valuation, if you fancy they are thrown out by that, you are much mistaken. When I got to the Cour des Comptes the day after the disappointment, I found friend Védrine planted before an easel, absorbed in pleasure, sketching upon a large canvas the curious wild vegetation on the burnt building. Behind him were his wife and son in ecstasy, and Madame Védrine, with the little girl in her arms, said to me in a serious undertone, 'We are so happy; Monsieur Védrine has at last got to oils.' Is it not laughable? Is it not touching?

This piecemeal letter, dear, will show you in what a bustle and fever I live since I have been working at my candidature. I go here and go there, to 'at homes,' to dinner parties, to evening parties. I am even supposed to be 'zebra' to good Madame Ancelin, because I am constant at her drawing-room on Fridays, and on Tuesday evenings in her box at the Français. A very countrified 'zebra,' I am sure, in spite of the changes I have had made to give myself a graver and more fashionable appearance. You must look for a surprise when I come back. Last Monday there was a select party at the Duchess Padovani's, where I had the honour to be presented to the Grand-Duke Leopold. His Highness complimented me on my last book, and all my books, which he knows as well as I do. It is marvellous what foreigners do know. But it is at the Astiers' that I am most comfortable. It is such a primitive, simple, united family. One day, after breakfast, there arrived a new Academic coat for the master, and we tried it on together. I say 'we,' for he wanted to see how the palm leaves looked upon me. I put on the coat, hat, and sword, a real sword, my dear, which comes out, and has a groove in the middle for the blood to run away, and I assure you I was struck with my appearance; but this I tell you only to show the intimacy of this invaluable friendship.

When I come back to my peaceful, if narrow, quarters, if it is too late to write to you, I always do a little counting. On the full list of the Académie I tick those of whom I am sure, and those who stand by Dalzon. Then I do various sums in subtraction and addition. It is an excellent amusement, as you will see when I show you. As I was telling you, Dalzon has the 'dukes,' but the writer of the 'House of Orleans,' who is received at Chantilly, is to introduce me there before long. If I get on there—and with this object I am diligently studying a certain engagement at Rocroy; so you see your brother is becoming deep—well, if I get on, the author of 'Without the Veil, printed at Eropolis,' loses his strongest support. As for my opinions, I do not disavow them. I am a Republican, but not extreme, and more particularly I am a Candidate! Immediately after this little expedition I quite expect to come back to my darling Germaine, who will, I do hope, bear up and think of the happiness of the triumph! We will do it, dear! We will get into the 'goose's garden,' as it is called by that Bohemian Védrine; but we shall need endurance.

Your loving brother,

Abel de Freydet.

I have opened my letter again to say that the morning papers announce the death of Loisillon. The stroke of fate is always affecting, even when fully expected. What a sad event! What a loss to French literature! And unhappily, dear, it will keep me here still longer. Please pay the labourers. More news soon.

CHAPTER VIII.

DESTINY had willed that Loisillon, fortunate always, should be fortunate in dying at the right moment. A week later, when houses were closed, society broken up, the Chamber and the Institute not sitting, his funeral train would have been composed of Academicians attentive to their tallies, followed only by deputies from the numerous societies of which he was Secretary or President. But business-like to the last and after, he went off to the moment, just before the Grand Prix, choosing a week entirely blank, when, as there was no crime, or duel, or interesting lawsuit, or political event, the sensational obsequies of the Permanent Secretary would be the only pastime of the town.

The funeral mass was to be at twelve o'clock, and long before that hour an immense crowd was gathering round St. Germain des Prés. The traffic was stopped, and no carriages but those of persons invited were allowed to pass within the rails, strictly kept by a line of policemen posted at intervals. Who Loisillon was, what he had done in his seventy years' sojourn among mankind, what was the meaning of the capital letter embroidered in silver on the funeral drapery, was known to but few in the crowd. The one thing which struck them was the arrangement of the protecting line, and the large space left to the dead, distance, room, and emptiness being the constant symbols of respect and grandeur. It had been understood that there would be a chance of seeing actresses and persons of notoriety, and the cockneys at a distance were putting names to the faces they recognised among the groups conversing in front of the church.

Under the black-draped porch. Page 147.

There, under the black-draped porch, was the place for hearing the true funeral oration on Loisillon, quite other than that which was to be delivered presently at Mont Parnasse, and the true article on the man and his work, very different from the notices ready for to-morrow's newspapers. His work was a 'Journey in Val d'Andorre,' and two reports published at the National Press, relating to the time when he was Superintendent at the Beaux-Arts. The man was a sort of shrewd attorney, creeping and cringing, with a permanent bow and an apologetic attitude, which seemed to ask your pardon for his decorations, your pardon for his insignia, your pardon for his place in the Académie—where his experience as a man of business was useful in fusing together a number of different elements, with none of which he could well have been classed—your pardon for the amazing success which had raised so high such a worthless winged grub. It was remembered that at an official dinner he had said of himself complacently, as he bustled round the table with a napkin on his arm, 'What an excellent servant I should have made!' And it might have been written on his tomb.

And while they moralised upon the nothingness of his life, his corpse, the remains of nothing, was receiving the honours of death. Carriage after carriage drew up at the church; liveries brown and liveries blue came and disappeared; long-frocked footmen bowed to the pavement with a pompous banging of doors and steps; the groups of journalists respectfully made way, now for the Duchess Padovani, stately and proud, now for Madame Ancelin, blooming in her crape, now for Madame Eviza, whose Jewish eyes shone through her veil with blaze enough to attract a constable—all the ladies of the Académie, assembled in full congregation to practise their worship, not so much by a service to the memory of Loisillon, as by contemplation of their living idols, the 'deities' made and fashioned by the cunning of their little hands, the work upon which, as women, they had employed the superabundance of their energy, artfulness, ambition, and pride. Some actresses had come too, on the pretext that the deceased had been the president of some sort of Actors' Orphanage, but moved in reality by the frantic determination 'not to be out of it,' which belongs to their class. Their expressions of woe were such that they might have been taken for near relations. A carriage suddenly drawing up set down a distracted group of black veils, whose sorrow was distressing to witness. The widow, at last? No, it is Marguerite Oger, the great sensational actress, whose appearance excites all round the square a prolonged stir and much pushing about. From the porch a journalist ran forward to meet her, and taking her hands besought her to bear up. 'Yes,' she said, 'I ought to be calm; I will,' Whereupon, drying her tears and forcing them back with her handkerchief, she entered, or it should rather be said 'went on,' into the darkness of the nave, with its background of glimmering tapers, fell down before a desk on the ladies' side in a prostration of self-abandonment, and rising with a sorrowful air said to another actress at her side, 'How much did they take at the Vaudeville last night?' '168L. 18s.,' answered her friend, with the same accent of grief.

Lost in the crowd at the edge of the square, Abel de Freydet heard the people round him say, 'It's Marguerite. How well she did it!' But being a small man, he was trying in vain to make his way, when a hand was laid upon his shoulder. 'What, still in Paris? It must be a trial for your poor sister,' said Védrine, as he carried him along. Working his way with his strong elbows through the stream of people who only came up to his shoulder, and saying occasionally, 'Excuse me, gentlemen—members of the family,' he brought to the front with him his country friend, who, though delighted at the meeting, felt some embarrassment, as the sculptor talked after his fashion, freely and audibly. 'Bless me, what luck Loisillon has! Why there weren't more people for Béranger. This is the sort of thing to keep a young man's pecker up.' Here Freydet, seeing the hearse approaching, took off his hat. 'Good gracious, what have you done to your head? Turn round. Why you look like Louis Philippe!' The poet's moustache was turned down, his hair brushed forward, and his pleasant face showed its complexion of ruddy brown between whiskers touched with grey. He drew up his short figure with a stiff dignity, whereat Védrine laughing said, 'Ah, I see. Made up for the grandees at Chantilly? So you are still bent upon the Académie! Why, just look at the exhibition yonder.'

In the sunlight and on the broad enclosure the official attendants immediately behind the hearse made a shocking show. Chance might seem to have chosen them for a wager among the most ridiculous seniors in the Institute, and they looked especially-ugly in the uniform designed by David, the coat embroidered with green, the hat, the Court sword, beating against legs for which the designer was certainly not responsible. First came Gazan; his hat was tilted awry by the bumps of his skull, and the vegetable green of the coat threw into relief the earthy colour and scaly texture of his elephantine visage. At his side was the grim tall Laniboire with purple apoplectic veins and a crooked mouth. His uniform was covered by an overcoat whose insufficient length left visible the end of his sword and the tails of the frock, and gave him an appearance certainly much less dignified than that of the marshal with his black rod, who walked before. Those that followed, such as Astier-Réhu and Desminières, were all embarrassed and uncomfortable, all acknowledged by their apologetic and self-conscious bearing the absurdity of their disguise, which, though it might pass in the chastened light of their historic dome, seemed amid the real life of the street not less laughable than a show of monkeys. 'I declare one would like to throw some nuts to see if they would go after them on all fours,' said Freydet's undesirable companion. But Freydet did not catch the impertinent remark. He slipped away, mixed with the procession, and entered the church between two files of soldiers with arms reversed. He was in his heart profoundly glad that Loisillon was dead. He had never seen or known him; he could not love him for his work's sake, as he had done no work; and the only thing for which he could thank him was that he had left his chair empty at such a convenient moment. But he was impressed notwithstanding. The funeral pomp to which custom makes the old Parisian indifferent, the long line of knapsacks, the muskets that fell on the flags with a single blow (at the command of a boyish little martinet, with a stock under-his chin, who was probably performing on this occasion his first military duty), and, above all, the funeral music and the muffled drums, filled him with respectful emotion: and as always happened when he felt keenly, rimes began to rise. He had actually got a good beginning, presenting a grand picture of the storm and electric agitation and mental eclipse produced in the atmosphere of a nation when one of its great men disappears. But he broke off his thoughts to make room for Danjou, who, having arrived very late, pushed on amid the looks and whispers of the ladies, gazing about him coldly and haughtily and passing his hand over his head as he habitually does, doubtless to ascertain the safety of his back hair.

'He did not recognise me,' thought Freydet, hurt by the crushing glance with which the Academician relegated to the ranks the nobody who had ventured to greet him; 'it's my whiskers, I suppose.' The interruption turned the thoughts of the candidate from his verses, and he began to consider his plan of operations, his calls, his official announcement to the Permanent Secretary. But what was he thinking of? The Permanent Secretary was dead! Would Astier-Réhu be appointed before the vacation? And when would the election be? He proceeded to consider all the 'details, down to his coat. Should he go to Astier's tailor now? And did the tailor supply also the hat and sword?

Pie Jesu, Domine, sang a voice behind the altar, the swelling notes of an opera singer, asking repose for Loisillon, whom it might be thought the Divine Mercy had destined to special torment, for all through the church, loud and soft, in every variety of voice, solo and in unison, came the supplication for 'repose, repose.' Ah, let him sleep quietly after his many years of turmoil and intrigue! The solemn stirring chant was answered in the nave by women's sobbing, above which rose the tragic convulsive gasp of Marguerite Oger, the gasp so impressive in the fourth act of 'Musidora.' All this lamentation touched the kind-hearted candidate and linked itself in his feelings to other lamentations and other sorrows. He thought of relatives who had died, and of his sister who had been a mother to him, and who was now given up by all the doctors, and knew it, and spoke of it in every letter. Ah! would she live even to see the day of his success? Tears blinded him, and he was obliged to wipe his eyes.

'Don't come it too strong, it won't seem genuine,' said the sneering voice of fat Lavaux, grinning close at his ear. He turned round angrily; but here the young officer gave at stentorian pitch the command 'Carry—arms!' and the bayonets rattled on the muskets while the muffled tones of the organ rolled out the 'Dead March.' The procession began to form for leaving the church, headed as before by Gazan, Laniboire, Desminières, and Freydet's old master, Astier-Réhu. They all looked superb now, the parrot green of their laced coats being subdued by the dim religious light of the lofty building as they walked down the central aisle, two and two, slowly, as if loth to reach the great square of daylight seen through the open doors. Behind came the whole Society, headed by its senior member, the wonderful old Jean Réhu, looking taller than ever in a long coat, and holding up the little brown head, carved, one might fancy, out of a cocoa-nut, with an air of contemptuous indifference telling that 'this was a thing he had seen' any number of times before. Indeed in the course of the sixty years during which he had been in receipt of the tallies of the Académie, he must have heard many such funeral chants, and sprinkled much holy water on illustrious biers.

But if Jean Réhu was a 'deity,' whose miraculous immortality justified the name, it could only be applied in mockery to the band of patriarchs who followed him. Decrepit, bent double, gnarled as old apple trees, with feet of lead, limp legs, and blinking owlish eyes, they stumbled along, either supported on an arm or feeling their way with outstretched hands; and their names whispered by the crowd recalled works long dead and forgotten. Beside such ghosts as these, 'on furlough from the cemetery,' as was remarked by a smart young soldier in the guard of honour, the rest of the Academicians seemed young. They posed and strutted before the delighted eyes of the ladies, whose bright gleams reached them through the black veils, the ranks of the crowd, and the cloaks and knapsacks of the bewildered soldiers. On this occasion again Freydet, bowing to two or three 'future colleagues,' encountered cold or contemptuous smiles, like those which a man sees when he dreams that his dearest friends have forgotten him. But he had not time to be depressed, being caught and turned about by the double stream which moved up the church and towards the door.

'Well, my lord, you will have to be stirring now,' was the advice of friendly Picheral, whispered in the midst of the hubbub and the scraping of chairs. It sent the candidate's blood tingling through his veins. But just as he passed before the bier Danjou muttered, without looking at him, as he handed him the holy-water brush, 'Whatever you do, be quiet, and let things slide.' His knees shook beneath him. Bestir yourself! Be quiet! Which advice was he to take? Which was the best? Doubtless his master, Astier, would tell him, and he tried to reach him outside the church. It was no easy task in the confusion of the court, where they were forming the procession, and lifting the coffin under its heap of countless wreaths. Never was a scene more lively than this coming out from the funeral into the brilliant daylight; everywhere people were bowing and talking gossip quite unconnected with the ceremony, while the bright expression on every face showed the reaction after a long hour's sitting still and listening to melancholy music. Plans were made, meetings arranged; the hurrying stream of life, stopped for a brief while, impatiently resumed its course, and poor Loisillon was left far behind in the past to which he belonged.

'At the Français to-night, don't forget; it's the last Tuesday,' simpered Madame Ancelin, while Paul said to Lavaux, 'Are you going to see it through?'

'No; I'm taking Madame Eviza home.'

'Then come to Keyser's at six. We shall want freshening after the speeches.'

The mourning coaches were drawing up one after the other, while the private carriages set off at a trot. People were leaning out of all the windows in the square, and over towards the Boulevard Saint-Germain men standing on the stationary tramcars showed tier after tier of heads rising in dark relief against the blue sky. Freydet, dazzled by the sun, tilted his hat over his eyes and looked at the crowd, which reached as far as he could see. He felt proud, transferring to the Académie the posthumous glory which certainly could not be ascribed to the author of the 'Journey in Val d'Andorre,' though at the same time he was distressed at noticing that his dear 'future colleagues' obviously kept him at a distance, became meditative when he drew near, or turned away, making little groups to keep out the intruder. And these were the very men who only two days ago at Voisin's had said to him, 'When are you going to join us?' But the heaviest blow was the desertion of Astier-Réhu.

'What a calamity, sir!' said Freydet, coming up to him and putting on a doleful expression for the purpose of saying something sympathetic. Astier-Réhu, standing by the hearse, made no answer, but went on turning over the leaves of the oration he would shortly have to deliver. 'What a calamity!' repeated Freydet.

'My dear Freydet, you are indecent,' said his master, roughly, in a loud voice. And with one harsh snap of the jaw he betook himself again to his reading.

Indecent! What did he mean? The poor man looked himself over, but could find no explanation of the reproach. What was the matter? What had he done?

For some minutes he was quite dazed. Vaguely he saw the hearse start under its shaking pyramid of flowers, with green coats at the four corners, more green coats behind, then all the Society, and immediately following, but at a respectful distance, another group, in which he found himself involved and carried along he knew not how. Young men, old men, all terribly gloomy and depressed, all marked on the brow with the same deep furrow, set there by one fixed idea, all expressing with their eyes the same hatred and distrust of their neighbours. When he had got over his discomfiture, and was able to identify these persons, he recognised the faded, hopeless face of old Moser, the candidate everlasting; the honest expression of Dalzon, the author of 'that book,' who had failed at the last election; and de Salêles!—and Guérineau!—Why, they were the 'fish in tow'! They were the men about whom the Académie 'does not trouble itself,' whom it leaves, hanging on to a strong hook, to be drawn along in the wake of the ship of fame. There they all were—all of them, poor drowned fish!—some dead and under the water; others still struggling, turning up sad and greedy eyes full of an eager craving, never to be appeased. And while he vowed to himself to avoid a similar fate, Abel de Freydet followed the bait and dragged at the line, too firmly struck already to get himself free.

Far away, along the line cleared for the procession, muffled drums alternated with the blast of trumpets, bringing crowds of bystanders on the pavement and heads to every window. Then the music again took up the long-drawn strains of the Hero's March. In the presence of so impressive a tribute as this national funeral, this proud protest on the part of humanity, crushed and overcome by death but decking defeat in magnificence, it was hard to realise that all this pomp was for Loisillon, Permanent Secretary of the Académie Française—for nothing, servant to nothing.

CHAPTER IX.

EVERY day between four and six, earlier or later according to the time of year, Paul Astier came to take his *douche* at Keyser's hydropathic establishment at the top of the Faubourg Saint-Honoré Twenty minutes' fencing, boxing, or single-stick followed by a bath and a cold *douche*; then a little halt at the flower-shop, as he came out, to have a carnation stitched in his buttonhole; then a constitutional as far as the Arc de l'Etoile, Stenne and the phaeton following close to the footway. Finally came a turn in the Bois, where Paul, thanks to his observance of fashionable hygiene, displayed a feminine delicacy of colouring and a complexion rivalling any lady's. By this visit to Keyser's he also saved himself the trouble of reading the papers. Gossip went on between one dressing-room and another, or on the lounges of the fencing-room, where the visitors sat in fencing dress or flannel dressing-gowns, or even outside the doctor's door while awaiting the *douche*. From clubs, drawing-rooms, the Chamber, the Bourse, or the Palais de Justice came in the news of the day, and there it was proclaimed freely in loud tones, to the accompaniment of the clashing of swords and sticks, shouts for the waiter, resounding slaps on bare backs, creaking of wheel-chairs for rheumatic patients, heavy plunges re-echoing under the reverberating roof of the swimming-bath, while above the various sounds of splashing and spurting water rose the voice of worthy Dr. Keyser, standing on his platform, and the ever-recurring burden, 'Turn round.'

On this occasion Paul Astier was 'turning round' under the refreshing shower with great enjoyment; he was getting rid of the dust and fatigue of his wearisome afternoon, as well as of the lugubrious sonorities of Astier-Réhu's Academic regret 'His hour sounded upon the bell'... 'the hand of Loisillon was cold'... 'he had drained the cup of happiness'... &c, &c. Oh Master! Master! oh, respected papa! It took a good deal of water, showers, streams, floods of it, to wash off all that grimy rubbish.

He passed a tall figure bent double. Page 161.

As he went away with the water running off him, he passed a tall figure bent double, coming up from the swimming bath, which gave him a shivering nod from under a huge gutta-percha cap covering the head and half the face. The man's lean pallor and stiff stooping walk made Paul take him for one of the poor invalids who attend the establishment regularly, and whose apparition, silent as night-birds in the fencing-room where they come to be weighed, contrasts so strangely with the healthy laughter and superabundant vigour of the rest of the company. But the contemptuous curve of the large nose and the weary lines round the mouth vaguely recalled some face he knew in society. In his dressing-room he asked the man who was shampooing him, 'Who was that, Raymond, who bowed to me just now?'

'Why, that's the Prince d'Athis, sir,' replied Raymond, with a plebeian's satisfaction in uttering the word 'prince.' 'He has been taking *douches* for some time past, and generally comes in the morning. But he is later to-day, on account of a burial, so he told Joseph.'

The door of Paul's dressing-room was partly open during this dialogue, and in the room on the opposite side of the passage was visible La vaux. As he pulled on and buckled his long clerical hose, he said, 'I say, Paul, did you see Sammy coming to freshen himself up a bit?'

'Freshen himself up?' said Paul. 'What for?'

'He's going to be married in a fortnight, you know.'

'Oh! And when does he go to his Embassy?'

'Why, now, at once. The Princess has started. They are to be married out there.'

Paul had a horrid presentiment. 'The Princess?' he asked. 'Whom is he going to marry?'

'Where have you been? It's been the talk of Paris for the last two days! Colette, of course; Colette the inconsolable. I should like to see what the Duchess looks like. At the Loisillon affair she carried herself well, but never lifted her veil or spoke a word. It's a tough bit to swallow, eh? When you think that only yesterday I was helping her to choose materials for the room he was to have at St. Petersburg!'

The ill-natured unctuous voice of the fashionable scandalmonger went on with the story as he finished buckling his garters, accompanied by the sound of a *douche* two boxes off, and the Prince's voice saying, 'Harder, Joseph, harder, don't be afraid.' Freshening himself up, was he?

Paul had crossed the passage as soon as Lavaux began to talk, that he might hear better. He was seized with a wild desire to kick in the door of the Prince's room, spring on him, and have an explanation face to face with the scoundrel who was stealing the fortune almost in his grasp. Suddenly he perceived that he had nothing on, reflected that his wrath was ill-timed, and went back to his room, where he calmed down a little as he realised that the first thing to do was to have a talk with his mother and find out exactly how matters stood.

That afternoon, for once, he had no flower in his buttonhole, and while, as the stream of carriages went past, the ladies looked languidly for the charming young man in the usual row, he was driving rapidly to the Rue de Beaune. There he was greeted by Corentine with bare arms and a dirty apron. She had taken the opportunity of her mistress's absence to have a great clean-up.

'Do you know where my mother is dining?'

No, her mistress had not told her. But the master was upstairs, rummaging in his papers. The little staircase leading to the paper-room creaked under Léonard Astier's heavy tread.

'Is that you, Paul?' he asked.

The dim light of the passage and his own agitation prevented the young man from noticing his father's extraordinary appearance and the dazed sound of his voice when he answered.

'How's the Master?' said the son—'So mamma's not in?'

'No, she is dining with Madame Ancelin and going on to the Français; I am to join them in the evening.'

After this the father and son had nothing further to say to each other. They met like two strangers, like two men of hostile races. On this occasion, indeed, Paul in his impatience was half inclined to ask Leonard whether he knew anything about the marriage; but he thought the next minute, 'No, he is too stupid; mother would never say a word to him.' His father, who was also strongly tempted to put a question, called him back with an air of embarrassment.

'Paul,' he said, 'I have lost—I can't find——'

'Can't find what?' asked the son.

Astier-Réhu hesitated a moment; but after looking closely at the pretty face, whose expression, on account of the bend in the nose, was never perfectly straightforward, he added in a gloomy, surly tone—

'No, nothing; it does not matter. I won't keep you.'

There was nothing for it but to meet his mother at the theatre in Madame Ancelin's box. That meant two or three hours to be got through first. Paul dismissed his carriage and ordered Stenne to bring him his dress things at his club. Then he started for a stroll through the city in a faint twilight, while the clipped shrubs of the Tuileries Gardens assumed brighter colours as the sky grew dark around them. It was the mystic hour so precious to people pursuing dreams or making plans. The carriages grow fewer, the shadowy figures hurry by and touch the stroller lightly. There is no interruption to the flow of a man's thoughts. So the ambitious young fellow, who had quite recovered his presence of mind, carried on his reflections clearly. His thoughts were like those of Napoleon at the last hour of the battle of Waterloo: after a long day of success defeat had come with night. What was the reason? What mistake had he made? He replaced the pieces on the chessboard, and looked for the explanation of failure, but in vain. It had perhaps been rash of him to let two days pass without seeing her. But it was the most elementary rule that after such a scene as that in the cemetery a woman should be left to herself to recover. How was he to foresee this sudden flight? Suddenly a hope flashed upon him. He knew that the Princess changed her plan as often as a bird its perch. Perhaps she might not yet have gone; perhaps he should find her in the midst of preparations, unhappy, undecided, asking Herbert's portrait for advice, and should win her back by one embrace. He understood and could follow now all the capricious turns of the romance which had been going on in her little head.

He took a cab to the Rue de Courcelles. Nobody there. The Princess had gone abroad, they told him, that very morning. A terrible fit of despair came over him, and he went home instead of to the club, so as not to have to talk and answer questions. His spirits sank even lower at the sight of his great mediaeval erection and its front, in the style of the *Tour de la Faim*, all covered with bills; it suggested the piles of overdue accounts. As he felt his way in, he was greeted by a smell of fried onions filling the whole place; for his spruce little valet on nights when his master dined at the club would cook himself a tasty dish. A gleam of daylight still lingered in the studio, and Paul flung himself down on a sofa. There, as he was trying to think by what ill-luck his artfullest, cleverest designs had been upset, he fell asleep for a couple of hours and woke up another man. Just as memory gains in sharpness during the sleep of the body, so had his determination and talent for intrigue gone on acting during his short rest. He had found a new plan, and moreover a calm fixity of resolution, such as among the modern youth of France is very much more rarely met with than courage under arms.

He dressed rapidly and took a couple of eggs and a cup of tea; and when, with a faint odour of the warm curling-iron about his beard and moustaches, he entered the Théâtre Français and gave Madame Ancelin's name at the box-office, the keenest observer would have failed to detect any absorbing preoccupation in the perfect gentleman of fashion, and would never have guessed the contents of this pretty drawing-room article, black-and-white lacquered, and well locked.

Madame Ancelin's worship of official literature had two temples, the Académie Française and the Comédie Française. But the first of these places being open to the pious believer only at uncertain periods, she made the most of the second, and attended its services with great regularity. She never missed a 'first night,' whether important or unimportant, nor any of the Subscribers' Tuesdays. And as she read no books but those stamped with the hall-mark of the Académie, so the actors at the Comédie were the only players to whom she listened with enthusiasm, with excited ejaculations and rapturous amazement. Her exclamations began at the box-office, at the sight of the two great marble fonts, which the good lady's fancy had set up before the statues of Rachel and Talma in the entrance to the 'House of Molière.'

'Don't they look after it well? Just look at the door-keepers! What a theatre it is!'

The jerky movements of her short arms and the puffing of her fat little body diffused through the passage a sense of noisy gleefulness which made people say in every box, 'Here's Madame Ancelin!' On Tuesdays especially, the fashionable indifference of the house contrasted oddly with the seat where, in supreme content, leaning half out of the box, sat and cooed this good plump pink-eyed pigeon, piping away audibly, 'Look at Coquelin! Look at De-launay! What perennial youth! What an admirable theatre!' She never allowed her friends to talk of anything else, and in the *entr'actes* greeted her visitors with exclamations of rapture over the genius of the Academic playwright and the grace of the Actress-Associate.

At Paul Astier's entrance the curtain was up; and knowing that the ritual of Madame Ancelin required absolute silence at such a time, he waited quietly in the little room, separated by a step from the front of the box, where Madame Ancelin was seated in bliss between Madame Astier and Madame Eviza, while behind were Danjou and De Freydet looking like prisoners. The click, which the box-door made and must make in shutting, was followed by a 'Hush!' calculated to appal the intruder who was disturbing the service. Madame Astier half turned round, and felt a shiver at the sight of her son. What was the matter? What had Paul to say to her of such pressing importance as to bring him to that haunt of boredom—Paul, who never let himself be bored without a reason? Money again, no doubt, horrid money! Well, fortunately she would soon have plenty; Sammy's marriage would make them all rich. Much as she longed to go up to Paul and reassure him with the good news, which perhaps he had not heard, she was obliged to stay in her seat, look on at the play, and join as chorus in her hostess's exclamations, 'Look at Coquelin! Look at De-launay! Oh! Oh!' It was a hard trial to her to have to wait So it was to Paul, who could see nothing but the glaring heat of the footlights, and in the looking-glass at the side the reflection of part of the house, stalls, dress-circle, boxes, rows of faces, pretty dresses, bonnets, all as it were drowned in a blue haze, and presenting the colourless ghostly appearance of things dimly seen under water. During the *entr'acte* came the usual infliction of indiscriminate praise.

'Monsieur Paul! Di' y' see Reichemberg's dress? Di' y' see the pink-bead apron? and the ribbon ruching? Di' y' see? This is the only place where they know how to dress, that it is!'

Visitors began to come, and the mother was able to get hold of her son and carry him off to the sofa. There, in the midst of wraps and the bustle of people going out, they spoke in low voices with their heads close together.

'Answer me quickly and clearly,' began Paul 'Is Sammy going to be married?'

'Yes, the Duchess heard yesterday. But she has come here to-night all the same. Corsican pride!'

'And whom has he caught? Can you tell me now?'

'Why, Colette, of course! You must have had a suspicion.'

'Not the least,' said Paul. 'And what shall you get for it?'

She murmured triumphantly, 'Eight thousand pounds!'

"Well, by your schemes I have lost a million!" Page 171.

'Well, by your schemes I have lost a million!—a million, and a wife!' He grasped her by the wrists in his anger, and hissed into her face, 'You selfish marplot!'

The news took away her breath and her senses. It was Paul then, Paul, from whom proceeded the force which acted, as she had occasionally perceived, against her influence; it was Paul whom the little fool was thinking of when she said, sobbing in her arms, 'If you only knew!' And now, just at the end of the mines which with so much cunning and skilful patience they had each been driving towards the treasure, one last stroke of the axe had brought them face to face, empty-handed! They sat silent, looking at each other, with corresponding crooks in their noses and the same fierce gleam in both pairs of grey eyes, while all around them were the stir of people coming and going and the buzz of conversation. Rigid indeed is the discipline of society, seeing that it could repress in these two creatures all the cries and groans, all the desire to roar and slay, which filled and shook their hearts. Madame Astier was the first to express her thoughts aloud:

'If only the Princess were not gone!'

And she writhed her lips with rage at the thought that the sudden departure had been her own suggestion.

'We will get her back,' said Paul.

'How?'

Without answering her question, he asked, 'Is Sammy here to-night?'

'Oh, I don't think so, as *she* is—— Where are you going? what do you mean to do?'

'Keep quiet, won't you? Don't interfere. You are too unlucky for me.'

He left with a crowd of visitors who were driven away by the end of the *entr'acte*, and she went back to her seat on Madame Ancelin's left. Her hostess worshipped with the same ecstasy as before, and it was one perpetual giving of thanks.

'Oh, look at Coquelin! What humour he has! My dear, do look at him!'

'My dear' was indeed not attending; her eyes wandered, and on her lips was the painful smile of a dancer hissed off the boards. With the excuse that the footlights dazzled her, she was turning every moment towards the audience to look for her son. Perhaps there would be a duel with the Prince, if he was there. And all her fault—all through her stupid bungling.

'Ah, there's Delaunay! Di' y' see him? Di' y' see?'

No, she had seen nothing but the Duchess's box, where some one had just come in, with a youthful elegant figure, like her Paul. But it was the little Count Adriani, who had heard of the rupture like the rest of Paris and was already tracking the game. Through the rest of the play the mother ate her heart out in misery, turning over innumerable confused plans for the future, mixed in her thoughts with past events and scenes which ought to have forewarned her. Stupid, how stupid of her! How had she failed to guess?

At last came the departure, but oh how long it took! She had to stop every moment, to bow or smile to her friends, to say good-bye. 'What are you going to do this summer? Do come and see us at Deauville.' All down the narrow passage crammed with people, where ladies finish putting on their wraps with a pretty movement to make sure of their ear-rings, all down the white marble staircase to the men-servants waiting at the foot, the mother, as she talks, still watches, listens, tries to catch in the hum of the great fashionable swarm dispersing for some months a word or hint of a scene that evening in a box. Here comes the Duchess, haughty and erect in her long white and gold mantle, taking the arm of the young officer of the Papal Guard. She knows the shabby trick her friend has played her, and as the two women pass they exchange a cold expressionless glance more to be dreaded than the most violent expletive of a fishwoman. They know now what to think of each other; they know that in the poisoned warfare, which is to succeed their sisterly intimacy, every blow will tell, will be directed to the right spot by practised hands. But they discharge the task imposed by society, and both wear the same mask of indifference, so that the masterful hate of the one can meet and strike against the spiteful hate of the other without producing a spark.

Downstairs, in the press of valets and young clubmen, Léonard Astier was waiting, as he had promised, for his wife. 'Ah, there is the great man!' exclaimed Madame Ancelin; and with a final dip of her fingers into the holy water she scattered it around her broadcast, over the great Astier-Réhu, the great Danjou, and Coquelin, you know! and Delaunay, you know! Oh! Oh! Oh!—Astier did not reply, but followed with his wife on his arm and his collar turned up against the draught. It was raining. Madame Ancelin offered to take them home; but it was only with the conventional politeness of a 'carriage' lady afraid of tiring her horses and still more afraid of her coachman's temper (she has invariably the best coachman in Paris). Besides, 'the great man' had a cab; and without waiting for the lady's benediction—'Ah, well, we know you two like to be alone. Ah! what a happy household!'—he dragged off Madame Astier along the wet and dirty colonnade.

When, at the end of a ball or evening party, a fashionable couple drive off in their carriage, the question always suggests itself, 'Now what will they say?' Not much usually, for the man generally comes away from this kind of festivity weary and knocked up, while the lady continues the party in the darkness of the carriage by inward comparisons of her dress and her looks with those she has just seen, and makes plans for the arrangement of her drawing-room or a new costume. Still the restraint of feature required by society is so excessive, and fashionable hypocrisy has reached such a height, that it would be interesting to be present at the moment when the conventional attitude is relaxed, to hear the real natural tone of voice, and to realise the actual relations of the beings thus suddenly released from trammels and sent rolling home in the light of their brougham lamps through the empty streets of Paris. In the case of the Astiers the return home was very characteristic. The moment they were alone the wife laid aside the deference and pretended interest exhibited towards the Master in society, and spoke her mind, compensating herself in so doing for the attention with which she had listened for the hundredth time to old stories which bored her to death. The husband, kindly by disposition and accustomed to think well of himself and everyone else, invariably came home in a state of bliss, and was horrified at the malicious comments of his wife on their hosts and the guests they had met. Madame Astier would utter calmly the most shocking accusations, exaggerating gossip in the light unconscious way which is characteristic of Parisian society. Rather than stimulate her he would hold his tongue and turn round in his corner to take a little doze. But on this evening Léonard sat down straight, regardless of the sharp 'Do mind my dress!' which showed that somebody's skirts were being crumpled. What did he care about her dress? 'I've been robbed!' he said, in such a tone that the windows rattled.

Oh dear, the autographs! She had not been thinking of them, least of all just now, when tormented by very different anxieties, and there was nothing feigned in her surprise.

Robbed—yes, robbed of his 'Charles-the-Fifths,' the three best things in his collection! But the assurance which made his attack so violent died out of his voice, and his suspicion hesitated, at the sight of Adelaide's surprise. Meanwhile she recovered her self-possession. 'But whom do you suspect?' Corentine, she thought, was trustworthy. Teyssèdre? It was hardly likely that an ignorant——

Teyssèdre! He exclaimed at it, the thing seemed so obvious. Helped by his hatred for the man of polish, he soon began to see how the crime had come about, and traced it step by step from a chance allusion at dinner to the value of his documents, heard by Corentine and repeated in all innocence. Ah, the scoundrel! Why, he had the skull of a criminal! Foolish to struggle against the intimations of instinct! There must be something out of the common, when a floor-polisher could arouse so strange an antipathy in a member of the Institute! Ah, well, the dolt was done for now! He should catch it! 'My three Charleses! Only fancy!' He wanted to inform the police at once, before going home. His wife tried to prevent him. 'Are you out of your mind? Go to the police-station after midnight?' But he insisted, and thrust his great numskull out into the rain to give orders to the driver. She was obliged to pull him back with an effort, and feeling too much exhausted to carry on the lie, to let him say his say and bring him round gradually, she came out with the whole truth.

'It's not Teyssèdre—it's I! There!' At one breath she poured out the story of her visit to Bos, the money she had got, the 800L., and the necessity for it. The silence which ensued was so long that at first she thought he had had a fit of apoplexy. It was not that; but like a child that falls or hits itself, poor Crocodilus had opened his mouth so wide to let out his anger, and taken so deep a breath, that he could not utter a sound. At last came a roar that filled the Carrousel, where their cab was at that minute splashing through the pools.

'Robbed, robbed! Robbed by my wife for the sake of her son!' In his insane fury he jumbled together indiscriminately the abusive patois of his native hillside, '*Ah la garso! Ah li bongri!*' with the classical exclamations of Harpagon bewailing his casket, *Justice, justice du ciel!* and other select extracts often recited to his pupils. It was as light as day in the bright rays of the tall electric lamps standing round the great square, over which, as the theatres were emptying, omnibuses and carriages were now passing in all directions.

'Do be quiet,' said Madame Astier; 'everyone knows you.'

'Except you, Madame!'

She thought he was going to beat her, and in the strained condition of her nerves it might perhaps have been a relief. But under the terror of a scandal he suddenly quieted down, swearing finally by his mother's ashes that as soon as he got home he would pack up his trunk and go straight off to Sauvagnat, leaving his wife to depart with her scoundrelly prodigal and live on their spoils.

Once more the deep old box with its big nails was brought hastily from the anteroom into the study. A few billets of wood were still left in it from the winter's supply, but the 'deity' did not change his purpose for that. For an hour the house resounded with the rolling of logs and the banging of cupboard doors, as he flung among the sawdust and bits of dry bark linen, clothes, boots, and even the green coat and embroidered waistcoat of the Academic full dress, carefully put away in napkins. His wrath was relieved by this operation, and diminished as he filled his trunk, till his last resentful grumblings died away when it occurred to him that, fixed as he was to his place, to uproot himself was utterly impossible. Meanwhile Madame Astier, sitting on the edge of an armchair in her dressing-gown, with a lace wrap round her head, watched his proceedings and murmured between yawn and yawn with placid irony, 'Really, Léonard, really!'

CHAPTER X.

'My notion is that people, like things, have a right and a wrong way up, and there's always a place to get hold of, if you want to have a good control and grasp of them. I know where the place is, and that's my power! Driver, to the Tête Noire.' At Paul Astier's order the open carriage, in which the three tall hats belonging to Freydet, Védrine, and himself rose in funereal outline against the brightness of the afternoon landscape, drew up on the right-hand side of the bridge at St. Cloud, in front of the inn he had named. Every jolt of the hired conveyance over the paving of the square brought into sight an ominous long case of green baize projecting beyond the lowered hood of the carriage. Paul had chosen, as seconds for this meeting with D'Athis, first the Vicomte de Freydet, on account of his title and his 'de,' and with him the Count Adriani. But the Papal Embassy was afraid of adding another scandal to the recent affair of the Cardinal's hat, and he had been obliged to find a substitute for Pepino in the sculptor, who would perhaps allow himself at the last minute to be described in the official statement as 'Marquis.' The matter, however, was not supposed to be serious, only a quarrel at the club over the card-table, where the Prince had taken a hand for a last game before leaving Paris. The affair could not be hushed up; it was specially impossible to cave in to a fighting man like Paul Astier, who had a great reputation in fencing rooms, and whose records were framed and hung in the shooting-gallery in the Avenue d'Antin.

While the carriage waited by the terrace of the *restaurant* and the waiters unobtrusively bestowed on it knowing glances, down a steep little path came rolling a short, fat man, with the white spats, white tie, silk hat, and captivating air of the doctor of a fashionable watering-place. He made signals from the distance with his sunshade, there's Gomes,' said Paul. Doctor Gomes, formerly on the resident staff of one of the Paris hospitals, had been ruined by play and an old attachment. Now he was 'Uncle Gomes,' and had an irregular practice; not a bad fellow, but one who would stick at nothing, and had made a specialty of affairs like the present. Fee, two guineas and breakfast. Just now he was spending his holiday with Cloclo at Ville d'Avray, and came puffing to the meeting place, carrying a little bag which held his instrument case, medicines, bandages, splints—enough to set up an ambulance.

'Is it to be scratch or wound?' he asked, as he took his seat in the carriage opposite Paul.

'Scratch, of course, doctor, scratch, with swords of the Institute. The Académie Française against the Sciences Morales et Politiques.'

Gomès smiled as he steadied his bag between his knees.

'I did not know, so I brought the big apparatus.'

'Well, you must display it; it will impress the enemy,' suggested Védrine, in his quiet way.

The doctor winked, a little put out by the two seconds, whose faces were unknown to the boulevards, and to whom Paul Astier, who treated him like a servant, did not even introduce him.

As the carriage started, the window of a room on the first floor opened, and a pair came and looked at them curiously. The girl was Marie Donval, of the Gymnase, whom the doctor recognised and named in a loud voice. The other was a deformed little creature, whose head was barely visible above the window-sill. Freydet, with much indignation, and Védrine, with some amusement, recognised Fage.

'Are you surprised, M. de Freydet?' said Paul. And hereupon he launched into a savage attack upon woman. Woman! A disordered child, with all a child's perversity and wickedness, all its instinctive desire to cheat, to lie, to tease, all its cowardice. She was greedy, she was vain, she was inquisitive. Oh yes, she could serve you a hash of somebody else, but she had not an idea of her own; and in argument, why, she was as full of holes, twists, and slippery places as the pavement on a frosty night after a thaw. How was conversation possible with a woman? Why, there was nothing in her, neither kindness nor pity nor intellect—not leven common sense. For a fashionable bonnet or one of Spricht's gowns she was capable of stealing, of any trick however dirty; for at bottom the only thing she cares for is dress. To know the strength of this passion a man must have gone, as Paul had, with the most elegant ladies of fashion to the rooms of the great man-milliner. They were hand-and-glove with the forewomen, asked them to breakfast at their country houses, knelt to old Spricht as if he were the Pope himself. The Marquise de Roca-Nera took her young daughters to him, and all but asked him to bless them!

'Just so,' said the doctor, with the automatic jerk of a hireling whose neck has been put out of joint by perpetual acquiescence. Then followed an awkward pause, the conversation being, as it were, thrown out of gear by this sudden and unexpectedly violent effusion from a young fellow usually very civil and self-possessed. The sun was oppressive, and was reflected off the dry stone walls on each side of the steep road, up which the horses were toiling painfully, while the pebbles creaked under the wheels.

'To show the kindness and pity of woman, I can vouch for the following.' It was Védrine who spoke, his head thrown back and swaying as it rested on the hood of the carriage, his eyes half shut as he looked at some inward vision. 'It was not at the great milliner's. It was at the Hôtel-Dieu, in Bouchereau's department. A rough, white-washed cell, an iron bedstead with all the clothes thrown off, and on it, stark naked, covered with sweat and foam, contorted and twisted like a clown with sudden springs and with yells that re-echoed through the fore-court of Notre Dame, a madman in the last agony. Beside the bed two women, one on either side, the Sister, and one of Bouchereau's little lady-students, both quite young, yet with no disgust and no fear, both leaning over the poonwretch whom no one dared go near, wiping from his brow and mouth the sweat of his agony and the suffocating foam. The Sister was praying all the time; the other was not. But in the inspired look in the eyes of both, in the gentleness of the brave little hands which wiped away the madman's foam right from under his teeth, in the heroic and maternal beauty of their unwearied movements, you felt that they were both very women. There is woman! It was enough to make a man fall on his knees and sob.'

'Thank you, Védrine,' said Freydet under his breath; he had been choking with the recollection of the dear one at Clos Jallanges. The doctor began his jerk and his 'just so,' but was cut short by the dry, incisive tones of Paul Astier.

'Oh yes, sick nurses, I'll allow. Sickly themselves, nothing gives them such pleasure as nursing, dressing, bathing their patients, handling hot towels and basins; and then there's the power they exercise over the suffering and the weak.' His voice hissed and rose to the pitch of his mother's, while from his cold eye darted a little gleam of wickedness which made his companions wonder 'what is up,' and suggested to the doctor the sage reflection, 'All very well to talk about a scratch, and swords of the Institute, but I should not care to be in the Prince's skin.'

'Now I'll paint you a pendant to our friend's chromo,' sneered Paul. 'As a specimen of feminine delicacy and faithfulness, take a little widow, who even in the burial vault of the departed, and on his very tombstone——'

'*The Ephesian Matron!*' broke in Védrine, 'you want to tell us that!' The discussion grew animated and ran on, still to an accompaniment of the jolting wheels, upon the never-failing topics of masculine discussion, woman and love.

'Gentlemen, look,' said the doctor, who from his place on the front seat saw two carriages coming up the hill at a quick trot. In the first, an open victoria, were the Prince's seconds. Gomes stood up, and as he sat down again named them in a low and respectful tone, 'the Marquis d'Urbin and General de Bonneuil of the Jockey Club—very good form—and my brother-surgeon, Aubouis.' This Doctor Aubouis was another low-caste of the same stamp as Gomes; but as he had a ribbon his fee was five guineas. Behind was a little brougham in which, along with the inseparable Lavaux, was concealed D'Athis, desperately bored with the whole business. During five minutes the three vehicles went up the hill one behind another like a wedding or funeral procession, and nothing was heard but the sound of the wheels and the panting or snorting of the horses as they rattled their bits.

'Pass them,' said a haughty nasal voice.

'By all means,' said Paul, 'they are going to see to our quarters.' The wheels grazed on the narrow road, the seconds bowed, the doctors exchanged professional smiles. Then the brougham went by, showing behind the window glass, pulled up in spite of the heat, a morose motionless profile, as pale as a corpse. 'He won't be paler than that an hour hence, when they take him home with a hole in his side,' thought Paul, and he pictured the exact thrust, feint No. 2, followed by a direct lunge straight in between the third and fourth ribs.

At the top of the hill the air was cooler, and laden with the scent of lime-flowers, acacias, and roses warm in the sun. Behind the low park railings sloped great lawns over which moved the mottled shadows of the trees. Presently was heard the bell of a garden gate.

'Here we are,' said the doctor, who knew the place. It was where the Marquis d'Urbin's stud used to be, but for the last two years it had been for sale. All the horses were gone, except a few colts gambolling about in fields separated by high barriers.

The duel was to take place at the further end of the estate, on a wide terrace in front of a white brick stable. It was reached by sloping paths all overgrown with moss and grass, along which both parties walked together, mingling, but not speaking, proper as could be; except that Védrine, unable to support these fashionable formalities, scandalised Freydet, who carried his high collar with much gravity, by exclaiming, 'Here's a lily of the valley,' or pulling off a bough, and presently, struck with the contrast between the splendid passivity of nature and the futile activity of man, ejaculated, as he gazed on the great woods that climbed the opposite hill-side, and the distance composed of clustered roofs, shining water and blue haze, 'How beautiful, how peaceful!' With an involuntary movement he pointed to the horizon, for the benefit of some one whose patent leather boots came squeaking behind him. But oh, what an outpouring of contempt, not only upon the improper Védrine, but upon the landscape and the sky! The Prince d'Athis was unsurpassed in contempt. He expressed it with his eye, the celebrated eye whose flash had always overcome Bismarck; he expressed it with his great hooked nose, and with the turned down corners of his mouth; he expressed it without reason, without inquiry, study, or thought, and his rise in diplomacy, his successes in love and in society, were all the work of this supposed contempt!

In reality 'Sammy 'was an empty-headed bauble, a puppet picked by a clever woman's compassion out of the refuse and oyster shells of the supper-tavern, raised by her higher and higher, prompted by her what to say and, more important still, what not to say, lessoned and guided by her, till the day when, finding himself at the top of the ladder, he kicked away the stool which he no longer wanted. Society thought him a very clever fellow, but Védrine did not share the general opinion; and the comparison of Talleyrand to a 'silk stocking full of mud' came into his mind as he watched this highly respectable and proper personage stalk majestically past him. Evidently the Duchess had her wits about her when she disguised his emptiness by making him both diplomatist and academician, and cloaking him for the official carnival with the double thickness of both the two thread-bare, though venerable, dominos, to which society continues to bow. But how she could have loved such a hollow, stony-hearted piece of crockery, Védrine did not understand. Was it his title? But her family was as good as his. Was it the English cut of his clothes, the frock coat closely fitted to his broken-down shoulders, and the mud-coloured trousers that made so crude a bit of colour among the trees? One might almost think that the young villain, Paul, was right in his contemptuous remarks on woman's taste for what is low, for deformity in morals or physique!

The Prince had reached the three-foot fence which divided the path from the meadow, and either because he mistrusted his slender legs, or because he thought a vigorous movement improper for a man of his position, he hesitated, particularly bothered by the sense that 'that huge artist fellow' was just at his back. At last he made up his mind to step out of his way to a gap in the wooden fence. Védrine winked his little eyes. 'Go round, my good sir,' was his thought, 'go round; make the road as long as you will, it must bring you in the end to the front of the white building yonder. And when you get there, you may possibly have to pay a heavy reckoning for all your scoundrelly tricks. There is always a reckoning to pay in the end.' Having relieved his mind by this soliloquy, he jumped clean over the fence without so much as putting a hand on it (a proceeding extremely improper), and joined the knot of seconds busily engaged in casting lots for places and swords. In spite of the dandified solemnity of their aspect, they looked, as they all bent to see whether the toss fell head or tail, or ran to pick up the coins, like big school-boys in the playground, wrinkled and grey. During a discussion on a doubtful pitch, Védrine heard his name called by Astier, who, with perfect self-possession, was taking off his coat and emptying his pockets behind the little building. 'What's that stuff the General is talking? Wants to have his walking-stick within reach of our swords, to prevent accidents? I won't have that sort of thing, do you hear? This is not a lower school fight. We are both old hands, fifth form.' In spite of his light words, his teeth were clenched and his eye gleamed fiercely. 'It's serious then?' asked Védrine, looking at him hard.

'Couldn't be more so.'

'Ah! Somehow I thought as much,' and the sculptor returned to convey the message to the General, commander of a cavalry division, looking all leg from his heels to his pointed ears, which in brilliancy of colour vied with Freydet's. At Védrine's intimation these ears flushed suddenly scarlet, as if the blood boiled in them. 'Right, Sir! 'Course, Sir!' His words cut the air like the lash of a whip. Sammy was being helped by Doctor Aubouis to turn up his shirt sleeves. Did he hear? or was it the aspect of the lithe, cat-like, vigorous young fellow as he came forward with neck and arms bare and round as a woman's, and with that pitiless look. Be the reason what it may, D'Athis, who had come to the ground as a social duty without a shade of anxiety, as befitted a gentleman who was not inexperienced and knew the value of two good seconds, suddenly changed countenance, turned earthy pale, while his beard scarcely concealed the twitch of his jaw in the horrible contortion of fear. But he kept his self-control, and put himself on the defensive bravely enough.

'Now, gentlemen.'

Yes, there is always a reckoning to pay. He realised that keenly as he faced that pitiless sword-point, which sought him, felt him at a distance, seemed to spare him now only to make more sure of hitting presently. They meant to kill him; that was certain. And as he parried the blows with his long, thin arm stretched out, amid the clashing of the hilts he felt, for the first time, a pang of remorse for his mean desertion of the noble lady who had lifted him out of the gutter and given him once more a decent place in the world; he felt too that her merited wrath was in some way connected with this present encompassing peril, which seemed to shake the air all about him, to send round and round in a glancing, vanishing vision the expanse of sky overhead, the alarmed faces of the seconds and doctors, and the remoter figures of two stable boys wildly beating off with their caps the gambolling horses that wanted to come and look on. Suddenly came exclamations, sharp and peremptory: 'Enough! Stop, stop!' What has happened? The peril is gone, the sky stands still, everything has resumed its natural colour and place. But at his feet over the torn and trampled ground spreads a widening pool of blood, which darkens the yellow soil, and in it lies Paul Astier helpless, with a wound right through his bare neck, stuck like a pig. In the still pause of horror which followed the disaster was heard the shrill, unceasing noise of insects in the distant meadow, while the horses, no longer watched, gathered together a little way off and stretched out inquisitive noses towards the motionless body of the vanquished.

Yet he was a skilful swordsman. His fingers had a firm grasp of the hilt and could make the whistling blade flash, hover, and descend where he pleased, while his adversary encountered him with a wavering cowardly spit. How had it come about? The seconds will say, and the evening papers repeat, and tomorrow all Paris will take up the cue, that Paul Astier slipped as he made his thrust and ran on his opponent's point. A full and accurate account will no doubt be given: but in life it usually happens that decision of language varies inversely with certainty of knowledge. Even from the spectators, even from the combatants themselves, a certain mist and confusion will always veil the crucial moment, when, against all reasonable calculation, the final stroke was given by intervening fate, wrapped in that obscure cloud which by epic rule closes round the end of a contest.

Carried into a small coachman's room adjoining the stable, Paul, on opening his eyes after a long swoon, saw first from the iron bedstead on which he lay a lithographic print of the Prince Imperial pinned to the wall over the drawers, which were covered with surgical instruments. As consciousness returned to him through the medium of external objects, the poor melancholy face with its faded eyes, discoloured by the damp of the walls, suggested a sad omen of ill-fated youth. But besides ambition and cunning, Paul had his full share of courage; and raising with difficulty his head and its cumbrous wrapping of bandages, he asked in a voice broken and weak, though fleeting still, 'Wound or scratch, doctor?' Gomes, who was rolling up his medicated wool, waved to him to keep quiet, as he answered, 'Scratch, you lucky dog; but a near shave. Aubouis and I thought the carotid was cut.' A faint colour came into the young man's cheeks, and his eyes sparkled. It is so satisfactory not to die! Instantly his ambition revived, and he wanted to know how long he should take to get well again. 'From three weeks to a month.' Such was the doctor's judgment, announced in an indifferent tone with an amusing shade of contempt. He was really very much annoyed and mortified that his patient had got the worst of it. Paul with his eyes on the wall was making calculations. D'Athis would be gone and Colette married before he was even out of bed. Well, that business had failed; he must look out for something else.

The door was opened, and a great flood of light poured into the miserable room. How delightful was life and the warm sunshine! Védrine, coming in with Freydet, went up to the bed and held out his hand joyously, saying 'You did give us a fright!' He was really fond of his young rascal, and cherished him as a work of art. 'Ah, that you did!' said Freydet, wiping his brow with an air of great relief. His eyes had seen all his hopes of election to the Académie lying on the ground in that pool of blood. How could Astier, the father, ever have come out as the champion of a man connected with such a fatal event? Not but that Freydet had a warm heart, but the absorbing thought of his candidature brought his mind, like a compass needle, always round to the same point; howsoever shaken and turned about, it came back still to the Academic Pole. And as the wounded man smiled at his friends, feeling a little foolish at finding himself, for all his cleverness, lying there at full length, Freydet dilated with admiration on the 'proper' behaviour of the seconds, whom they had just assisted in framing the report, of Doctor Aubouis, who had offered to stay with his professional friend, of the Prince, who had gone off in the victoria and left for Paul his well-hung carriage, which having only one horse could be brought right up to the door of the little building. Every one had behaved most properly.

'How he bores one with his proprieties!' said Védrine, seeing the face Paul had not been able to help making.

'It really is very odd,' murmured the young fellow in a vague and wandering voice. So it would be he, and not the other fellow, whose pale, bloodstained face would be seen by the doctors side through the window of the brougham as it went slowly home. Well, he had made a mess of it! Suddenly he sat up, in spite of the doctor's protest, rummaged in his card-case for a card, and scribbled on it with pencil in a shaky hand, 'Fate is as faithless as man. I wanted to avenge you, but could not. Forgive me.' He signed his name, read it over, reflected, read it again, then fastened up the envelope, which they had found in a dusty drawer, a nasty scented envelope from some rural stores, and directed it to the Duchess Padovani. He gave it to Freydet, begging him to deliver it himself as soon as possible.

'It shall be there within an hour, my dear Paul.'

He made with his hand a sign of thanks and dismissal, then stretched himself out, shut his eyes, and lay quiet and still till the departure, listening to the sound which came from the sunny meadow around—a vast shrill hum of insects, which imitated the pulsation of approaching fever. Beneath the closed lids his thoughts pursued the windings of this second and quite novel plot, conceived by a sudden inspiration on 'the place of defeat.

Was it a sudden inspiration? There perhaps the ambitious young man was wrong; for the spring of our actions is often unseen, lost and hidden amid the internal disturbance of the crisis, even as the agitator who starts a crowd himself disappears in it. A human being resembles a crowd; both are manifold, complicated things, full of confused and irregular impulses, but there is an agitator in the background; and the movements of a man, like those of a mob, passionate and spontaneous as they may appear, have always been preconcerted. Since the evening when on the terrace of the Hôtel Padovani Lavaux had suggested the Duchess to the young Guardsman, the thought had occurred to Paul that, if Madame de Rosen failed him, he might fall back on the fair Antonia. It had recurred two nights ago at the Français, when he saw Adriani in the Duchess's box; but it took no definite shape, because all his energy was then turned in another direction, and he still believed in the possibility of success. Now that the game was completely lost, his first idea on returning to life was 'the Duchess.' Thus, although he scarcely knew it, the resolution reached so abruptly was but the coming to light of what grew slowly underground. 'I wanted to avenge you, but could not.' Warm-hearted, impulsive, and revengeful as he knew her to be, 'Mari' Anto,' as her Corsicans called her, would certainly be at his bedside the next morning. It would be his business to see that she did not go away.

Védrine and Freydet went back together in the landau, without waiting for Sammy's brougham, which had to come slowly for the sake of the wounded man. The sight of the swords lying in their baize cover on the empty seat opposite suggested reflection. 'They don't rattle so much as they did going, the brutes,' said Védrine, kicking them as he spoke. 'Ah, you see they are his!' said Freydet, giving words to his thoughts. Then, resuming the air of gravity and propriety appropriate to a second, he added, 'We had everything in our favour, the ground, the weapons, and a first rate fencer. As he says, it is very odd.'

Presently there was a pause in the dialogue, while their attention was fixed by the gorgeous colour of the river, spread in sheets of green and purple under the setting sun. Crossing the bridge the horses trotted fast up the street of Boulogne. 'Yes,' Védrine went on, as if there had been no long interruption of silence; 'yes, after all, in spite of apparent successes, the fellow is unlucky at bottom. I have now seen him more than once fighting with circumstances in one of those crises which are touchstones to a man's fate, and bring out of him all the luck he has. Well, let him plot as cunningly as he will, foresee everything, mix his tints with the utmost skill, something gives way at the last moment, and without completely ruining him prevents him from attaining his object. Why? Very likely, just because his nose is crooked. I assure you, that sort of crookedness is nearly always the sign of a twist in the intellect, an obliquity in the character. The helm's not straight, you see!'

They laughed at the suggestion; and Védrine, pursuing the subject of good and bad luck, told an odd story of a thing which had happened almost under his eyes when he was staying with the Padovani in Corsica. It was on the coast at Barbicaglia, just opposite the lighthouse on the Sanguinaires. In this lighthouse lived an old keeper, a tried servant, just on the eve of retirement. One night when he was on duty the old fellow fell asleep and dozed for five minutes at the most, stopping with his outstretched leg the movement of the revolving light, which ought to change colour once a minute. That very night, just at that moment, the inspector-general, who was making his annual round in a Government boat, happened to be opposite the Sanguinaires. He was amazed to see a stationary light, had the boat stopped, investigated and reported the matter, and the next morning the official boat brought a new keeper to the island and notice of instant dismissal to the poor old man. 'It seems to me,' said Védrine, 'a curiosity in ill-luck that, in the chances of darkness, time, and space, the inspector's survey should have coincided with the old man's nap.' Their carriage was just reaching the Place de la Concorde, and Védrine pointed with one of his slow calm movements to a great piece of sky overhead where the dark green colour was pierced here and there by newly-appearing stars, visible in the waning light of the glorious day.

A few minutes later the landau turned into the Rue de Poitiers, a short street, already in shadow, and stopped in front of the high iron gates bearing the Padovani shield. All the shutters of the house were closed, and there was a great chattering of birds in the garden. The Duchess had gone for the summer to Mousseaux. Freydet stood hesitating, with the huge envelope in his hand. He had expected to see the fair Antonia and give a graphic account of the duel, perhaps even to slip in a reference to his approaching candidature. Now he could not make up his mind whether he should leave the letter, or deliver it himself a few days hence, when he went back to Clos Jallanges. Eventually he decided to leave it, and as he stepped back into the carriage he said, 'Poor fellow! He impressed upon me that the letter was urgent.'

'Quite so,' said Védrine, as the landau carried them along the quays, now beginning to glimmer with rows of yellow lights, to the meeting place arranged with D'Athis's seconds; 'quite so. I don't know what the letter is about, but for him to take the trouble to write it at such a moment, it must be something very smart, something extremely ingenious and clever. Only there you are! Very urgent—and the Duchess has left.'

And pushing the end of his nose on one side between two fingers, he said with the utmost gravity, 'That's what it is, you see.'

CHAPTER XI.

The sword-thrust which had so nearly cost Paul Astier his life made peace for the time between his parents. In the emotion produced by such a shock to his natural feelings, the father forgave all; and as for three weeks Madame Astier remained with her patient, coming home only on flying visits to fetch linen or change her dress, there was no risk of the covert allusions and indirect reproaches, which will revive, even after forgiveness and reconciliation, the disagreement of husband and wife. And when Paul got well and went, at the urgent invitation of the Duchess, to Mousseaux, the return of this truly academic household, if not to warm affection, at least to the equable temperature of the 'cold bed,' was finally secured by its establishment in the Institute, in the official lodgings vacated by Loisillon, whose widow, having been appointed manager of the school of Ecouen, removed so quickly, that the new secretary began to move in within a very few days of his election.

It was not a long process to settle in rooms which they had surveyed for years with the minute exactness of envy and hope, till they knew the very utmost that could be made of every corner. The pieces of furniture from the Rue de Beaune fell into the new arrangement so smartly, that it looked as if they were merely returning after a sojourn in the country, and finding their fixed habitat and natural place of adhesion by the marks of their own forms upon the floors or panels. The redecoration was limited to cleaning the room in which Loisillon died, and papering what had been the reception-room of Villemain and was now taken by Astier for his study, because there was a good light from the quiet court and a lofty bright little room, immediately adjoining, for his MSS., which were transferred there in three journeys of a cab, with the help of Fage the bookbinder.

With the help of Fage, the bookbinder. Page 204.

Every morning, with a fresh delight, he enjoyed the convenience of a 'library' scarcely inferior to the Foreign Office, which he could enter without stooping or climbing a ladder. Of his kennel in the Rue de Beaune he could not now think without anger and disgust. It is the nature of man to regard places in which he has felt pain with an obstinate and unforgiving dislike. We can reconcile ourselves to living creatures, which are capable of alteration and differences of aspect, but not to the stony unchange-ableness of things. Amid the pleasures of getting in, Astier-Réhu could forget his indignation at the offence of his wife, and even his grievances against Teyssèdre, who received orders to come every Wednesday morning as before. But at the mere remembrance of the slope-roofed den, into which he was lately banished for one day in each week, the historian ground his teeth, and the jaw of 'Crocodilus' reappeared.

Teyssèdre, incredible as it may be, was very little excited or impressed by the honour of polishing the monumental floors of the Palais Mazarin, and still shoved about the table, papers, and numberless refaits of the Permanent Secretary with the calm superiority of a citizen of Riom over a common fellow from 'Chauvagnat.' Astier-Réhu, secretly uncomfortable under this crushing contempt, sometimes tried to make the savage feel the dignity of the place upon which his wax-cake was operating. 'Teyssèdre,' said he to him, one morning, 'this was the reception-room of the great Villemain. Pray treat it accordingly;' but he instantly offered satisfaction to the Arvernian's pride by saying weakly to Corentine, 'Give the good man a glass of wine.' The astonished Corentine brought it, and the polisher, leaning on his stick, emptied it at a draught, his pupils dilating with pleasure. Then he wiped his mouth with his sleeve and, setting down the glass with the mark of his greedy lips upon it, said, 'Look you, *Meuchieu Astier*, a glass of good wine is the only real good in life.' There was such a ring of truth in his voice, such a sparkle of contentment in his eyes, that the Permanent Secretary, going back into his library, shut the door a little sharply.

A glass of good wine is the only good thing in life. Page 206.

It was scarcely worth while to have scrambled from his low beginning to his present glory as head of literature, historian of the 'House of Orleans,' and keystone of the Académie Française, if a glass of good wine could give to a boor a happiness worth it all. But the next minute, hearing the polisher say with a sneer to Corentine that 'mooch 'e cared for the 'ception-room of the great Villemain,' Léonard Astier shrugged his shoulders, and at the thought of such ignorance his half-felt envy gave way to a deep and benign compassion.

Meanwhile Madame Astier, who had been brought up in the building, and recognised with remembrances of her childhood every stone in the court and every step in the dusty and venerable Staircase B, felt as if she had at last got back to her home. She had, moreover, a sense far keener than her husband's of the material advantages of the place. Nothing to pay for rent, for lighting, for fires, a great saving upon the parties of the winter season, to say nothing of the increase of income and the influential connection, so particularly valuable in procuring orders for her beloved Paul. Madame Loisillon in her time, when sounding the praises of her apartments at the Institute, never failed to add with emphasis, 'I have entertained there even Sovereigns.' 'Yes, in the *little* room,' good Adelaide would answer tartly, drawing up her long neck. It was the fact that not unfrequently, after the prolonged fatigue of a Special Session, some great lady, a Royal Highness on her travels, or a leader influential in politics, would go upstairs to pay a little particular visit to the wife of the Permanent Secretary. To this sort of hospitality Madame Loisillon was indebted for her present appointment as school-manager, and Madame Astier would certainly not be less clever than her predecessor in utilising the convenience. The only drawback to her triumph was her quarrel with the Duchess, which made it impossible for her to follow Paul to Mousseaux. But an invitation, opportunely arriving at this moment, enabled her to get as near to him as the house at Clos Jallanges; and she had hopes of recovering in time the favour of the fair Antonia, towards whom, when she saw her so kind to Paul she began again to feel quite affectionate.

Léonard could not leave Paris, having to work off the arrears of business left by Loisillon. He let his wife go however, and promised to come down to their friends for a few hours now and then, though in truth he was resolved not to separate himself from his beloved Institute. It was so comfortable and quiet! He had to attend two meetings in the week, just on the other side of the court—summer meetings, where a friendly party of five or six 'tallymen' dozed at ease under the warm glass. The rest of the week he was entirely free, and the old man employed it industriously in correcting the proofs of his 'Galileo,' which, finished at last, was to come out at the opening of the season, as well as a second edition of 'The House of Orleans,' improved to twice its value by the addition of new and unpublished documents. As the world grows old, history, which being but a collective memory of the race is liable to all the lapses, losses, and weaknesses of memory in the individual, finds it ever more necessary to be fortified with authentic texts, and if it would escape the errors of senility, must refresh itself at the original springs. With what pride, therefore, with what enjoyment did Astier-Réhu, during those hot August days, revise the fresh and trustworthy information displayed in his beloved pages, as a preparation for returning them to his publisher, with the heading on which, for the first time, appeared beneath his name the words 'Secretaire perpétuel de l'Académie Française.' His eyes were not yet accustomed to the title, which dazzled him on each occasion, like the sun upon the white courtyard beneath his windows. It was the vast Second Court of the Institute, private and majestic, silent, but for sparrows or swallows passing rarely overhead, and consecrated by a bronze bust of Minerva with ten *termini* in a row against the back wall, over which rose the huge chimney of the adjoining Mint.

Towards four o'clock, when the helmeted shadow of the bust was beginning to lengthen, the stiff mechanical step of old Jean Réhu woould be heard upon the flags. He lived over the Astiers, and went out regularly every day for a long walk, watched from a respectful distance by a servant, whose arm he persistently refused. Within the barrier of his increasing deafness his faculties, under the great heat of this summer, had begun to *give* way, and especially his memory, no longer effectually guided by the reminding pins upon the lappets of his coat. He mixed his stories, and lost himself, like old Livingstone in the marshes of Central Africa, among his recollections, where he scrambled and floundered till some one assisted him. Such a humiliation irritated his spleen, and he now therefore seldom spoke to anyone, but talked to himself as he went along, marking with a sudden stop and a shake of the head the end of an anecdote and the inevitable phrase, 'That's a thing that I have seen.' But he still carried himself upright, and was as fond of a hoax as in the days of the Directory. It was his amusement to impose abstinence from wine, abstinence from meat, and every ridiculous variety of regimen upon cits enamoured of life, crowds of whom wrote to him daily, asking by what diet he had so miraculously extended his. He would prescribe sometimes vegetables, milk, or cider, sometimes shell-fish exclusively, and meanwhile ate and drank without restriction, taking after each meal a siesta, and every evening a good turn up and down the floor, audible to Leonard Astier in the room below.

Two months, August and September, had now elapsed since the Permanent Secretary came in—two clear months of fruitful, delightful peace; such a pause in the climb of ambition as perhaps in all his life he had never enjoyed before. Madame Astier, still at Clos Jallanges, talked of returning soon; the sky of Paris showed the grey of the first fogs; the Academicians began to come home; the meetings were becoming less sociable; and Astier, during his working hours in the reception-room of the great Villemain, found it no longer necessary to screen himself with blinds from the blazing reflection of the court. He was at his table one afternoon, writing to the worthy De Freydet a letter of good news about his candidature, when the old cracked door-bell was violently rung. Corentine had just gone out, so he went to the door, where, to his astonishment, he was confronted by Baron Huchenard and Bos the dealer in manuscripts. Bos dashed into the study wildly waving his arms, while breathless ejaculations flew out of his red tangle of beard and hair: 'Forged! The documents are forged! I can prove it! I can prove it!'

Astier-Réhu, not understanding at first, looked at the Baron, who looked at the ceiling. But when he had picked up the meaning of the dealer's outcry—that the three autograph letters of Charles V., sold by Madame Astier to Bos and by him transferred to Huchenard, were asserted not to be genuine—he said with a disdainful smile, that he would readily repurchase them, as he regarded them with a confidence not to be affected by any means whatsoever.

'Allow me, Mr. Secretary, allow me. I would ask you,' said Baron Huchenard, slowly unbuttoning his macintosh as he spoke, and drawing the three documents out of a large envelope, 'to observe this.' The parchments were so changed as scarcely to seem the same; their smoky brown was bleached to a perfect whiteness; and upon each, clear and legible in the middle of the page, below the signature of Charles V., was this mark,

    BB.

    Angoulême 1836.

'It was Delpech, the Professor of Chemistry, our learned colleague of the Académie des Sciences, who—' but of the Baron's explanation nothing but a confused murmur reached poor Léonard. There was no colour in his face, nor a drop of blood left at the tips of the big heavy fingers, in whose hold the three autographs shook.

'The 800L. shall be at your house this evening, M. Bos,' he managed to say at last with what moisture was left in his mouth.

Bos protested and appealed. The Baron had given him 900L.

'900L., then,' said Astier-Réhu, making a great effort to show them out. But in the dimly-lighted hall he kept back his colleague, and begged him humbly, as a Member of the Académie des Inscriptions, and for the honour of the whole Institute, to say nothing of this unlucky affair.

'Certainly, my dear sir, certainly, on one condition.'

'Name it, name it.'

'You will shortly receive notice that I am a candidate for Loisillon's chair.' The Secretary's answer was a firm clasp of hand in hand, which pledged the assistance of himself and his friends.

Once alone, the unhappy man sank down before the table with its load of proofs, on which lay outspread the three forged letters to Rabelais. He gazed at them blankly, and mechanically read: '*Maître Rabelais, vous qu'avez l'esprit fin et subtil!*' The characters seemed to go round and round in a mixture of ink, dissolved into broad blots of sulphate of iron, which to his imagination went on spreading, till they reached his whole collection of originals, ten or twelve thousand, all unhappily got from the same quarter. Since these three were forged, what of his 'Galileo'?—what of his 'House of Orleans'?—the letter of Catherine II. which he had presented to the Grand Duke?—the letter of Rotrou, which he had solemnly bestowed upon the Académie? What? What? A spasm of energy brought him to his legs. Fage! He must at once see Fage!

His dealings with the bookbinder had begun some years before, when the little man had come one day to the Library of the Foreign Office to request the opinion of its learned and illustrious Keeper respecting a letter from Marie de Médicis to Pope Urban VIII. in favour of Galileo. It happened that Petit-Séquard had just announced as forthcoming, among a series of short light volumes on history, entitled 'Holiday Studies,' a 'Galileo' by Astier-Réhu of the Académie Française. When therefore the librarian's trained judgment had assured him that the MS. was genuine, and he was told that Fage possessed also the letter of the Pope in reply, a letter of thanks from Galileo to the Queen, and others, he conceived instantaneously the idea of writing, instead of the 'slight trifle,' a great historical work. But his probity suggesting at the same moment a doubt as to the source of these documents, he looked the dwarf steadily in the face, and after examining, as he would have examined an original, the long pallid visage and the reddened, blinking eye-lids, said, with an inquisitorial snap of the jaw, 'Are these manuscripts your own, M. Fage?'

'Oh no, sir,' said Fage. He was merely acting on behalf of a third person, an old maiden lady of good birth, who was obliged to part gradually with a very fine collection, which had belonged to the family ever since Louis XVI. Nor had he been willing to act, till he had taken the opinion of a scholar of the highest learning and character. Now, relying upon so competent a judgment, he should go to rich collectors, such as Baron Huchenard, for instance—but Astier-Réhu stopped him, saying, 'Do not trouble yourself. Bring me all you have relating to Galileo. I can dispose of it.' People were coming in and taking their places at the little tables, the sort of people who prowl and hunt in libraries, colourless and taciturn as diggers from the mines, with an air as if they had themselves been dug up out of somewhere close and damp. 'Come to my private room, upstairs, not here,' whispered the librarian in the big ear of the humpback as he moved away, displaying his gloves, oiled hair, and middle parting with the self-sufficiency often observable in his species.

The collection of Mademoiselle du Mesnil-Case, a name disclosed by Albin Fage only under solemn promise of secrecy, proved to be an inexhaustible treasure of papers relating to the sixteenth and seventeenth centuries, which threw all sorts of interesting lights upon the past, and sometimes, by a word or a date, overturned completely the established opinions about facts or persons. Whatever the price, Léonard Astier took and kept every one of the documents, which almost always fitted in with his commenced or projected works. Without a shadow of doubt he accepted the little man's account of the masses of originals that were still accumulating dust in the attic of an ancient mansion at Ménilmontant. If, after some venomous criticism from 'the first collector' in France, his trust was slightly disturbed the suspicion could not but vanish when the book-binder, seated at his table or watering his vegetables in the quiet grass-grown yard, met it with perfect composure, and offered in particular a quite natural explanation of certain marks of erasure and restoration, visible on some of the pages, as due to the submergence of the collection in sea-water, when it was sent to England during the emigration. After this fresh assurance Astier-Réhu would go back to the gate with a lively step, carrying off each time a purchase for which he had given, according to its historical value, a cheque for twenty, forty, or even as much as eighty pounds.

These extravagances, unsuspected as yet by those around him, were prompted, whatever he might say to quiet his conscience, not so much by the motives of the historian as by those of the collector. This, even in a place so ill-adapted for seeing and hearing as the attic in the Rue de Beaune, where the bargains were usually struck, would have been patent to any observer. The tone of pretended indifference, the 'Let me see' muttered with dry lips, the quivering of the covetous fingers, marked the progress from passion to mania, the growth of the hard and selfish cyst, which was feeding its monstrous size upon the ruin of the whole organism. Astier was becoming the intractable Harpagon of the stage, pitiless to others as to himself, bewailing his poverty and riding in the omnibus, while in two years nearly 6500L. of his savings dropped secretly into the pocket of the humpback. To account to Madame Astier, Corentine, and Teyssèdre for the frequent visits of the little man, he received from the Academician pamphlets to bind, which he took away and brought back ostentatiously. They corresponded by a sort of private code. Fage would write on a post-card, 'I have some new tooling to show you, sixteenth century, in good condition and rare.' Astier would temporise: 'Not wanted, thanks. Perhaps later.' Then would come 'My dear Sir, Do not think of it. I will try elsewhere,' and to this the Academician invariably answered 'Early to-morrow morning. Bring the tooling.' Here was the torment of the collector's pleasure. He must buy and buy, or else let pass to Bos, Huchenard, or some other rival the treasures of Ménilmontant. Sometimes the thought of the time when money must fail would put him into a grim rage, and infuriated by the calm, self-satisfied countenance of the dwarf, he would exclaim 'More than 6400L. in two years! And still you say, the lady is in want of money! How on earth does she get rid of it?' At such moments he longed for the death of the old maid, the annihilation of the bookbinder, even a war, revolution, or general catastrophe, which might swallow up both the treasure and the relentless speculators who worked it.

And now the catastrophe was indeed near, not the catastrophe desired, for destiny never finds to her hand precisely the thing we asked for, but a turn of things so sudden and appalling as to threaten his work, his honour, fortune, and fame, all that he was and all that he had. As he strode away towards the Cour des Comptes, deadly pale and talking to himself, the booksellers and print-dealers along the quay scarcely recognised the Astier-Réhu who, instead of looking right into the shop for a bow, now passed them without recognition. To him neither person nor thing was visible. In imagination he was grasping the humpback by the throat, shaking him by his pin-bespangled scarf, and thrusting under his nose the autographs dishonoured by the chemistry of Delpech, with the question, 'Now then, what is your answer to that?'

When he reached the Rue de Lille, he dashed through the door of rough planks in the fence which surrounds the ruins, went up the steps, and rang the bell once and again. He was struck by the gloomy look of the building, now that no flowers or greenery covered the nakedness of the gaping, crumbling masonry and the confusion of the twisted iron-work and leafless creepers. The sound of pattens came slowly across the chilly court, and the caretaker appeared, a solid woman, who, broom in hand and without opening the gate, said, 'You want the bookbinder; but he isn't here now.' Not here! Yes, Fage had gone, and left no address. In fact, she was just cleaning up the cottage for the man who was to have the appointment to the Cour des Comptes, which Fage had resigned.

Astier-Réhu, for appearance' sake, stammered out a word or two, but his voice was lost in the harsh and mournful cries of a great flight of black birds, which made the arches echo as they descended upon the court. 'Why, here are the Duchess's rooks!' said the woman, with a respectful wave of the hand towards the bare plane-trees of the Hôtel Padovani, visible over the roof opposite. 'They are come before the Duchess this year, and that means an early winter!'

He went away, with horror in his heart.

CHAPTER XII.

The day following that on which the Duchess Padovani, to show herself smiling under the blow which had fallen upon her, had appeared at the theatre, she went, as she usually did at that time of year, to Mousseaux. She made no change in her plans. She had sent out her invitations for the season, and did not cancel them. But before the arrival of the first instalment of visitors, during the few days' solitude usually spent in superintending in detail the arrangements for entertaining her guests, she passed the whole time from morning to night in the park at Mousseaux, whose slopes stretched far and wide on the banks of the Loire. She would go madly along, like a wounded and hunted animal, stop for a moment from exhaustion, and then at a throb of pain start off again. 'Coward! coward! wretch!' She hurled invectives at the Prince as though he had been by her side, and still she walked with the same fevered tread the labyrinth of green paths which ran down in long shady windings to the river. Here, forgetting her rank and her position, flinging off her mask and able to be natural at last, she would give vent to her despair, a despair perhaps something less than her wrath, for the voice of pride spoke louder within her than any other, and the few tears which escaped her lids did not flow, but leaped and sparkled like flames. Revenge, revenge! She longed for a revenge of blood, and sometimes pictured one of her foresters, Bertoli or Salviato, going off abroad to put a bullet into him on his wedding-day. Then she changed her mind. No, she would deal the blow herself, and feel the joy of the *vendetta* in her own grasp. She envied the women of lower class who wait behind a doorway for the traitor, and fling in his face a bottle full of vitriol with a storm of hideous curses. Why did she not know some of the horrible names that relieve the heart, some foul insult to shriek at the mean treacherous companion who rose before her mind with the hesitating look and false constrained smile he wore at their last meeting? But even in her savage Corsican patois the great lady knew no 'nasty words,' and when she had cried 'Coward! coward! wretch!' her beautiful mouth could only writhe in helpless rage.

In the evening after her solitary dinner in the vast hall, whose panelling of old leather was gilt by the setting sun, her wild pacing to and fro began again. Now it was on the gallery overhanging the river, quaintly restored by Paul Astier, with open arcades like lace-work and two pretty corbel-turrets. Below on the Loire, outspread like a lake, there still lingered a delicate silvery light from the departing day, while the hazy evening air exaggerated the distances between the willow beds and islands out towards Chaumont. But poor Mari' Anto did not look at the view when, worn out with retracing the steps of her grief, she leant both elbows on the balustrade and gazed into the dimness. Her life appeared before her, waste and desolate, at an age when it is difficult to make a fresh start. A faint sound of voices rose from Mousseaux, a group of two or three small houses on the embankment; the chain of a boat creaked as the night breeze rose. How easy it would be! Grief had bowed down her head so low, that if she were but to lean forward a little farther.... But then what would the world say? A woman of her rank and age could not kill herself like any little grisette! The third day Paul's note arrived, and with it the newspapers' detailed report of the duel. It gave her the same delight as a warm pressure of the hand. So some one still cared for her, and had wanted to avenge her at the risk of his life! Not that Paul's feeling was love, she supposed, but only a grateful affection, the reminiscence of kindnesses done by her to him and his family, perhaps an imperative desire to atone for his mother's treachery. Generous, brave fellow! If she had been in Paris, she would have gone to him at once, but as her guests were just due, she could only write and send him her own doctor.

Every hour came fresh arrivals from Blois and from Onzain, Mousseaux lying half way between the two stations. The landau, the victoria, and two great breaks set down at the steps in the great court, amid the incessant ringing of the bell, many illustrious members of the Duchess's set, academicians and diplomatists, the Count and Countess Foder, the Comte de Brétigny and his son the Vicomte, who was a Secretary of Legation, M. and Madame Desminières, Laniboire the philosopher, who had come to the castle to draw up his report on the award of the *Prix de vertu*, the young critic of Shelley, who was 'run' by the Padovani set, and Danjou, handsome Danjou, all by himself, though his wife had been asked. Life at Mousseaux was exactly what it had been the year before. The day passed in calls, or work in the separate rooms, meals, general conversation, afternoon naps; then, when the great heat was passed, came long drives through the woods, or sails on the river in the little fleet of boats anchored at the bottom of the park. Parties would be made to picnic on an island, and some of the guests would repair to the fish preserves, which were always well stocked with lively fish, as the keeper took care to replenish them from his nets before each expedition. Then every one came back to the ceremonious dinner, after which the gentlemen, when they had smoked in the billiard room or on the gallery, joined the ladies in a splendid apartment, which had been the council-chamber of Catherine de Médicis.

All round the huge room were depicted in tapestry the loves of Dido and her despair at the departure of the Trojan ships. The irony of this strange coincidence was not remarked by any one, so little do people in society regard their surroundings, less for want of observation than because they are always and fully occupied with their personal behaviour and the effect they are to produce. But there was a striking contrast between the tragic despair of the abandoned queen, gazing with arms uplifted and streaming eyes as the little black speck disappeared, and the smiling serenity of the Duchess, as she presided in the drawing-room, maintaining her supremacy over the other ladies, whose dress and whose reading were guided by her taste, or joining in the discussions between Laniboire and the young critic, and in the disputes waged over the candidates for Loisillon's seat by Desminières and Danjou. Indeed, if the Prince d'Athis, the faithless Sammy, whose name was in every one's thoughts, though on no one's lips, could have seen her, he would have been mortified to find how small was the gap left in a woman's life by hisabsence, and how busy was the turmoil throughout the royal castle of Mousseaux, where in all the long front there were but three windows shut up, those belonging to what were called 'the Prince's rooms.'

'She takes it well,' said Danjou the first evening. And neither little Countess Foder, from whose massy lace protruded a very sharp inquisitive little nose, nor sentimental Madame Desminières, who had looked forward to lamentations and confidences, could get over such amazing courage. In truth they were as much amazed at her as if going to a long-expected play they had found the house 'closed for the day'; while the men took Ariadne's equanimity as an encouragement to would-be successors. The real change in the Duchess's life lay in the attitude observed towards her by all or nearly all the men; they were less reserved, more sedulous, more eager to please her, and fluttered round her chair with an obvious desire, not merely to merit her patronage, but to attract her regard.

Never indeed had Maria Antonia been more beautiful. When she entered the dining-room the tempered brilliancy of her complexion and her shoulders in their light summer robe made a bright place at the table, even when the Marquise de Roca Nera had come over from her neighbouring country seat on the other side of the Loire. The Marquise was younger, but no one would have thought so to look at them. Laniboire, the philosopher, was strongly attracted to the Duchess. He was a widower, well on in years, with heavy features and apoplectic complexion, but he did his best to captivate his hostess by the display of a manly and sportsmanlike activity which led him into occasional mishaps. One day, in a boat, as he tried to make a great display of biceps over his rowing, he fell into the river; another time, as he was prancing on horseback at the side of the carriage, his mount squeezed his leg so hard against the wheel that he had to keep his room and be bandaged for several days. But the finest spectacle was to see him in the drawing-room, 'dancing,' as Danjou said, 'before the Ark.' He stretched and bent his unwieldy person in all directions. He would challenge to a philosophic duel the young critic, a confirmed pessimist of three-and-twenty, and overwhelm him with his own imperturbable optimism. Laniboire the philosopher had one particular reason for this good opinion of the world; his wife had died of diphtheria caught from nursing their children; both his children had died with their mother; and each time that he repeated his dithyramb in praise of existence, the philosopher concluded his statement with a sort of practical demonstration, a bow to the Duchess, which seemed to say, 'How can a man think ill of life in the presence of such beauty as yours?'

The young critic paid his court in a less conspicuous and sufficiently cunning fashion. He was an immense admirer of the Prince d'Athis, and being at the age when admiration shows itself by imitation, he no sooner made his entry into society than he copied Sammy's attitudes, his walk, even the carriage of his head, his bent back, and vague mysterious smile of contemptuous reserve. Now he increased the resemblance by details of dress, which he had observed and collected with the sharpness of a child, from the way of pinning his tie just at the opening of the collar to the fawn-coloured check of his English trousers. Unfortunately he had too much hair and not a scrap of beard, so that his efforts were quite thrown away, and revived no uncomfortable memories in the Duchess, who was as indifferent to his English checks as she was to the languishing glances of Brétigny *fils*, or the significant pressure of Brétigny *père*, as he gave her his arm to dinner. But all this helped to surround her with that atmosphere of gallantry to which she had long been accustomed by D'Athis, who played the humble servant to the verge of servility, and to save her woman's pride from the conscious humiliation of abandonment.

Amidst all these aspirants Danjou kept somewhat aloof, amusing the Duchess with his green-room stories and making her laugh, a way of self-recommendation in certain cases not unsuccessful. But the time came when he thought matters sufficiently advanced: and one morning when she was starting for her rapid solitary walk with her dogs through the park, in the hope of leaving her wrath behind in the thickets with the waking birds, or of cooling and tempering it among the dewy lawns and dripping branches—suddenly, at a turn in the path, appeared Danjou, ready for the attack. Dressed from head to foot in white flannels, his trousers tucked into his boots, with a picturesque cap and a well-trimmed beard, he was trying to find a *dénouement* for a three-act drama, to be ready for the Français that winter. The name was 'Appearances,' and the subject a satire on society. Everything was written but the final scene.

He began to ta'k of his love.   Page 228

'Well, let us try what we can do together,' said the Duchess brightly, as she cracked the long lash of the short-handled whip with silver whistle, which she used to call in her dogs. But the moment they turned to walk together, he began to talk of his love, and how sad it would be for her to live alone; and ended by offering himself, after his own fashion, straight out and with no circumlocutions. The Duchess, with a quick movement of pride, threw up her head, grasping her whip handle tightly, as if to strike the insolent fellow who dared to talk to her as he might to a super at the opera. But the insult was also a compliment, and there was pleasure as well as anger in her blush. Danjou steadily urged his point, and tried to dazzle her with his polished wit, pretending to treat the matter less as a love affair than as an intellectual partnership. A man like himself and a woman like her might command the world.

'Many thanks, my dear Danjou; such specious reasoning is not new to me. I am suffering from it still.' Then with a haughty wave of her hand, which allowed no reply, she pointed out the shady path which the dramatist was to follow, and said, 'Look for your *dénouement*; I am going in.' He stood where he was, completely disconcerted, and gazed at her beautiful carriage as she walked away.

'Not even as zebra?' he said, in a tone of appeal.

She looked round, her black brows meeting. 'Ah, yes, you are right; the post is vacant,' Her thoughts went to Lavaux, the base underling for whom she had done so much, and without a smile she answered in a weary voice, 'Zebra, if you like.'

Then she vanished behind a little group of fine yellow roses a little overblown, whose leaves would be scattered at the first fresh breeze.

It was something to boast of that the proud Mari' Anto' had heard him through. Probably no other man, not even her Prince, had ever spoken to her thus. Full of the inspiration of hope, and stimulated by the fine speeches he had just thrown off, the dramatist soon hit upon his final scene. He was going back to write it out before breakfast, when he stopped short in surprise at seeing through the branches 'the Prince's' windows open to the sunlight Who was coming? What favourite guest was to be honoured with those convenient and luxurious rooms, looking over the river and the park? He made inquiries, and was reassured. It was her Grace's architect; he was coming to the castle after an illness. Considering the intimacy between the lady and the Astiers, nothing was more natural than that Paul should be entertained like a son of the house in a mansion which he had more or less created. Still, when the new arrival took his seat at breakfast, his chastened delicacy of feature, his paleness—the paler by a white silk kerchief—his duel, his wound, and the general flavour of romance surrounding him seemed to make so keen an impression on the ladies, and called forth such affectionate interest and care on the part of the Duchess herself, that handsome Danjou, being one of those all-engrossing persons to whom any other man's success seems a personal loss, if not downright robbery, felt a jealous pang. With his eyes on his plate he took advantage of his position by the hostess to murmur some depreciatory remarks upon the pretty young fellow, unfortunately so much disfigured by his mother's nose. He made merry over his duel, his wound, and his reputation in the fencing-room, the kind of bubble which bursts at the first prick of a real sword. He added, not knowing how near he was to the truth, 'The quarrel at cards was of course a mere pretext; there was a woman at the bottom of it.'

'Of the duel? Do you think so?' His nod said 'I am sure of it.' Much admiring his own cleverness, he turned to the company, and dazzled them with his epigrams and anecdotes. He never went into society without providing himself with a store of these pocket squibs. Paul was no match for him here, and the ladies' interest soon reverted to the brilliant talker, especially when he announced that, having got his *dénouement* and finished his play, he would read it in the drawing-room while it was too hot to go out. A universal exclamation of delight from the ladies welcomed this invaluable relief to the day's monotony. What a precious privilege for them, proud as they were already of dating their letters from Mousseaux, to be able to send to all their dear friends, who were not there, accounts of an unpublished play by Danjou, read by Danjou himself, and then next winter to be in a position to say when the rehearsals were going on, 'Oh, Danjou's play! I know it; he read it to us at the castle.'

As the company rose, full of excitement at this good news, the Duchess went towards Paul, and taking his arm with her graceful air of command said, 'Come for a turn on the gallery; it is stifling here.' The air was heavy even at the height of the gallery, for there rose from the steaming river a mist of heat, which overspread and blurred the irregular green outlines of its banks and of its low floating islands. She led the young man away from the smokers right to the end of the furthest bay, and then clasping his hand said, 'So it was for me; it was all for me.'

'Yes, Duchess, for you.'

And he pursed his lips as he added, 'And presently we shall have another try.'

'You must not say that, you naughty boy.'

She stopped, as an inquisitive footstep came towards them. Danjou!'

'Yes, Duchess.'

'My fan... on the dining-room table... would you be so kind?...' When he was some way off, she said, 'I will not have it, Paul. In the first place, the creature is not worth fighting. Ah, if we were alone—if I could tell you!' The fierceness of her tone and the clenching of her hands betrayed a rage that amazed Paul Astier. After a month he had hoped to find her calmer than this. It was a disappointment, and it checked the explosion, 'I love you—I have always loved you,' which was to have been forced from him at the first confidential interview. He was only telling the story of the duel, in which she was very much interested, when the Academician brought her fan. 'Well fetched, zebra!' she said by way of thanks. With a little pout he answered in the same strain but a lowered voice, 'A zebra on promotion, you know!'

'What, wanting to be raised already!' She tapped him with her fan as she spoke, and anxious to put him in a good temper for his reading, let him escort her back to the drawing-room, where his manuscript was lying ready on a dainty card-table in the full light of a high window partly open, showing the flower-garden and the groups of great trees.

Danjou read like a genuine "Player" of Picheral's classification. Page 234

'*Appearances. A Drama in Three Acts. Dramatis Personæ....*'

The ladies, getting as close round as they could, drew themselves together with the charming little shiver which is their way of anticipating enjoyment. Danjou read like a genuine 'Player' of Picheral's classification, making lengthy pauses while he moistened his lips with his glass of water, and wiped them with a fine cambric handkerchief. As he finished each of the long broad pages, scribbled all over with his tiny handwriting, he let-it fall carelessly at his feet on the carpet Each time Madame de Foder, who hunts the 'lions' of all nations, stooped noiselessly, picked up the fallen sheet, and placed it reverently upon an armchair beside her, exactly square with the sheets before, contriving, in this subtle and delicate way, to take a certain part in the great man's work. It was as if Liszt or Rubinstein had been at the piano and she had been turning over the music. All went well till the end of Act I., an interesting and promising introduction, received with a *furore* of delighted exclamations, rapturous laughter, and enthusiastic applause. After a long pause, in which was audible from the far distance of the park the hum of the insects buzzing about the tree-tops, the reader wiped his moustache, and resumed:

Act II The scene represents... But here his voice began to break, and grew huskier with every speech. He had just seen an empty chair among the ladies in the first row; it was Antonia's chair; and his glances strayed over his eye-glass searching the whole huge room. It was full of green plants and screens, behind which the auditors had ensconced themselves to hear—or to sleep—

undisturbed. At last, in one of the numerous and regular intervals provided by his glass of water, he caught a whisper, then a glimpse of a light dress, then, at the far end, on a sofa, he saw the Duchess with Paul beside her, continuing the conversation interrupted on the gallery. To one like Danjou, spoiled with every kind of success, the affront was deadly. But he nerved himself to finish the Act, throwing his pages down on the floor with a violence which made them fly, and sent little Madame de Foder crawling after them on all fours. At the end of the Act, as the whispering still went on, he left off, pretending that he was suddenly taken hoarse and must defer the rest till the next day. The Duchess, absorbed in the duel, of which she could not hear enough, supposed the play concluded, and cried from the distance, clapping her little hands, 'Bravo, Danjou, the *dénouement* is delicious.'

That evening the great man had, or said he had, a bilious attack, and very early next morning he left Mousseaux without seeing any one again. Perhaps it was only the vexation of an author; perhaps he truly believed that young Astier was going to succeed the Prince. However that may be, a week after he had gone Paul had not got beyond an occasional whispered word. The lady showed him the utmost kindness, treated him with the care of a mother, asked after his health, whether he did not find the tower looking south too hot, whether the shaking of the carriage tired him, whether it was not too late for him to stay on the river. But the moment he tried to mention the word 'love,' she was off without seeming to understand. Still he found her a very different creature from the proud Antonia of other years. Then, haughty and calm, she would show impertinence its place by a mere frown. It was the serenity of a majestic river flowing between its embankments. But now the embankment was giving way; there seemed to be a crack somewhere, through which was breaking the real nature of the woman. She had fits of rebellion against custom and social convention, which hitherto she had respected scrupulously, sudden desires to go somewhere else, and to tire herself in some long excursion. She planned festivities, fireworks, great coursing expeditions for the autumn, in which she would take the lead, though it was years since she had been on horseback. Paul watched carefully the vagaries of her excitement, and kept his sharp hawk's-eye upon everything; he had quite made up his mind not to dangle for two years, as he had round Colette de Rosen.

One night the party had broken up early, after a tiring day of driving in the neighbourhood. Paul had gone up to his room, and having thrown off his coat was sitting in his slippers smoking a cigar and writing to his mother a carefully studied epistle. Mamma was staying at Clos Jallanges, and wearing her eyes out with looking across the winding river into the extreme distance for a glimpse of the four towers of Mousseaux: and he had to convince her that there was no chance of a reconciliation at present between her and her friend, and that they had better not meet. (No, no! His good mother was much too fond of fishing on her own hook to be a desirable associate!) He had to remind her of the bill due at the end of the month, and her promise to send the money to good little Stenne, who had been left in the Rue Fortuny as sole garrison of the mediaeval mansion. If Sammy's money had not yet come in, she might borrow of the Freydets, who would not refuse to advance it for a few days. That very morning the Paris papers in their foreign news had announced the marriage of the French Ambassador at St. Petersburg, mentioned the presence of the Grand Duke, described the bride's dresses, and given the name of the Polish Bishop who had bestowed his blessing on the happy pair. Mamma might imagine how the breakfast party at Mousseaux was affected by this news, known to every one, and read by the hostess in the eyes of her guests and in their persistent conversation on other topics.

The poor Duchess, who had hardly spoken during the meal, felt, when it was over, that she must rouse herself, and in spite of the heat had carried off all her visitors in three carriages to the Château de la Poissonnière, where the poet Ronsard was born. Ten miles' drive in the sun on a road all cracks and dust, for the pleasure of hearing that hideous old Lani-boire, hoisted on to an old stump as decayed as himself, recite 'Mignonne, allons voir si la rose.' On the way home they had paid a visit to the Agricultural Orphanage and Training School founded by old Padovani. Mamma must know it all well; they had been over the dormitory and laundry, and inspected the implements and the copy-books; and the whole place was so hot and smelly; and Laniboire made a speech to the Agricultural Orphans, cropped like convicts, in which he assured them that the world was good. To finish themselves up they stopped again at the furnaces near Onzain, and spent an hour between the heat of the setting sun and the smoke and smell of coal from three huge belching brick chimneys, stumbling over the rails and dodging the trucks and shovels full of molten metal in gigantic masses, which dropped fire like dissolving blocks of red ice, All the time the Duchess went on unwearied, but looked at nothing, listened to nothing. She seemed to be having an animated discussion with old Brétigny, whose arm she had taken, and paid as little attention to the furnaces and forges as to the poet Ronsard or the Agricultural Orphanage.

Paul had reached this point in his letter, painting with terrible force, to console his mother for her absence, the dullness of life this year at Mousseaux, when he heard a gentle knock at his door. He thought it was the young critic, or the Vicomte de Brétigny, or perhaps Laniboire, who had been very unquiet of late. All these had often prolonged the evening in his room, which was the largest and most convenient, and had a dainty smoking-room attached to it. He was very much surprised on opening his door to see by the light of the painted windows that the long corridor of the first floor was absolutely silent and deserted, right away to the guard-room, where a ray of moonlight showed the outline of the carving on the massive door. He was going back to his seat, when there came another knock. It came from the smoking-room, which communicated by a little door under the hangings with a narrow passage in the thickness of the wall leading to the rooms of the Duchess. The arrangement, dating much earlier than the restorations, was not known to him: and, as he remembered certain conversations during the last few days, when the men were alone, and especially some of the stories of old Laniboire, his first thought was 'Whew! I hope she did not hear us.' He drew the bolt and the Duchess passed him without a word, and laying down on the table where he had been writing a bundle of yellowish papers, with which her delicate fingers played nervously, she said in a serious voice:

'I want you to give me your advice; you are my friend, and I have no one else to confide in.'

No one but him—poor woman! And she did not take warning from the cunning watchful predatory glance, which shifted from the letter, imprudently left open on the table where she might have read it, to herself as she stood there with her arms bare and heavy hair coiled round and round her head. He was thinking, 'What does she want? What has she come for?' She, absorbed in the requickened wrath which had been rising and choking her since the morning, panted out in low broken sentences, 'Just before you came, he sent Lavaux—he did! he sent Lavaux—to ask for his letters!—I gave his impudent cheeks such a reception that he won't come again.—His letters, indeed!—these are what he wanted.'

She held out the roll, her brief, as it might be called, against the partner of her affections, showing what she had paid to raise the man out of the gutter.

'Take them, look at them! They are really quite interesting! 'He turned over the odd collection, smelling now of the boudoir, but better suited to Bos's shop-front; there were mortgageable debts to dealers in curiosities, private jewellers, laundresses, yacht-builders, agents for imitation-champagne from Touraine, receipts from stewards and club-waiters, in short, every device of usury by which a man about Paris comes to bankruptcy. Mari' Anto muttered under her breath, 'The restoration of this gentleman cost more than Mousseaux, you see!... I have had all these things in a drawer for years, because I never destroy anything; but I solemnly declare that. I never thought of using them. Now I have changed my mind. He is rich. I want my money and interest. If he does not pay, I will take proceedings. Don't you think I am justified?'

'Entirely justified,' said Paul, stroking the point of his fair beard, 'only—was not the Prince d'Athis incapable of contracting when he signed these bills?'

'Yes, yes, I know... Brétigny told me about that... for as he could get nothing through Lavaux, he wrote to Brétigny to ask him to arbitrate. A fellow Academician, you know!' She laughed a laugh of impartial scorn for the official dignities of the Ambassador and the ex-Minister. Then she burst out indignantly, 'It is true that I need not have paid, but I chose he should be clean. I don't want any arbitration. I paid and will be paid back, or else I go into court, where the name and title of our representative at St. Petersburg will be dragged through the dirt. If I can only degrade the wretch, I shall have won the suit I care about.'

'I can't understand,' said Paul as he put down the packet so as to hide the awkward letter to Mamma, 'I can't understand how such proofs should have been left in your hands by a man as clever——'

'As D'Athis?'

The shrug of her shoulders sufficiently completed the interjection. But the madness of a woman's anger may always lead to something, so he drew her on. 'Yet he was one of our best diplomatists.'

'It was I who put him up to it. He knows nothing of the business but what I taught him.'

She hid her face, as for shame, in her hands, checking her sobs and gasping with fury. 'To think, to think, twelve years of my life to a man like that! And now he leaves me; he casts me off! Cast off by him! Cast off by him!'

It is some hours later, and she is still there. The young man is upon his knees and is whispering tenderly: 'When you know that I love you—when you know that I loved you always. Think, think!' The striking of a clock is heard in the far distance and wakening sounds go by in the growing light. She flies in dismay from the room, not caring so much as to take with her the brief of her intended revenge.

Revenge herself now? On whom? and what for? There was an end of her hatred now, for had she not her love? From this day she was another woman, such an one as when she is seen with her lover or her husband, supporting her unhasty steps upon the tender cradle of his arm, makes the common people say, 'Well, *she* has got what she wants.' There are not so many of them as people think, particularly in society. Not that the mistress of a great house could be thinking exclusively of her own happiness; there were guests going away and other guests arriving and settling in, a second instalment, more numerous and less intimate, the whole in fact of the Academic set. There were the Duke de Courson-Launay, the Prince and Princess de Fitz-Roy, the De Circourts, the Huchenards, Saint-Avol the diplomatist, Moser and his daughter, Mr. and Mrs. Henry of the American embassy. It was a hard task to provide entertainment and occupation for all these people and to fuse such different elements. No one understood the business better than she, but just now it was a burden and a weariness to her. She would have liked to keep quiet and meditate on her happiness, to think of nothing else: and she could devise no other amusements for her guests than the invariable. visit to the fish preserves, to Ronsard's castle, and to the Orphanage. Her own pleasure was complete when her hand touched Paul's, as accident brought them together in the same boat or the same carriage.

In the course of one such pompous expedition on the river, the little fleet from Mousseaux, sailing on a shimmering mirror of silken awnings and ducal pennons, had gone somewhat further than usual. Paul Astier was in the boat in front of his lady's. He was sitting in the stern beside Laniboire, and was receiving the Academician's confidences. Having been invited to stay at Mousseaux till his report was finished, the old fool fancied that he was making good progress towards the coveted succession; and as always happens in such cases, he chose Paul as the confidant of his hopes. After telling him what he had said and what she had answered, and one thing and another, he was just saying, 'Now, young man, what would you do, if you were me?' when a clear voice of low pitch rang over the water from the boat behind them.

'Monsieur Astier!'

'Yes, Duchess.'

'See yonder, among the reeds. It looks like Védrine.'

Védrine it was, painting away, with his wife and children at his side, on an old flat-bottomed boat moored to a willow branch alongside of a green islet, where the wagtails were chirping themselves hoarse. The boats drew quickly up beside him, any novelty being a break to the everlasting tedium of fashionable society: and while the Duchess greeted with her sweetest smile Madame Védrine, who had once been her guest at Mousseaux, the ladies looked with interest at the artist's strange home and the beautiful children, born of its light and its love, as they lay in the shelter of their green refuge on the clear, placid stream, which reflected the picture of their happiness. After the first greetings, Védrine, palette in hand, gave Paul an account of the doings at Clos Jallanges, which was visible through the mists of the river, half-way up the hill side—a long low white house with an Italian roof. 'My dear fellow, they have all gone crazy there! The vacancy has turned their heads. They spend their days ticking votes—your mother, Picheral, and the poor invalid in her wheelchair. She too has caught the Academic fever, and talks of moving to Paris, entertaining and giving parties to help her brother on.' So Védrine, to escape the general madness, camped out all day and worked in the open air—children and all; and pointing to his old boat he said, with a simple unresentful laugh, 'My dahabeeah, you see; my trip to the Nile.'

All at once the little boy, who in the midst of so many people, so many pretty ladies and pretty dresses, had eyes for no one but old Laniboire, addressed him in a clear voice, 'Please, are you the gentleman of the Académie who is going to be a hundred?' The philosopher, occupied in showing off his boating for the benefit of the fair Antonia, was all but knocked off his seat: and when the peals of laughter had somewhat subsided, Védrine explained that the child was strangely interested in Jean Réhu, whom he did not know and had never seen, merely because he was nearly a hundred years old. Every day the handsome little boy asked about the old man and inquired how he was. Child as he was, he admired such length of days with something of a personal regard. If others had lived to a hundred, why not he?

But a sudden freshening of the breeze filled the sails of the little craft, and fluttered all the tiny pennons; a mass of clouds was moving up from over Blois, and towards Mousseaux a film of rain dimmed the horizon, while the four lights on the top of the towers sparkled against the black sky.

There was a moment of hurry and confusion. Then the vessels went away between the banks of yellow sand, one behind the other in the narrow channels; while Védrine, pleased by the brightness of the colours beneath the stormy sky and by the striking figures of the boatmen, standing in the bows and leaning hard on their long poles, turned to his wife, who was kneeling in the punt packing in the children, the colour-box, and the palette, and said, 'Look over there, mamma. I sometimes say of a friend, that we are in the same boat. Well, there you may see what I mean. As those boats fly in line through the wind, with the darkness-coming down, so are we men and workers, generation after generation. It's no use being shy of the fellows in your own boat; you know them, you rub up against them, you are friends without wishing it or even knowing it, all sailing on the same tack. But how the fellows in front do loiter and get in the way! There's nothing in common between their boat and ours. We are too far off, we cannot catch what they say. We never trouble about them except to call out "Go ahead; get on, do!" Meanwhile youth in the boat behind is pushing *us*; they would not mind running us down; and we shout to them angrily, "Easy there! Where's the hurry?" Well, as for me,' and he drew himself to his full height, towering above the line of coast and river, 'I belong, of course, to my own beat and I am fond of it. But the boat just ahead and the one coming up interest me not less. I would hail them, signal to them, speak to them all. All of us alike, those before and those behind, are threatened by the same dangers, and every boat finds the current strong, the sky treacherous, and the evening quick to close in... Now, my dears, we must make haste; here comes the rain!'

CHAPTER XIII.

'Pray for the repose of the soul of the most noble Lord, the Duke Charles Henri François Padovani, Prince d'Olmitz, formerly Member of the Senate, Ambassador and Minister, Grand Cross of the Legion of Honour, who departed this life September 20, 1880, at his estate of Barbicaglia, where his remains have been interred. A mass for the deceased will be celebrated on Sunday next in the private chapel, where you are invited to attend.'

This quaint summons was being proclaimed on both banks of the Loire, between Mousseaux and Onzain, by mourners hired from Vafflard's, wearing tall hats with crape mufflers that reached the ground, and ringing their heavy bells as they walked. Paul Astier, hearing the words as he came downstairs to the midday breakfast, felt his heart beat high with joy and pride. Four days ago the news of the Duke's death had startled Mousseaux as the report of a gun startles a covey of partridges, and had unexpectedly dispersed and scattered the second instalment of guests to various seaside and holiday resorts. The Duchess had had to set off at once for Corsica, leaving at the castle only a few very intimate friends. The melancholy sound of the voices and moving bells, carried to Paul's ear by a breeze from the river through the open panes of the staircase window, the antiquated and princely form of the funeral invitation, could not but invest the domain of Mousseaux with an impressive air of grandeur, which added to the height of its four towers and its immemorial trees. And as all this was to be his (for the Duchess on leaving had begged him to stay at the castle, as there were important decisions to be taken on her return), the proclamation of death sounded in his ears like the announcement of his approaching installation. 'Pray for the repose of the soul,' said the voices. At last he really had fortune within his grasp, and this time it should not be taken from him. 'Member of the Senate, Ambassador and Minister,' said the voices again.

'Those bells are depressing, are they not, Monsieur Paul?' said Mdlle. Moser who was sitting at breakfast between her father and the Academician Laniboire. The Duchess had kept these guests at Mousseaux, partly to amuse Paul's solitude and partly to give a little more rest and fresh air to the poor 'Antigone,' kept in bondage by the interminable candidature of her father. There was certainly no fear that the Duchess would find a rival in this woman, who had eyes like a beaten hound, hair without colour, and no other thought but her humiliating petition for the unattainable place in the Académie. But on this particular morning she had taken more pains than usual with her appearance, and wore a bright dress open at the neck. The poor neck was very thin and lean, but—there was no higher game. So Laniboire, in high spirits, was teasing her with a gay freedom. No, he did not think the death-bells at all depressing, nor the repetition of 'Pray for the repose,' as it died away in the distance. No, life seemed to him by contrast more enjoyable than usual, the *Vouvray* sparkled more brightly in the decanters, and his good stories had a telling echo in the huge half-empty dining-room. The sodden subservient face of Moser the candidate wore a fawning smile, though he wished his daughter away. But the philosopher was a man of great influence in the Académie.

After coffee had been served on the terrace, Laniboire, with his face coloured like a Redskin, called out, 'Now let's go and work, Mdlle. Moser; I feel quite in the humour. I believe I shall finish my report to-day.' The gentle little lady, who sometimes acted as his secretary, rose with some regret. On a delicious day like this, hazy with the first mists of autumn, a good walk, or perhaps a continuation on the gallery of her talk with the charming and well-mannered M. Paul, would have pleased her better than writing at old M. Laniboire's dictation commendations of devoted hospital-nurses or exemplary attendants. But her father urged her to go, as the great man wanted her. She obeyed and went upstairs behind Laniboire, followed by old Moser, who was going to have his afternoon nap.

Laniboire may have had Pascal's nose, but he had not his manners. When Paul came back from cooling his ambitious hopes by a long walk in the woods, he found the break waiting at the foot of the steps in the great court. The two fine horses were pawing the ground, and Mdlle. Moser was inside, surrounded by boxes and bags, while Moser, looking bewildered, stood on the doorstep, feeling in his pockets and bestowing coins on two or three sneering footmen. Paul went up to the carriage, 'So you are leaving us, Mademoiselle.' She gave him a thin clammy hand, on which she had forgotten to put a glove, and without saying a word, or removing the handkerchief with which she was wiping her eyes under her veil, she bent her head in sign of good-bye. He learnt little more from old Moser, who stammered out in a low voice, as he stood vexed and gloomy, with one foot on the step of the carriage 'It's her doing: she *will* go. He was rude to her she says, but I can't believe it.' Then with a profound sigh, and knitting the wrinkle in his brow, the deep, red, scar-like wrinkle of the Academic candidate, he added, 'It's a very bad thing for my election.'

Laniboire stayed all the afternoon in his room, and at dinner, as he took his seat opposite Paul, he said, 'Do you know why our friends the Mosers went off so suddenly?'

'No, sir, do you?'

'It's very strange, very strange.'

He assumed an air of great composure for the benefit of the servants, but it was obvious that he was disturbed, worried, and in desperate fear of a scandal. Gradually he regained his serenity and satisfaction, not being able to think ill of life at dinner, and ended by admitting to his young friend that he had perhaps been a little too attentive. 'But it is her father's fault; he pesters me; and even an awarder of good-conduct prizes has his feelings, eh?' He lifted his glass of liqueur with a triumphant flourish, cut short by Paul's remark, 'What will the Duchess say? Of course Mdlle. Moser must have written to her to explain why she left.'

Laniboire turned pale. 'Really, do you think she did?'

Paul pressed the point, in the hopes of ridding himself of such a far from gay gallant. If the lady had not written, there was the chance that a servant might say something. Then, wrinkling his deceitful little nose, he said, 'If I were you, my dear sir——'

'Pooh, pooh! Nonsense! I may get a scolding, but it won't really do me any harm.'

But in spite of his assumed confidence, the day before the Duchess returned, upon the pretext that the election to the Académie was coming on, and that the damp evenings were bad for his rheumatism, he went off, taking in his portmanteau his completed report on the prizes for good-conduct.

The Duchess arrived for Sunday's mass, celebrated with great magnificence in the Renaissance chapel, where Védrine's versatility had restored both the fine stained glass and the wonderful carving of the reredos. A huge crowd from the villages of the neighbourhood filled the chapel to overflowing, and gathered in the great court. Everywhere were awkward fellows in hideous black coats, and long blue blouses shining from the iron, everywhere white caps and kerchiefs stiff with starch round sunburnt necks. All these people were brought together not by the religious ceremony, nor by the honours paid to the old Duke, who was unknown in the district, but by the open-air feast which was to follow the mass. The long tables and benches were arranged on both sides of the long lordly avenue; and here, after the service, between two and three thousand peasants had no difficulty in finding room. At first there was some constraint; the guests, overawed by the troop of servants in mourning and the rangers with crape on their caps, spoke in whispers under the shadow of the majestic elms. But as they warmed with the wine and the victuals, the funeral feast grew more lively, and ended in a vast merrymaking.

To escape this unpleasant carnival, the Duchess and Paul went for a drive, sweeping rapidly in an open carriage draped with black along the roads and fields, abandoned to the desertion of Sunday. The mourning cockades of the tall footmen and the long veil of the widow opposite reminded the young man of other similar drives. He thought to himself, 'My destiny seems to lie in the way of dead husbands.' He felt a touch of regret at the thought of Colette de Rosen's little curly head, contrasting so brightly with the black mass of her surroundings. The Duchess however, tired as she was by her journey, and looking stouter than usual in her improvised mourning, had a magnificence of manner entirely wanting in Colette, and besides, her dead husband did not embarrass her, for she was much too frank to feign a grief which ordinary women think necessary under such circumstances, even when the deceased has been cordially detested and completely abandoned. The road rang under the horses' hoofs, as it unrolled before them, climbing or descending gentle slopes, bordered now by little oak plantations, now by huge plains which, in the neighbourhood of the isolated mills, were swept by circling flights of crows. A pale sunlight gleamed through rare gaps in a sky soft, rainy, and low: and to protect them from the wind as they drove, the same wrap enveloped them both, so that their knees were closely pressed together under the furs. The Duchess was talking of her native Corsica, and of a wonderful *vocero* which had been improvised at the funeral by her maid.

'Matéa?'

'Yes, Matéa. She's quite a poet, fancy'—and the Duchess quoted some of the lines of the *voceratrice*, in the spirited Corsican dialect, admirably suited to her contralto voice. But to the 'important decision' she did not refer.

But it was the important decision that interested Paul Astier, and not the verses of the lady's-maid. No doubt it would be discussed that evening. To pass the time, he told her, in a low tone, how he had got rid of Laniboire. 'Poor little Moser,' said the Duchess, 'her father really must be elected this time.' After that they spoke but a word now and then. They only drew together, lulled, as it were, by the gentle movement of the carriage, while the daylight left the darkening fields, and let them see over towards the furnaces sudden flashes of flame and flickering gleams like lightning against the sky. Unfortunately the drive home was spoilt by the drunken cries and songs of the crowds returning from the feast. The peasants got among the wheels of the carriage like cattle, and from the ditches on either side of the road, into which they rolled, came snores and grunts, their peculiar fashion of praying for the repose of the soul of the most noble Lord Duke.

They walked, as usual, on the gallery, and the Duchess, leaning against Paul's shoulder to look out at the darkness between the massive pillars which cut the dim line of the horizon, murmured, 'This is happiness! Together, and alone!' Still not a word on the subject which Paul was waiting for. He tried to bring her to it, and with his lips in her hair asked what she was going to do in the winter. Should she go back to Paris? Oh, no! certainly not. She was sick of Paris and its false society, its disguises and its treachery! She was still undecided, however, whether to shut herself up at Mousseaux, or to set out on a long journey to Syria and Palestine. What did he think? Why, this must be the important decision they were to consider! It had been a mere pretext to keep him there! She had been afraid that if he went back to Paris, and away from her, some one else would carry him off! Paul, thinking that he had been taken in, bit his lips as he said to himself, 'Oh, if that's your game, my lady, we'll see!' Tired by her journey and a long day in the open air, the Duchess bid him good-night and went wearily up to her room.

The next day they hardly met. The Duchess was busy settling accounts with her steward and her tenants, much to the admiration of Maître Gobineau, the notary, who observed to Paul as they sat at breakfast, with slyness marked in every wrinkle of his shrivelled old face, 'Ah, it's not easy to get on the blind side of the Duchess!'

'Little he knows,' was the thought of the Duchess's young pursuer as he played with his light brown beard. But when he heard the hard cold tones which his lady's tender contralto could assume in a business discussion, he felt that he would have to play his cards carefully.

After breakfast there arrived some trunks from Paris with Spricht's forewoman and two fitters. And at last, about four o'clock, the Duchess appeared in a marvellous costume, which made her look quite young and slim, and proposed a walk in the park. They went along briskly, side by side, keeping to the bye-paths to avoid the noise of the heavy rakes. Three times a day the gardeners struggled against the accumulation of the falling leaves. But in vain; in an hour the walks were again covered by the same Oriental carpet, richly coloured with purple, green, and bronze; and their feet rustled in it as they walked under the soft level rays of the sun. The Duchess spoke of the husband who had brought so much sorrow into her youth; she was anxious to make Paul feel that her mourning was entirely conventional and did not affect her feelings. Paul understood her object, and smiled coldly, determined to carry out his plan.

At the lower end of the park they sat down, near a little building hidden behind maples and privet, where the fishing nets and oars of the boats were kept. From their seat they looked across the sloping lawns and the plantations and shrubberies showing patches of gold. The castle, seen in the background, with its long array of closed windows and deserted terraces, lifting its towers and turrets proudly to the sky, seemed withdrawn, as it were, into the past, and grander than ever.

'I am sorry to leave all that,' said Paul, with a sigh. She looked at him in amazement with storm in her knitted brows. Go away? Did he mean to go away? Why?

'No help. Such is life.'

'Are we to part? And what is to become of me?—and the journey we were to make together?'

'I could not interrupt you——' he said. But how could a poor artist like him afford himself a journey to Palestine? It was an impossible dream, like Védrine's dahabeeah ending in a punt on the Loire.

She shrugged her aristocratic shoulders, and said, 'Why, Paul, what nonsense! You know that all I have is yours.'

'Mine? By what right?'

It was out! But she did not see yet what he was driving at. Fearing that he had gone too far, he added, 'I mean, what right, in the prejudiced view of society, shall I have to travel with you?'

'Well then, we will stay at Mousseaux.'

He made her a little mocking bow as he said, 'Your architect has finished his work on the castle.'

'Oh, we will find him something to do, if I have to set fire to it to-night!'

She laughed her open-hearted tender laugh, leant against him, and taking his hands pressed them against her cheeks—fond trifling this, not the word which he was waiting for, and trying to make her say. Then he burst out, 'If you love me, Antonia, let me go. I must make a living for myself and mine. Society would not forgive my living on the bounty of a woman who is not and never will be my wife.'

She understood, and closed her eyes as if on the brink of an abyss. In the long silence that followed was heard all over the park the falling of the leaves in the breeze, some still heavy with sap, dropping in bunches from bough to bough, others stealing down with a scarcely audible sound, like the rustling of a dress. Round the little hut, under the maples, it was more like the pattering footsteps of some voiceless crowd which moved around. She rose with a shiver. 'It is cold; let us go in.' She had made her sacrifice. It would kill her, very probably, but the world should not see the degradation of the Duchess Padovani into Madame Paul Astier, who had married her architect.

Paul spent the evening in making the obvious arrangements for his departure. He gave orders about his luggage, bestowed princely gratuities upon the servants, and inquired about the time of the trains, chatting away without constraint, but quite unsuccessful in breaking through the gloomy silence of the fair Antonia, who read with absorbed attention a magazine, of which she did not turn the pages. But when he took his leave of her and thanked her for her prolonged and gracious hospitality, in the light of the huge lace lampshade he saw on her haughty face a look of anguish, and in her eyes, magnificent as those of a dying lion, a beseeching supplication.

When he reached his room the young man looked to see that the door to the smoking-room was bolted; then he put out his light and waited, sitting quite still on the divan close to the communication. If she did not come, he had made a mistake and must begin again. But there was a slight noise in the private passage, the sound of a gown, then after a momentary surprise at not being able to come straight in, a touch with the tip of a finger, scarcely a knock. He did not move, and paid no attention to a little significant coughing. Then he heard her go away, with an agitated, uneven step.

'Now,' thought he, 'she is mine. I can do what I like with her.' And he went quietly to bed.

'If I were called the Prince d'Athis, would you not have married me when your mourning was over? Yet D'Athis did not love you, and Paul Astier does. Proud of his love, he would gladly have proclaimed it abroad instead of hiding it as a thing to be ashamed of. Ah, Mari' Anto! I have awaked from a beautiful dream! Farewell for ever.'

She read his letter with her eyes hardly open, swollen with the tears she had been shedding all night. 'Is Monsieur Astier gone?' The maid who was leaning out of the window to fasten back the shutters that moment caught sight of the carriage that was taking away M. Paul, right at the end of the avenue, too far off to be called back. The Duchess sprang out of bed and flew to the clock. 'Nine o'clock.' The express did not reach Onzain till ten. 'Quick, a messenger—Bertoli, and the best of the horses!' By taking the short cut through the woods he could reach the station before the carriage. Whilst her orders were being hastily carried out she wrote a note, standing, without waiting to dress. 'Come back; all shall be as you wish.' No, that was too cold. That would not bring him back. She tore up the note, wrote another, 'What you will, so long as I am yours,' and signed it with her title. Then, wild at the thought that perhaps even that would not bring him, she cried, 'I'll go myself! My habit, quick!' And she called out of the window to Bertoli, whose horse was by this time waiting impatiently at the foot of the steps, and gave orders to saddle 'Mademoiselle Oger' for herself.

She had not ridden for five years. Her figure had grown stouter, the stitches of the habit gave way, some of the hooks were missing. 'Never mind, Matéa, never mind.' She went down the staircase with the train over her arm, between the footmen who stood with blank looks of astonishment, and set off full speed down the avenue, through the gate, into the road, into the wood, and down the cool green paths and long avenues, where the wild creatures fluttered and leapt away as she galloped madly by. She must and will have him. He is her death and life. She has tasted love; and what else does the world contain? Leaning forward, she listens for the sound of the train and watches in every distant view for the steam skirting the horizon. If only she is in time! Poor thing! She might let her horse walk, and yet she would overtake that handsome runaway He is her evil genius, and he is not to be escaped.

Down the cool, green paths and long avenues. Page 263.

CHAPTER XIV.

From the Vicomte de Freydet

To Mademoiselle Germaine de Freydet Villa Beauséjour, Paris-Passy.

Café d'Orsay: 11 A.M. at breakfast. EVERY two hours, and oftener if I can, I shall send you off an interim despatch like this, as much to relieve your anxiety, dearest, as for the pleasure of being with you throughout this great day, which I hope will end with the news of victory, in spite of defections at the last moment. Picheral told me just now of a saying of Laniboire's, 'When a man enters the Académie he wears a sword, but he does not draw it.' an allusion, of course, to the Astier duel. It was not I who fought, but the creature cares more for his jest than for his promise. Cannot count on Danjou, either. After having said so often to me, 'You must join us,' this morning in the secretary's office he came up to me and whispered, 'You should let us miss you,' perhaps the best epigram on his list. Never mind, I'm well ahead. My rivals are not formidable Fancy Baron Huchenard, the author of 'Cave Man,' in the Académie Française! Why, Paris would rise! As for M. Dalzon, I can't think how he has the face. I have got a copy of his too notorious book. I do not like to use it, but he had better be careful.

2 P.M.

At the Institute, in my good master's rooms, where I shall await the result of the voting. Perhaps it is pure imagination, but I fancy that my arrival, though they expected me, has put them out here a little. Our friends were finishing breakfast. There was a bustle and banging of doors, and Corentine, instead of showing me into the drawing-room, hustled me into the library, where my old master joined me with an embarrassed air, and in a low voice advised me to keep extremely quiet. He was quite depressed. I asked if he had any bad news. He said first, 'No, no, my dear boy,' and then, grasping my hand, 'Come, cheer up.' For some time past the poor man has been much altered. He is evidently ready to overflow with vexation and sorrow that he will not express. Probably some deep private trouble, quite unconnected with my candidature; but I am so nervous.

More than an hour to wait. I am amusing myself by looking across the court through the great bay window of the meeting-room at the long rows of busts. The Academicians! Is it an omen?

2.45 P.M.

I have just seen all my judges go by, thirty-seven of them, if I counted right. The full number of the Académie, since Epinchard is at Nice, Ripault-Babin in bed, and Loisillon in the grave. It was glorious to see all the distinguished men come into the court; the younger walking slowly with serious looks and head bent as if under the weight of a responsibility too heavy for them, the old men carrying themselves well and stepping out briskly. A few gouty and rheumatic, like Courson-Launay, drove up to the foot of the steps and leant on the arm of a colleague. They stood about before going up, talking in little knots, and I watched the movements of their backs and shoulders and the play of their open hands. What would I not give to hear the last discussion of my prospects! I opened the window gently, but just then a carriage covered with luggage came clattering into the court, and out got a traveller wrapped in furs and wearing an otter-skin cap. It was Epinchard; just think, dear, Epinchard arriving from Nice on purpose to vote for me. Good fellow! Then my old master went by, his broad-brimmed hat down over his *eyes*; he was turning over the copy of 'Without the Veil,' which I gave him, to be used if necessary. Well, self-defence is always legitimate.

Now there's nothing to see but two carriages waiting and the bust of Minerva keeping guard. Goddess, protect me! They must be beginning the calling of names, and the interrogatory. Each Academician has to state to the President that his vote is not promised. It's a mere formality, as you may suppose, and they all reply by a smile of denial or a little shake of the head like a Chinese mandarin.

A most amazing thing has just happened! I had given my letter to Corentine and was getting a breath of fresh air at the window and trying to read the secret of my fate in the gloomy front of the building opposite, when at the next window to mine I caught sight of Huchenard, airing himself too, quite close to me. Huchenard, my rival—Astier-Réhu's worst enemy, installed in his study! We were, both equally amazed, bowed, and withdrew at the same moment. But there he is, I can hear him, I feel that he is on the other side of the partition. No doubt, like me, he is waiting to hear the decision of the Académie, only he has all the space of 'Villemain's reception-room,' while I am suffocating in this hole crammed full of papers! Now I understand the confusion caused by my arrival. But what is it all about? What is going on? My dear Germaine, my head is going! Which of us is the fool?

Lost! And by treachery, by some mean Academic intrigue which I do not yet understand!

FIRST COUNTING.

Baron Huchenard.......... 17 votes.

Dalzon................... 15 "

Vicomte de Freydet....... 5 "

Moser.................1 vote.

SECOND COUNTING.

Baron Huchenard.......... 19 votes.

Dalzon................... 15 "

Vicomte de Freydet....... 3 "

Moser................... 1 vote.

THIRD COUNTING.

Baron Huchenard.......... 33 votes.

Dalzon................... 4 "

Vicomte de Freydet....... 0 "(!!)

Moser................... . 1 vote.

It is clear that between the second and third taking of votes the copy of 'Without the Veil' must have been sent round in the interest of Baron Huchenard. An explanation I must and will have. I won't leave the place till I get it.

4 P.M.

Dearest sister, you may guess my feelings when, after I had heard in the next room M. and Madame Astier, old Réhu, and a stream of visitors congratulating the author of 'Cave Man,' the door of the library opened and my old master came in, reaching out his hands and saying, 'My dear boy, forgive me'—between heat and emotion he was nearly speechless—'forgive me, that man had a hold over me. I had to do it, I had to do it. I thought I could avert the disaster which threatens me, but destiny is not to be escaped, no, not even by a base act—' He held out his arms and I embraced him without the least anger, without indeed quite understanding the mystery of this bitter grief.

After all, my own loss is easily retrieved. I have first-rate news of Ripault-Babin. He can hardly live through the week. One more campaign, dear, one more. Unfortunately the Hôtel Padovani will be closed all the winter, owing to the Duchess's deep mourning. So for our scene of operations we shall have the 'at home' days of Madame Astier, Madame Ancelin, and Madame Eviza, of whose fashion there is no question since the visit of the Grand Duke. But the first thing, dear Germaine, will be to move. Passy is too far off; the Académie will not go there. You will say I am dragging you about again, but it is so important. Just look at Huchenard. He had no claim whatever but his parties. I dine with my dear master; don't wait for me.

Your affectionate brother,

Abel de Freydet.

Moser's solitary vote in each counting was given by Laniboire, the man who reports for the good conduct prizes. They tell a queer story about it There are strange things under the dome!

CHAPTER XV.

'It's a scandal.'

'There must be a reply. The Académie cannot be silent under the attack.'

'What are you thinking of? On the contrary, the dignity of the Académie demands——'

'Gentlemen, gentlemen, the real feeling of the Académie is——'

In their private assembly room, in front of the great chimney-piece and the full-length portrait of Cardinal Richelieu, the 'deities' were engaged in a discussion preliminary to the meeting. The cold smoke-stained light of a Parisian winter's day, falling through the great lantern overhead, gave effect to the chill solemnity of the marble busts ranged in row along the walls; and the huge fire in the chimney, nearly as red as the Cardinal's robe, was not enough to warm the little council-chamber or court-house, furnished with green leather seats, long horse-shoe table in front of the desk, and chain-bedecked usher, keeping the entrance near the place of Picheral, the Secretary.

Generally the best part of the meeting is the quarter of an hour's grace allowed to late-comers. The Academicians gather in groups with their backs to the fire and their coat tails turned up, chatting familiarly in undertones. But on this afternoon the conversation was general and had risen to the utmost violence of public debate, each new comer joining in from the far end of the room, while he signed the attendance list. Some even before entering, while they were still depositing their great coats, comforters, and overshoes in the empty room of the Académie des Sciences, opened the door to join in the cries of 'Shame!' and 'Scandalous!'

The cause of all the commotion was this. There had appeared in a morning paper a reprint of a highly disrespectful report made to the Académie of Florence upon Astier-Réhu's 'Galileo' and the manifestly apocryphal and absurd (sic) historical documents which were published with it. The report had been sent with the greatest privacy to the President of the Académie Française, and for some days there had been considerable excitement at the Institute, where Astier-Réhu's decision was eagerly awaited. He had said nothing but, 'I know, I know; I am taking the necessary steps.' And now suddenly here was this report which they believed to be known only to themselves, hurled at them like a bomb-shell from the outer sheet of one of the most widely circulated of the Parisian newspapers, and accompanied by remarks insulting to the Permanent Secretary and to the whole Society.

Furious was the indignant outcry against the impudence of the journalist and the folly of Astier-Réhu, which had brought this upon them. The Académie has not been accustomed to such attacks, since it has prudently opened its doors to 'gentlemen of the Press.' The fiery Laniboire, familiar with every kind of 'sport,' talked of cutting off the gentleman's ears, and it took two or three colleagues to restrain his ardour.

'Come, Laniboire; we wear the sword, but we do not draw it Why, it's your own epigram, confound you, though adopted by the Institute.'

'Gentlemen, you remember that Pliny the Elder, in the thirteenth book of his "Natural History"'—here arrived Gazan, who came in puffing with his elephantine trot—'is one of the first writers who mentions counterfeit autographs; amongst others, a false letter of Priam's on papyrus'—

'Monsieur Gazan has not signed the list,' cried Picheral's sharp falsetto.

'Oh, I beg your pardon.' And the fat man went off to sign, still discoursing about papyrus and King Priam, though unheard for the hubbub of angry voices, in which the only word that could be distinguished was 'Académie.' They all talked about the Académie as if it were an actual live person, whose real view each man believed himself alone to know and to express. Suddenly the exclamations ceased, as Astier-Réhu entered, signed his name, and quietly deposited at his place as Permanent Secretary the ensign of his office, carried under his arm. Then moving towards his colleagues he said:

'Gentlemen, I have bad news for you. I sent to the Library to be tested the twelve or fifteen thousand documents which made what I called my collection. Well, gentlemen, all are forgeries. The Académie of Florence stated the truth. I am the victim of a stupendous hoax.'

As he wiped from his brow the great drops of sweat wrung out by the strain of his confession, some one asked in an insolent tone:

'Well, and *so*, Mr. Secretary'—

'So, M. Danjou, I had no other choice but to bring an action—which is what I have done. There was a general protest, all declaring that a lawsuit was out of the question and would bring ridicule upon the whole Society, to which he answered that he was exceedingly sorry to disoblige his colleagues, but his mind was made up. 'Besides, the man is in prison and the proceedings have commenced.'

Never had the private assembly-room heard a roar like that which greeted this statement. Laniboire distinguished himself as usual among the most excited by shouting that the Académie ought to get rid of so dangerous a member. In the first heat of their anger some of the assembly began to discuss the question aloud. Could it be done? Could the Académie say to a member who had brought the whole body into an undignified position, 'Go! I reverse my judgment. Deity as you are, I relegate you to the rank of a mere mortal'? Suddenly, either having caught a few words of the discussion, or by one of those strange intuitions which seem occasionally to come as an inspiration to the most hopelessly deaf, old Réhu, who had been keeping to himself, away from the fire for fear of a fit, remarked in his loud unmodulated voice, 'During the Restoration, for reasons merely political, we turned out eleven members at once.' The patriarch gave the usual little attesting movement of the head, calling to witness his contemporaries of the period, white busts with vacant eyes standing in rows on pedestals round the room.

'Eleven! whew!' muttered Danjou amid a great silence. And Laniboire, cynical as before, said 'All societies are cowardly; it's the natural law of self-preservation.' Here Epinchard, who had been busy near the door with Picheral the Secretary, rejoined the rest, and observed in a weak voice, between two fits of coughing, that the Permanent Secretary was not the only person to blame in the matter, as would appear from the minutes of the proceedings of July 8, 1879, which should now be read. Picheral from his place, in his thin brisk voice, began at a great pace: *On July 8, 1879, Léonard-Pierre-Alexandre Astier-Réhu presented to the Académie Française a letter from Rotrou to Cardinal Richelieu respecting the statutes of the Society. The Académie, after an examination of this unpublished and interesting document, passed a vote of thanks to the donor, and decided to enter the letter of Rotrou upon the minutes. The letter is appended* (at this point the Secretary slackened his delivery and put a malicious stress upon each word) *with all the errors of the original text, which, being such as occur in ordinary correspondence, confirm the authenticity of the document.* All stood motionless in the faded light that came through the glass, avoiding each other's eyes and listening in utter amazement.

'Shall I read the letter too?' asked Picheral with a smile. He was much amused.

'Yes, read the letter too,' said Epinchard. But after a phrase or two there were cries of 'Enough, enough, that will do!' They were ashamed of such a letter of Rotrou. It was a crying forgery, a mere schoolboy's imitation, the sentences misshapen, and half the words not known at the supposed date. How could they have been so blind?

'You see, gentlemen, that we could scarcely throw the whole burden upon our unfortunate colleague,' said Epinchard; and turning to the Permanent Secretary begged him to abandon proceedings which could bring nothing but discredit upon the whole Society and the great Cardinal himself.

But neither the fervour of the appeal nor the magnificence of the orator's attitude, as he pointed to the insignia of the Sacred Founder, could prevail over the stubborn resolution of Astier-Réhu. Standing firm and upright before the little table in the middle of the room, which was used as a desk for the reading of communications, with his fists clenched, as if he feared that his decision might be wrung out of his hands, he repeated that 'Nothing, I assure you, nothing' would alter his determination. He struck the hard wood angrily with his big knuckles, as he said, 'Ah, gentlemen, I have waited, for reasons like these, too long already! I tell you, my "Galileo" is a bone in my throat! I am not rich enough to buy it up, and I see it in the shop windows, advertising me as the accomplice of a forger.' What was his object! Why, to tear out the rotten pages with his own hand and burn them before all the world! A trial would give him the opportunity. 'You talk of ridicule? The Académie is above the fear of it; and as for me, a butt and a beggar as I must be, I shall have the proud satisfaction of having protected my personal honour and the dignity of history. I ask no more.' Honest Crocodilus! In the beat of his rhetoric was a sound of pure probity, which rang strangely where all around was padded with compromise and concealment. Suddenly the usher announced, 'Four o'clock, gentlemen.' Four o'clock! and they had not finished the arrangements for Ripault-Babin's funeral.

'Ah, we must remember Ripault-Babin!' observed Danjou in a mocking voice. 'He has died at the right moment!' said Laniboire with mournful emphasis. But the point of his epigram was lost, for the usher was crying, 'Take your places'; and the President was ringing his bell On his right was Desminières the Chancellor, and on his left the Permanent Secretary, reading quietly with recovered self-possession the report of the Funeral Committee, to an accompaniment of eager whispers and the pattering of sleet on the glass.

'How late you went on to-day!' remarked Coren-tine, as she opened the door to her master. Corentine was certainly to be reckoned with those who had no great opinion of the Institute. 'M. Paul is in your study with Madame. You must go through the library; the drawing-room is full of people waiting to see you.'

The library, where nothing was left but the frame of the pigeon-holes, looked as if there had been a fire or a burglary. It depressed him, and he generally avoided it But to-day he went through it proudly, supported by the remembrance of his resolve, and of how he had declared it at the meeting. After an effort, which had cost him so much courage and determination, he felt a sweet sense of relief in the thought that his son was waiting for him. He had not seen him since just after the duel, when he had been overcome by the sight of his gallant boy, laid at full length and whiter than the sheet. He was thinking with delight how he would go up to him with open arms, and embrace him, and hold him tight, a long while, and say nothing— nothing! But as soon as he came into the room and saw the mother and son close together, whispering, with their eyes on the carpet, and their everlasting air of conspiracy, the affectionate impulse was gone.

'Here you are at last!' cried Madame Astier, who was dressed to go out. And in a tone of mock solemnity, as if introducing the two, she said, 'My dear— the Count Paul Astier.'

'At your service, Master,' said Paul, as he bowed.

Astier-Réhu knitted his thick brows as he looked at them. '*Count* Paul Astier?' said he.

The young fellow, as charming as ever, in spite of the tanning of six months spent in the open air, said he had just indulged in the extravagance of a Roman title, not so much for his own sake as in honour of the lady who was about to take his name.

'So you are going to be married,' said his father, whose suspicions increased. 'And who is the lady?'

'The Duchess Padovani.'

'You must have lost your senses! Why she is five-and-twenty years older than you, and besides—and besides—' He hesitated, trying to find a respectful phrase, but at last blurted right out, 'You can't marry a woman who to every one's knowledge has belonged to another for years.'

'A fact, however, which has never prevented our dining with her regularly, and accepting from her all kinds of favours,' hissed Madame Astier, rearing her little head as to strike. Without bestowing on her a word or a look, as holding her no judge in a question of honour, the man went up to his son, and said in earnest tones, the muscles of his big cheeks twitching with emotion, 'Don't do it, Paul. For the sake of the name you bear, don't do it, my boy, I beg you.' He grasped his son's shoulder and shook him, voice and hand quivering together. But the young fellow moved away, not liking such demonstrations, and objected generally that 'he didn't see it; it was not his view.' The father felt the impassable distance between himself and his son, saw the impenetrable face and the look askance, and instinctively lifted up his voice in appeal to his rights as head of the family. A smile which he caught passing between Paul and his mother, a fresh proof of their joint share in this discreditable business, completed his exasperation. He shouted and raved, threatening to make a public protest, to write to the papers, to brand them both, mother and son, 'in his history.' This last was his most appalling threat. When he had said of some historical character, 'I have branded him in my history,' he thought no punishment could be more severe. Madame Astier, almost as familiar with the threat of branding as with the dragging of his trunk about the passage, contented herself with saying as she buttoned her gloves: 'You know every word can be heard in the next room.' In spite of the curtains over the door, the murmur of conversation was audible from the drawing-room.

Then, repressing and swallowing his wrath, 'Listen to me, Paul,' said Léonard Astier, shaking his forefinger in the young man's face, 'if ever this thing you are talking of comes to pass, do not expect to look upon me again. I will not be present on your wedding day; I will not have you near me, not even at my death-bed; You are no longer a son of mine; and you go with my curse upon you.' Moving away instinctively from the finger which almost touched him, Paul replied with great calmness, 'Oh, you know, my dear father, that sort of thing is never done now-a-days! Even on the stage they have given up blessing and cursing.'

'But not punishing, you scoundrel!' growled the old man, lifting his hand. There was an angry cry of 'Léonard!' from the mother, as with the prompt parry of a boxer Paul turned the blow aside, quietly as if he had been in Keyser's gymnasium, and without letting go the wrist he had twisted under, said beneath his breath, 'No, no; I won't have that.'

The tough old hillsman struggled violently, but, vigorous as he still was, he had found his master. At this terrible moment, while father and son stood face to face, breathing hate at one another, and exchanging murderous glances, the door of the drawing-room opened a little and showed the good-natured doll-like smile of a fat lady bedecked with feathers and flowers. 'Excuse me, dear master, I want just to say a word—why, Adelaide is here, and M. Paul too. Charming! delightful! Quite a family group!' Madame Ancelin was right. A family group it was, a picture of the modern family, spoilt by the crack which runs through European society from top to bottom, endangering its essential principles of authority and subordination, and nowhere more remarkable than here, under the stately dome of the Institute, where the traditional domestic virtues are judged and rewarded.

CHAPTER XVI.

People were still coming in through the entrance lobby. Page 285.

It was stifling in the Eighth Chamber, where the Fage case was just coming on after interminable preliminaries and great efforts on the part of influential persons to stop the proceedings. Never had this court-room, whose walls of a mouldy blue and diamond pattern in faded gilding reeked with the effluvium of rags and misery, never had this court seen squeezed on its dirty seats and packed in its passages such a press and such a crowd of fashionable and distinguished persons, so many flower-trimmed bonnets and spring costumes by the masters of millinery art, to throw into relief the dead black of the gowns and caps. People were still coming in through the entrance lobby, where the double doors were perpetually swinging as the tide flowed on, a wavy sea of throning faces upturned beneath the whitish light of the landing. Everyone was there, all the well-known, well-worn, depressingly familiar personages that figure at every Parisian festivity, fashionable funeral, or famous 'first night.' There was Marguerite Oger well to the fore, and the little Countess Foder, and beautiful Mrs. Henry of the American Embassy. There were the ladies belonging to the Academic confraternity, Madame Ancein in mauve on the arm of Raverand, the leader of the bar; Madame Eviza, a bush of little roses surrounded by a busy humming swarm of would-be barristers. Behind the President's bench was Danjou, standing with folded arms, and showing above the audience and the judges the hard angles of his regular stage-weathered countenance, everywhere to be seen during the last forty years as the type of social commonplace in all its manifold manifestations. With the exception of Astier-Réhu and Baron Huchenard, who were summoned as witnesses, he was the only Academician bold enough to face the irreverent remarks that might be expected in the speech of Fage's counsel, Margery, the dreaded wit, who convulses the whole assembly and the bench with the mere sound of his nasal 'Well.' Some fun was to be expected; the whole atmosphere of the place announced it, the erratic tilt of the barristers' caps, the gleam in the eyes and curl in the corners of the mouths of people giving one another little anticipatory smiles. There were endless anecdotes current about the achievements in gallantry of the little humpback who had just been brought to the prisoner's box and, lifting his long well-greased head, cast into the court over the bar the conquering glance of a manifest ladies' man. Stories were told of compromising letters, of an account drawn up by the prisoner mentioning right out the names of two or three well-known ladies of fashion, the regular names dragged again and again into every unsavoury case. There was a copy of the production going the rounds of the seats reserved for the press, a simple conceited autobiography containing none of the revelations imputed to it by public rumour. Fage had beguiled the tedium of confinement by writing for the court the story of his life. He was born, he said, near Vassy (Haute Marne), as straight as anybody—so they all say—but a fall from a horse at fifteen had bent and inflected his spine. His taste for gallantry had developed somewhat late in life when he was working at a bookseller's in the Passage des Panoramas. As his deformity interfered with his success, he tried to find some way of getting plenty of money. The story of his love affairs alternating with that of his forgeries and the means employed, with descriptions of ink and of parchment, resulted in such headings to his chapters as 'My first victim—For a red ribbon—The gingerbread fair—I make the acquaintance of Astier-Réhu—The mysterious ink—I defy the chemists of the Institute.' This brief epitome is enough to show the combination, the humpback's self-satisfaction *plus* the arrogance of the self-taught artisan. The general result of reading the production was utter amazement that the Permanent Secretary of the Académie Française and the official representatives of science and literature could have been taken in for two or three years by an ignorant dwarf with a brain crammed full of the refuse of libraries and the ill-digested parings of books. This constituted the extraordinary joke of the whole business, and was the explanation of the crowded court. People came to see the Académie pilloried in the person of Astier-Réhu, who sat among the witnesses, the mark of every eye. There he sat without moving, absorbed in his thoughts, not turning his head, and hardly answering the fulsome compliments of Freydet who was standing behind, with black gloves and a deep crape hat-band, having quite recently lost his sister. He had been summoned for the defence, and the Academic candidate was afraid that the fact might damage him in the eyes of his old master. He was apologising and explaining how he had come across the wretched Fage in Védrine's studio, and that was the reason of this unexpected call. But his whispers were lost in the noise of the court and the monotonous hum from the bench, as cases were called on and disposed of, the invariable 'This day week, this day week' descending like the stroke of the guillotine and cutting short the barrister's protest, and the entreaties of poor red-faced fellows mopping their brows before the seat of justice. 'But, Monsieur le Président...' 'This day week.' Sometimes from the back of the court would come a cry and a despairing movement of a pair of arms, 'I am here, M. le Président, but I can't get through, there's such a crowd...' 'This day week.' When a man has beheld such clearances as these, and seen the symbolic scales operate with such dexterity, he gets a vivid impression of French justice; it is not unlike the sensation of hearing the funeral service raced through in a hurry by a strange priest over a pauper's grave.

The voice of the President called for the Fage case. Complete silence followed in the court, and even on the staircase landing where people had climbed on to benches to see. Then after a short consultation on the bench the witnesses filed out through a dense crowd of gowns on their way to the little room reserved for them, a dreary empty place, badly lighted by glass windows that had once been red, and looking out on a narrow alley. Astier-Réhu, who was to be called first, did not go in, but walked up and down in the gloomy passage between the witness-room and the court. Freydet wished to stay with him, but he said in a colourless voice, 'No, no, let me alone, I want to be alone.' So the candidate joined the other witnesses who were standing in little knots—Baron Huchenard, Bos the palaeographer, Delpech the chemist, of the Académie des Sciences, some experts in handwriting, and two or three pretty girls, the originals of some of the photographs that adorned the walls of Fage's room, delighted at the notoriety that the proceedings would bring them, laughing loudly and displaying startling little spring hats strangely different from the linen cap and woollen mittens of the caretaker at the Cour des Comptes. Védrine also had been summoned, and Freydet came and sat by him on the wide ledge of the open window. The two friends, whirled apart in the opposing currents that divide men's lives in Paris, had not met since the summer before until the recent funeral of poor Germaine de Freydet Védrine pressed his friend's hand and asked how he was, how he felt after so terrible a blow. Freydet shrugged his shoulders, 'It's hard, very hard, but after all I'm used to it.' Then, as Védrine stared in wonder at his selfish stoicism, he added, 'Just think, that's twice in one year that I have been fooled.' The blow, the only blow, that he remembered, was his failure to get Ripault-Babin's seat, which he had lately missed, as he had missed Loisillon's before. Presently he understood, sighed deeply, and said, 'Ah, yes, poor Germaine!' She had taken so much trouble all the winter about his unlucky candidature. Two dinners a week! Up to twelve or one o'clock she would be wheeling her chair all over the drawing-room. She had sacrificed her remaining strength to it, and was even more excited and keen than her brother. And at the last, the very last, when she was past speaking, her poor twisted fingers went on counting upon the hem of the sheet 'Yes, Védrine, she died, ticking and calculating my chances of Ripault-Babin's seat. Oh, if only for her sake, I will get into their Académie, in defiance of them all, and in honour of her dear memory!' He stopped short, then in an altered and lower voice went on: 'Really I don't know why I talk like that. The truth is that, since they put the idea into my head, I can think of nothing else. My sister is dead and I have hardly given her a tear. I had to pay my calls and "beg for the Académie," as that fellow says. The thing takes the very life out of me. It's perfectly maddening.'

In the savage plainness of these words and the excited ring of the angry voice, the sculptor could scarcely recognise his gentle courteous friend, to whom mere living used to be a joy. The absent expression in his eye, the anxious wrinkle on his brow, and the heat of the hand which grasped Védrine's, all betrayed his subjection to one absorbing passion, one fixed idea. But the meeting with Védrine seemed to have relieved his nerves, and he asked affectionately, 'Well, what are you doing, and how are you getting on? How is your wife? And the children?' His friend answered with his quiet smile. All were doing well, thank God. The little girl was just going to be weaned. The boy continued to fulfil his function of looking lovely, and was waiting impatiently for old Réhu's centenary. As for himself, he was hard at work. He had two pictures in the Salon this year, not badly hung, and not badly sold. On the other hand a creditor, not less unwise than hard, had taken possession of the Knight, and he had passed from stage to stage, first lying much in the way in a fine suite of rooms on the ground floor in the Rue St. Pétersbourg, then packed off to a stable at Batignolles, and now shivering under a cowkeeper's shed at Levallois, where from time to time the sculptor and his family went to pay him a visit.

'So much for glory!' added Védrine with a laugh, as the voice of the usher called for the witness Astier-Réhu. The head of the Permanent Secretary showed for a moment, outlined against the dusty light of the court-room, upright and steady; but his back he had forgotten to control, and the shiver of his broad shoulders betrayed intense feeling. 'Poor man,' muttered the sculptor, 'he's got heavy trials to go through. This autograph business, and his son's marriage.'

'Is Paul Astier married?'

'Yes, three days ago, to the Duchess Padovani. It was a sort of morganatic marriage, with no guests but the young man's mamma and the four witnesses. I was one of them, as you may suppose, for a freak of fate seems to associate me with all the acts and deeds of the Astier family.'

And Védrine described the sorrowful surprise with which in the Mayor's room he had seen the Duchess Padovani appear, deathly pale, as haughty as ever, but withered and heart-broken, with a mass of grey hair, the poor beautiful hair that she no longer took the trouble to dye. By her side was Paul Astier, the Count, smiling, cold, and charming as before. They all looked at one another, and nobody had a word to say except the official who, after a good stare at the two old ladies, felt it incumbent upon him to remark with a gracious bow:

'We are only waiting for the bride.'

'The bride is here,' replied the Duchess, stepping forward with head erect and a bitter smile which spoilt and twisted her beautiful mouth.

From the Mayor's office, where the deputy on duty had the good taste to spare them an oration, they adjourned to the Catholic Institute in the Rue de Vaugirard, an aristocratic church, all over gilding and flowers and a blaze of candles, but not a soul there, nobody but the wedding party on a single row of chairs, to hear the Papal Nuncio, Monsignor Adriani, mumble an interminable homily out of an illuminated book. A fine thing it was, to hear the worldly prelate with large nose, thin lips, and hollow shoulders under his violet cape, talking of the 'honourable traditions of the husband and the charms of the wife,' with a sombre, cynical side-glance at the velvet cushions of the unhappy couple. Then came the departure; cold good-byes were exchanged under the arches of the little cloister, and a sigh of relief with 'Well, that's over,' escaped the Duchess, said in the despairing, disenchanted accent of a woman who has measured the abyss, and leaps in with her eyes open only to keep her word.

'Ah, well,' Védrine went on, 'I have seen gloomy and lamentable sights enough in the course of my life, but never anything so heart-breaking as Paul Astier's wedding.'

'He's a fine rascal, though, is our young friend,' said Freydet, between his closed teeth.

'Yes, a precious product of the "struggle for existence."'

The sculptor repeated the phrase with emphasis. A 'struggler for existence' was his name for the novel tribe of young savages who cite the necessity of 'nature's war' as an hypocritical excuse for every kind of meanness. Freydet went on:

'Well, anyhow, he's rich now, which is what he wanted. His nose has not led him astray this time.'

'Wait and see. The Duchess is not easy to get on with, and he looked devilish wicked at the Mayor's. If the old lady bores him too much, we may still see him some day at the Assize Court, son and grandson of divinities as he is.'

'The witness Védrine!' called the usher at the top of his voice.

At the same moment a huge roar of laughter ran over the thronging crowd and came through the door as it swung open. 'They don't seem bored in there,' said the municipal officer posted in the passage. The witnesses' room, which had been gradually emptying during the chat of the two schoolfellows, now contained only Freydet and the caretaker, who, scared at having to appear in court, was twisting the strings of her cap like a lunatic. The worthy candidate, on the contrary, thought he had an unparalleled opportunity of burning incense at the shrine of the Académie Française and its Permanent Secretary. Left alone, when the good woman's turn came, he paced up and down the room, planted himself in front of the window, and let off well-rounded periods accompanied by magnificent gestures of his black gloves. But he was misunderstood in the house opposite; and a fat hand at the end of a bare arm pulled aside a pink curtain and waved to him. Freydet, flushing crimson with shame, moved quickly away from the window, and took refuge in the passage.

'The Public Prosecutor is speaking now,' said the doorkeeper in a whisper, as a voice in a tone of assumed indignation rang through the heated air of the court—'You played,' it said, 'on the innocent passion of an old man.'

'But how about me?' said Freydet, thinking aloud.

'I expect you have been forgotten.'

Freydet was at first puzzled, but presently disgusted at the strange fate which prevented his coming forward in public as the champion of the Académie, and so getting himself talked about and seeing his name for once in the papers. Just then a shout of laughter greeted the enumeration of the forgeries in the Mesnil-Case collection; letters from kings, popes, empresses, Turenne, Buffon, Montaigne, La Boëtie, Clémence Isaure, and the mere mention of the absurd list showed the extraordinary simplicity of the historian who had been befooled by the little dwarf. But at the thought that this disrespectful laugh was a scoff at his master and protector, Freydet felt an indignation not altogether free from selfishness. He felt that he was himself hit by the recoil, and his candidature damaged again. He broke away, mingling in the stir of the general exodus amid a confusion of footmen running to and fro in the beautiful waning light of a fine June day, while the parasols, pink, white, mauve, or green opened like so many large flowers. Little explosions of laughter were still coming from the various groups, as if they had been seeing an amusing piece at the theatre. The little humpback had got it hot—five years' imprisonment and costs. But how comic Margery had been! Marguerite Oger was exclaiming in fits, 'Oh my dears, my dears!' and Danjou, escorting Madame Eviza to her carriage, said aloud in his cynical way, 'It's a slap in the face for the Académie, well planted—but it was cleverly done.'

Léonard Astier, who was walking alone, heard Danjou's remark as well as others, in spite of the warnings passed from mouth to mouth, 'Take care—there he is.' It signified to him the beginning of his fall in estimation, consequent on the general knowledge of his folly and the amusement of Paris.

'Take my arm, my dear master!' said Freydet, who had been carried to him by the strong impulse of affection.

'Ah, my dear friend, how much good you do me!' said the old man in a dull, broken voice.

They walked on in silence for some time. The trees on the quay cast a tracery of shade upon the stones below; the sounds of the street and the river echoed in the joyous air. It was one of those days on which human wretchedness seems to have been reprieved.

'Where are we going?' asked Freydet.

'Anywhere—except home,' answered the elder man, who felt a child's terror at the thought of the scene his wife would inflict on him at dinner.

They dined together at the Point-du-Jour after walking a long time by the river. When poor Astier returned home very late the friendly words of his old pupil and the sweetness of the air had succeeded in restoring his peace of mind. He had got over his five hours in the stocks on the bench of the Eighth Chamber—five hours to endure with bound hands the insulting laughter of the crowd and the vitriol squirt of the counsel. 'Laugh, apes, laugh! Posterity will judge!' was the thought with which he consoled himself as he crossed the large courts of the Institute, wrapped in slumber, with unlighted windows and great dark foursquare holes right and left where the staircases came down. He felt his way upstairs and reached his study noiselessly like a thief. Since Paul's marriage and his quarrel with his son he was in the habit of flinging himself down every night on a bed made up in the study, to escape the interminable midnight discussions in which the wife always comes off victorious, thanks to the never-failing support of her 'nerves', and the husband ends by giving way and promising everything for the sake of peace and permission to sleep.

Sleep! Never had he so much felt the need of it as now, at the end of his long day of emotion and fatigue, and the darkness of his study as he entered seemed the beginning of rest—when in the angle of the window he dimly distinguished a human figure.

'Well, I hope you are satisfied.' It was his wife! She was on the look out for him, waiting, and her angry voice stopped him short in the dark to listen. 'You have won your cause; you insisted on making yourself a mockery, and you have done it—daubed and drenched yourself with ridicule, till you won't be able to show yourself again! Much reason you had to cry out that your son was disgracing you, to insult and to curse your son! Poor boy, it is well he has changed his name, now that yours has become so identified with ignorance and gullibility that no one will be able to utter it without a smile. And all this, if you please, for the sake of your historical work! Why, you foolish man, who knows anything about your historical work? Who can possibly care whether your documents are genuine or forged? You know that nobody reads you.'

She went on and on, pouring out a thin stream of voice in her shrillest tone; and he felt as if he were back again in the pillory, listening to the official abuse as he had done all day, without interrupting, without even a threatening gesture, swallowing the insults as he had in court, and feeling that the authority was above attack and the judge one not to be answered. But how cruel was this invisible mouth which bit him, and wounded him all over, and slowly mangled in its teeth his pride as a man and a writer!

His books, indeed! Did he suppose that they had got him into the Académie? Why, it was to his wife alone that he owed his green coat! She had spent her life in plotting and manoeuvring to break open one door after another; sacrificed all her youth to such intrigues, and such intriguers, as made her sick with disgust. 'Why, my dear, I had to! The Académie is attained by talent, of which you have none, or a great name, or a high position. You had none of these things. So I came to the rescue.' And that there might be no mistake about it, that he might not attribute what she said only to the exasperation of a woman wounded and humiliated in her wifely pride and her blind maternal devotion, she recalled the details of his election, and reminded him of his famous remark about Madame Astier's veils that smelt of tobacco, though he never smoked, 'a remark, my dear, that has done more to make you notorious than your books.'

He gave a low deep groan, the stifled cry of a man who stays with both hands the life escaping from a mortal rent The sharp little voice went on unaltered. 'Ah well, pack your trunk, do, once for all! Let the world hear no more of you. Fortunately your son is rich and will give you your daily bread. For you need not be told that now you will find no publisher or magazine to take your rubbish, and it will be due to Paul's supposed infamy that you escape starvation.'

'This is more than I can bear,' muttered the poor man as he fled away, away from the lashing fury. And as he felt his way along the walls, and passed through the passage, down the stairs, across the echoing court, he muttered almost in tears, 'More than I can bear, more than I can bear.'

Whither is he going? Straight before him, as if in a dream. He crosses the square and is half over the bridge, before the fresh air revives him. He sits down on a bench, takes off his hat and pulls up his coat sleeves to still the beating of his pulses; and the regular lapping of the water makes him calmer. He comes to himself again, but consciousness brings only memory and pain. What a woman! what a monster! And to think that he has lived five-and-thirty years with her and not known her! A shudder of disgust runs over him at the recollection of all the horrors he has just heard. She has spared nothing and left within him nothing alive, not even the pride which still kept him erect, his faith in his work and his belief in the Académie. At the thought of the Académie he instinctively turned round. Beyond the deserted bridge, beyond the wider avenue which leads to the foot of the building, the pile of the Palais Mazarin, massed together in the darkness, up-reared its portico and its dome, as on the cover of the Didot books, so often gazed upon in his young days and in the ambitious aspirations of his whole life. That dome, that block of stone, had been the delusive object of his hopes, and the cause of all his misery.

It was there he sought his wife, feeling neither love nor delight, but for the hope of the Institute. And he has had the coveted seat, and he knows the price!

Just then there was a sound of steps and laughter on the bridge; it came nearer. Some students with their mistresses were coming back to their rooms. Afraid of being recognised, he rose and leant over the parapet; and while the party passed close to him without seeing him, he reflected with bitterness that he had never amused himself, never allowed himself such a fine night's holiday of song beneath the starlight. His ambition had always been fixed unbendingly on the approach to yonder dome, the dome, as it were, of a temple, whose beliefs and whose ritual he had respected in anticipation.

And what had yonder dome given him in return? Nothing, absolutely nothing. Even on the day of his admission, when the speeches were over and the double-edged compliments at an end, he had felt the sensation of emptiness and deluded hope. He had said to himself as he drove home to change his green coat, 'Have I really got in? Why, it can't be like this.' Since then, by dint of constant lying to himself and echoing, with his colleagues, that it was delightful, delicious, he had ended by believing so. But now the veil had fallen away, and he saw the truth; and he would have liked to proclaim with a thousand tongues to the youth of France, 'The Académie is a snare and a delusion. Go your way and do your work. Sacrifice nothing to the Académie, for it has nothing to offer you, neither gift, nor glory, nor the best thing of all, self-contentment. It is neither a retreat nor a refuge; it is a hollow idol, a religion that offers no consolations. The great troubles of life come upon you there as elsewhere; under that dome men have killed themselves, men have gone mad there! Those who in their agony have turned to the Académie, and weary of loving, or weary of cursing, have stretched forth their arms to her, have clasped but a shadow.'

The old schoolmaster was speaking aloud, bareheaded, grasping the parapet with both hands as in old days he used to hold the edge of his desk at lessons. The river rolled on below, tinged with hues of night, between its rows of winking lamps. An uncanny thing is the speechless life of light, moving, and looking, and never saying what it means. On the quay the song of a drunken man died quavering away in the distance, 'When Cupid... in the morn... awakes.' The accent showed that the merry singer was an Auvergnat making his way back to his coal-barge. It reminded him of Teyssèdre, the polisher, and his glass of good wine. He saw him wiping his mouth on his shirt-sleeve. 'It's the only real good in life.' Even a humble natural joy like that he had never known; he must needs envy even Teyssèdre. Absolutely alone, with no refuge, no breast on which to weep, he realised that 'that woman' was right, and 'the trunk had better be packed for good and all, Léonard.'

In the morning some policemen found on a bench on the Pont des Arts a wide-brimmed hat, one of those hats which preserve something of the expression of their owner. Inside was a large gold watch and a visiting card—'Léonard Astier-Réhu, Permanent Secretary of the Académie Française.' Right across the line of print had been written in pencil the words, 'I die here of my own will.' Of his own will indeed it was! Even better than the little phrase in the large, firm handwriting did the expression of his features—the set teeth, the projection of the lower jaw—declare his fixed determination to die, when after a morning's search the dredgers found the body caught in the wide meshes of an iron net surrounding some baths for women, quite close to the bridge.

The dredgers found the body. Page 305.

It was taken first to the emergency-station, where Picheral came to identify it, a strange sight himself, as he fluttered along the wide bank, with bare bald head and in a frock coat. It was not the first time that a Permanent Secretary had been taken out of the Seine; the same thing had occurred in the time of Picheral's father, under very similar circumstances. And Picheral the son did not seem much affected, only annoyed that he could not wait till the evening to carry Astier-Réhu home. But it was necessary to take advantage of the absence of Madame Astier (who was breakfasting with her son) so as to spare her too great a shock.

The clock of the Palais Mazarin was striking one, when with the heavy tramp of the bearers the stretcher from the station was brought under the archway, marking its road with ominous splashes of water. At the foot of Staircase B there was a halt to take breath. Over the dazzling court was a great sharp-lined square of blue sky. The covering of the stretcher had been raised, and the features of Léonard Astier-Réhu were visible for the last time to his colleagues on the Dictionary Committee, who had just broken up their meeting in sign of mourning. They stood round, with their hats off, not a little shocked. Other people also stopped to see what it was, workmen, clerks, and apprentices, for the Institute serves as a passage from the Rue Mazarin to the quay. Among them was kind-hearted Freydet, who, as he wiped his eyes, thought in his heart, and was ashamed to think it, that here was another vacancy. Old Jean Réhu was just coming downstairs for his daily constitutional.

He had heard nothing, seemed surprised to see the crowd beneath him as he stood on one of the lower steps, and came nearer to look, in spite of the scared gestures of those who tried to keep him back. Did he understand? Did he recognise the corpse? His face remained calm, so did his eyes, as expressionless as those of the bust of Minerva under her helmet of bronze. And after a long look, as they turned the striped canvas down over the poor dead face, he went on, upright and proud, with his tall shadow stalking beside him, a 'deity' deathless indeed, while a half-mad senile shake of the head seemed to say: 'That's another of the things I have seen.'

CPSIA information can be obtained
at www.ICGtesting.com
Printed in the USA
BVHW041839220822
645208BV00005B/328